the hockey problem

New York Times Bestselling Author

KENDALL RYAN

About the Book

He's the NHL's most guarded single dad.
She's the one woman who can't afford to fall for him.

Tori Wells didn't fight her way into the NHL just to become another cautionary tale. As a team physical therapist, she lives by strict rules: heal the players, protect her career, and never—ever—cross the line with a hockey player.

Then she's assigned to Zayden Bishop.

On the ice, he's untouchable—a French-Canadian superstar with a reputation for being cold, private, and impossible to read. Off the ice, he's a devoted single father running on discipline, stubbornness, and too little sleep. Until a serious shoulder injury threatens his season—and the stability he's built for his six-year-old daughter.

Tori is in charge of his rehab. Full oversight. Daily sessions.

No room for mistakes.

No room for attraction.

Except Zayden isn't what she expected.

The more time they spend together—early mornings, quiet road trips, late-night conversations—the harder it becomes to pretend this is just professional. Because Zayden doesn't just need his shoulder fixed. He needs someone who sees the man behind the jersey.

And Tori is dangerously close to becoming that someone.

Crossing the line could cost her everything she's worked for. And Zayden can't risk bringing anyone into his daughter's life unless he's certain they'll stay.

Perfect for fans of Meghan Quinn, Elle Kennedy, and Monica Murphy, this slow-burn, single dad, forced-proximity hockey romance brings the heat—and the heart—in all the best ways.
Book one in a brand-new hockey romance series. Each book can be read as a standalone.

1

IN WALKS TROUBLE

Tori

The file on my desk is three inches thick.

Zayden Bishop. Twenty-nine years old. Right winger for the New York Knights. Six-foot-two, two hundred and ten pounds of French-Canadian hockey prodigy who's been playing through what looks like a rotator cuff issue for at least six weeks, based on the game footage I reviewed last night.

I flip through his injury history while my coffee goes cold. Separated shoulder, 2021. Broken wrist, 2022. Concussion protocol twice in three years. The man treats his body like a rental car with full coverage insurance.

I'm sore just thinking about it.

Outside my window, January in New York is doing its thing—gray sky, bitter wind, cold that makes you question every life choice that led you to a city where the air physically hurts. The Knights' facility is shiny and modern, all glass and steel, but I can't focus on that. Not when I'm about to get hands-on with the most notorious player on the roster.

Dana Cross, Director of Athletic Performance and the reason I have this job, appears in my doorway. She's got her tablet tucked under her arm and that look on her face. The one that says *I'm about to ruin your morning*.

"You ready for Bishop?"

"Define ready."

She almost smiles. "He's essential to the playoff run. His shoulder's been bothering him for weeks. He's been hiding the severity."

"I noticed," I say, tapping the file. "You can see it from the nosebleeds. He's favoring his left side on every shot."

"Which is why you're taking point. Full oversight. Recovery plan, travel schedule, progress reports—all you."

I set down my coffee. "Dana."

"I know he's difficult."

"Difficult is an understatement. I've heard the stories." Everyone has. Zayden Bishop doesn't do interviews, doesn't do media days, doesn't do anything that isn't hockey or—according to the rumors—his kid. The tabloids call him cold. Unapproachable. The guy who looks through you like you're furniture.

"The stories are mostly bullshit," Dana says. "He's private, not hostile."

I raise a brow. "Is there a difference?"

"You'll see." She checks her watch. "He'll be in exam room two. Don't let him charm you."

I almost laugh. "Charm isn't exactly his reputation."

"No," she agrees, already walking away. "But he's got other tricks."

I have no idea what that means, and I don't have time to ask because my phone buzzes with a calendar reminder. *Bishop, Z. - Initial Assessment. 9:00 AM.*

Perfect. Another ego with a jersey number.

I grab my tablet, pull my hair back into a ponytail, and head down the hall.

Exam room two is bright, sterile—my kind of place. Fluorescent lights, adjustable table, wall of equipment I probably won't need today. I'm setting up my assessment forms when the door opens and Zayden Bishop walks in.

And he's... not what I expected. There's no swagger, no look-at-me energy. He enters like he'd rather not be here at all—shoulders tight, gaze scanning the room like he's searching for threats.

I wait for the arrogance. The *I'm a big deal* energy I've gotten from every other player who's sat on my table. It doesn't come.

He's wearing Knights athletic gear, black joggers and a hoodie pushed up to his elbows, and there's a tension in his jaw that tells me he's not happy to be here.

Second thing I notice: he's unfairly attractive in person.

I knew that, objectively. I've seen the photos, the game footage, the *Sports Illustrated* spread from three years ago that made every woman in America suddenly interested in hockey. But photos don't capture how massive he is in person—towering over me with all that bulky muscle. They don't capture how his eyes scan the room before landing on me, assessing, cataloging.

Dark hair. Darker eyes. A face that belongs on magazine covers, all sharp angles and stubble.

Stop it, I tell myself. *He's a patient. He's everything you promised yourself you'd never be stupid enough to want.*

"Mr. Bishop." I keep my voice clinical. "I'm Victoria Wells, Tori. I'll be handling your rehabilitation."

"Zayden," he says. Low voice, a little rough, with just a hint of an accent that betrays his Quebec roots.

"Have a seat on the table, Mr. Bishop. We'll begin with a full assessment."

Something flickers across his face—surprise, maybe, that I didn't immediately start fawning—but he doesn't argue. Just walks to the exam table and sits, movements careful, confirming what I already suspected. "Okay," he says. "But call me Zayden."

"Shirt off, please."

He pulls the hoodie over his head, then the T-shirt underneath, and I keep my face neutral through sheer willpower. He's built like a hockey player—broad shoulders, defined chest, functional muscle that comes from years of actual training, not vanity reps in front of a gym mirror. There's a scar on his left side, probably from the 2021 surgery. His skin is tan even in January, which either means good genetics or a spray tan habit I'm going to silently judge him for.

I wash my hands and then approach. "I'm going to palpate the shoulder. Tell me when it hurts."

He nods.

I start with the trapezius, working my way across to the deltoid. His muscles are tight—way too tight—and when I press into the junction of his neck and shoulder, his jaw clenches.

"That hurt?"

"It's fine."

"That's not what I asked." I press again, watching his face. "Scale of one to ten."

"Four."

I move to his rotator cuff, and when I find the spot I'm looking for—the one that's been causing all the problems—he sucks in a breath.

"Four?" I repeat.

"Maybe six."

"Mmhmm." I continue the assessment, cataloging every flinch he tries to hide, every compensation pattern his body has developed to work around the damage. By the time I'm done, I have a very clear picture of what we're dealing with.

I step back, and jot a few notes. "How long have you been playing through this?"

"Doesn't matter."

"It does to me. I can't fix what you won't admit is broken."

He looks at me then—really looks—those dark eyes assessing and I feel the weight of his attention like something physical. There's an intensity to him that's almost uncomfortable, like he's seeing more than you want him to see.

"Since October," he finally says.

"October." I don't bother hiding my disbelief.

"You've been playing through a rotator cuff impingement for three months."

"I've had worse."

"That's not the flex you think it is." I pick up my tablet, and start typing notes. "You have inflammation in the supraspinatus, early signs of tendinopathy, and your compensation patterns have put extra strain on your bicep tendon. If you'd come in when it first started hurting, we'd be talking about two weeks of modified training. Now we're looking at six to eight weeks of intensive rehab."

His expression doesn't change, but something in his posture shifts. "I don't have six to eight weeks."

"Then I suggest you follow my protocol exactly, because if you keep pushing through this, you're looking at surgery. And that's not six weeks. That's six months."

Silence.

I can see him doing the math—the games he'd miss, the playoff implications, whatever else is going on in his life that makes him treat his body like it's disposable. For a second, he looks tired. Not physically, but somewhere deeper. Somewhere he probably doesn't let most people see.

"Fine," he says. "What do you need me to do?"

"Ice, rest, and I'll see you tomorrow at eight AM. We'll start with mobility work and go from there." I pause. "And Zayden? When I ask if something hurts, I need the real answer. Not the tough-guy answer. I can't help you if you lie to me."

He holds my gaze for a beat longer than necessary. "You always this bossy?"

"With patients who hide injuries for three months? Yes."

The corner of his mouth twitches. Not quite a smile, but close. Closer than anything I've seen from him since he walked in.

He pulls his shirt back on, and I turn to my tablet, typing notes I don't actually need just to have something to do with my hands. The assessment is done. I should let him leave. That would be the professional thing to do.

"There's a place on Fifth that does recovery smoothies," he says.

I glance up. He's still by the exam table, hoodie in his hand, watching me.

"What?"

"If you're looking for post-workout fuel recommendations for players. The green one tastes like ass, but it works."

I give him a confused look. "I have a nutrition protocol."

"I'm sure you do." He shrugs into the hoodie. "Just saying. It works."

I go back to my notes. "Noted."

"You're not going to write that down?"

"I have a nutrition protocol," I repeat, but something's creeping into my voice. Something that sounds dangerously close to amusement.

He leans against the doorframe, arms crossed, watching me. "What about tacos?"

I look up again. "Excuse me?"

"Best tacos in the city. In your opinion." He tilts his head slightly. "Just to check your credibility."

"My credibility?" I blink.

"Tell me your favorite taco spot and I'll tell you if I can trust you."

I shouldn't engage. This is exactly how lines get blurry—the casual banter, the "we're just friendly" energy that slowly becomes something else, something dangerous. I have rules for a reason. Good reasons. Reasons I paid for in humiliation and tears and watching my reputation get shredded by a guy who smiled just like this one does.

But something about the way he's looking at me—not flirty, just genuinely curious, like my answer actually matters—makes me say, "Rosario's. On Twelfth."

He winces. Actually winces, like I've personally insulted his grandmother. "Rosario's? That tourist trap?"

"It's not a tourist trap. It's authentic."

"It's Instagram bait. You want real tacos, you go to Tito's. Cash only. No menu. You eat what they give you."

I lift one brow. "That sounds unsanitary."

"That sounds like you've never had a good taco."

"Still, not sure I'm willing to take my chances at *Tito's*."

I'm smiling now. Actually smiling, at a player, in my treatment room, and I can feel the ice I've carefully built around myself starting to crack at the edges.

"You want real food? Come to Montreal. I'll take you to Schwartz's for smoked meat. Then we'll talk."

"Let me guess… everything in Canada is better, according to you?"

"Not everything." He pauses, a smile tugging at his mouth. "Just most things."

Something about that smile—slow, a little smug, entirely too charming—makes me need to end this conversation immediately.

I clear my throat and straighten my posture. "I think we're done here, Mr. Bishop."

"Zayden."

"Mr. Bishop." I nod toward the door. "Ice, rest, and I'll see you tomorrow. Try not to do anything stupid before then."

He grins—just a flash, there and gone—and it transforms his whole face. Makes him look younger. Less guarded. Almost human.

"No promises," he says.

And then he's gone, the door swinging shut behind him, and I'm standing alone in the exam room wondering what the hell just happened.

I give myself sixty seconds to spiral. Zayden Bishop has a reputation. Cold. Difficult. The guy who doesn't waste words on anyone who isn't directly useful to him.

The man has a reputation for being a brick wall, and he just argued with me about tacos.

My phone buzzes in my pocket. A glance down confirms it's Dana.

He's yours. Full oversight. Don't let him self-destruct.

I type back:

Understood.

I gather my things and head back to my office, but I can't shake the weird, unsettled feeling in my chest. He was supposed to be easy to dismiss. Another arrogant athlete who thinks rules don't apply to him. Another entitled jerk who'd flirt and push and give me every reason to keep my walls exactly where they are.

Instead, he was quiet. Observant. Self-deprecating—which caught me completely off guard.

And he made me laugh.

I stop in the hallway, press my back against the wall, and take a breath of cold, recycled air.

Get it together, Tori. He's a patient. He's a player. He's literally everything you swore off.

The rules exist for a reason. I watched what happened to Carla when her relationship with a player went public—how fast she went from "rising star in sports medicine" to "the woman who slept with number forty-two." She was brilliant. Better than brilliant. None of it mattered once the story became about who she was sleeping with instead of what she could do.

I won't be that story.

I won't be anyone's story except my own.

My phone buzzes again. Winnie, my best friend, who has a sixth sense for when I'm having a moment.

Dinner tonight? That new Thai place?

I type back:

Yes. Need it.

I think about Zayden Bishop and his stupid taco opinions and the way his whole face changed when he smiled, and I hate that I noticed, hate that I'm still thinking about it, hate that some small, reckless part of me is already looking forward to tomorrow's session.

I pocket my phone and head to my office.

He's a patient. That's it. I just need to keep reminding myself of that.

2

PLAYING THROUGH THE PAIN

Zayden

My shoulder is on fire.

I knew it would be—the assessment wasn't gentle, and the new therapist has hands like she's trying to find every single thing I've been hiding. Which, apparently, she did. Six to eight weeks. The number keeps rattling around in my head as I pull out of the training facility parking lot and merge into Manhattan traffic.

Six to eight weeks I don't have.

The windshield wipers beat a steady rhythm against the freezing rain—not quite snow, not quite sleet, just that miserable hybrid that coats everything in a thin layer of ice. I crank the heat. January in New York is brutal, the kind of cold that seeps into your bones and makes old injuries ache. My shoulder throbs in agreement.

I flip on sports radio out of habit. They're talking about the Rangers' defensive line, which means they'll get to us eventually. I switch it off before they can. The last thing I need is to hear some analyst break down everything wrong with my game while I'm stuck in traffic on 47th.

I can't fix what you won't admit is broken.

Victoria Wells, but she goes by Tori, which she'd told me after calling me "Mr. Bishop" the entire session like she was making a point. Dark hair pulled back in a ponytail. Eyes that missed nothing. The kind of face that probably stops most guys in their tracks, all high cheekbones and full lips and zero interest in being looked at.

She didn't offer much of anything except sharp observations and zero tolerance for my bullshit.

I'm not used to that.

Most people look at me and see the jersey. The multi-million dollar contract. The headlines from three years ago that I'm still trying to outrun. They either want something from me or they're afraid of me.

She didn't seem like either.

She looked at me like I was a problem to solve. A body to fix. And when I lied about the pain—*four*, what a joke—she called me on it without blinking. Didn't back down when I tried to stare her into submission, which works on literally everyone else.

And then... tacos.

I don't know why I did that. Small talk isn't my thing. I've spent years perfecting the art of saying nothing, giving nothing, keeping everyone at arm's length so they can't disappoint me or leave me, or decide I'm not worth the effort.

But she was standing there with her tablet, all business, and something made me want to see if I could crack that professional mask. Just a little.

I still can't believe she said Rosario's, like that tourist trap is actual food.

And she smiled. Fought it the whole time, but I caught it—just a flash, just for a second—and it changed her whole face. Made her look less like a physical therapist who was about to ruin my season and more like... I don't know. Someone I'd want to talk to.

Which is dangerous.

I don't have time for dangerous. I have a season to salvage, a shoulder that's falling apart, and a six-year-old who needs me to keep my life together.

Speaking of which.

I check the clock on the dash. 3:15. School gets out at 3:20, and I'm still twelve blocks away. I'm going to be late. Again.

I weave through a yellow light and nearly clip a delivery truck. The driver lays on his horn—a long, angry blare that follows me down the block. Welcome to New York.

By some miracle of traffic lights, I pull up to Maple Street Elementary at 3:23. Not bad. Only three minutes of Maisie standing on the sidewalk wondering if today's the day I don't show up.

She's waiting by the fence when I get there, backpack hanging off one shoulder, clutching a piece of paper to her chest like it's classified information. Her teacher, Mrs. Patterson, waves at me with the tight smile of someone who's definitely noticed I'm late.

"Hey, Maze." I crouch down to her level. "Sorry I'm late. Traffic was—"

"It's okay." She's already walking toward the

car, paper still pressed against her coat.

Okay...

I open the back door for her, help her with the booster seat buckle, and try to get a look at whatever she's holding. She angles away from me.

"What's that?"

"Nothing."

"Doesn't look like nothing."

"It's homework."

"Since when do you hide homework from me?"

She doesn't answer. Just stares out the window as I pull away from the curb, her little jaw set in that stubborn way that reminds me so much of myself it hurts.

I let it go. For now.

The drive home takes twenty minutes through stop-and-go traffic, past bodegas with steamed-up windows and restaurants already setting up for the dinner rush. Maisie doesn't say a word the whole way, just stares out the window at the passing storefronts, her reflection a ghost in the glass.

I try the radio again. Kid-friendly station this time, the kind that plays sanitized pop songs and has DJs who sound aggressively cheerful. Maisie doesn't react. Doesn't sing along like she usually does. Doesn't even complain when a song she hates comes on.

By the time I pull into the driveway of our townhome—three bedrooms, small backyard, a swing set I put together myself using instructions that were definitely written by someone who hates humans—I'm starting to worry.

"Maze."

She looks at me in the rearview mirror.

"Whatever that paper is, you know you can show me, right? I'm not going to be mad."

She considers this. Then, quietly, "Promise?"

"I promise."

She hands it over.

It's a family tree. The kind of project every elementary school teacher assigns without thinking about the kids who don't have neat, simple families to draw. There's a trunk at the bottom with her name on it—MAISIE, written in careful purple crayon. Two branches extend upward.

On the left branch, there's me. She drew me with dark hair and a hockey stick, which is both accurate and kind of adorable.

On the right branch, there's nothing. Just an empty circle where "Mom" should be.

My chest tightens.

"I didn't know what to put," she says, voice small. "Mrs. Patterson said we have to fill in both sides, but I don't... I mean, I don't really..."

"Hey." I turn around in my seat to face her. "You can draw Grandma and Grandpa. Or Aunt Claire. Family doesn't have to mean—"

"It's supposed to be parents." She's not looking at me now. "That's what the worksheet says. Parents."

I take a breath. Let it out slow.

"Then draw what you have," I tell her. "Me. That's enough."

She finally meets my eyes, and the doubt I see there guts me. She's six years old, and she's already learned that some people leave. That promises don't always mean anything.

I did that to her. Me, and Sienna, and every choice we made that put this kid in the middle of our mess.

"Come on," I say, forcing my voice to stay steady. "Mrs. Hendricks is probably making dinner. I think I smell her famous mac and cheese."

Maisie unbuckles herself and climbs out of the car, the family tree clutched in her hand. She doesn't look convinced.

Neither am I.

Inside, Maisie kicks off her boots without untying them, a habit I've given up fighting. They land in a heap by the door, slowly forming a puddle of melted slush on the mat.

And in the kitchen, I find that Mrs. Hendricks is, in fact, making mac and cheese, which was entirely a lucky guess. But it's the from-scratch kind, with the breadcrumb topping Maisie loves. The kitchen smells like butter and comfort, and for a second, I let myself pretend everything is fine.

"There's my girl!" Mrs. Hendricks wipes her hands on her apron and bends down to Maisie's level. She's sixty-three, gray-haired, soft in all the ways that matter. She's been with us for two years, ever since the last nanny quit because my travel schedule was "incompatible with work-life balance." Which, *fair*. "How was school?"

"Fine," Maisie says, which is her answer for everything.

"Just fine? Nothing exciting?"

Maisie shrugs and heads for the living room, the family tree disappearing into her backpack.

Mrs. Hendricks and I exchange a look.

"Rough day?" she asks quietly.

"Family tree project."

"Ah." She nods, understanding immediately. "Poor thing."

I grab a water bottle from the fridge, mostly to have something to do with my hands. "She'll be okay. We'll figure it out."

"Speaking of figuring things out..." Mrs. Hendricks pauses, and I feel the shift in the air before she even continues. "My daughter called this morning. The baby's due in three weeks, but the doctor thinks it might come early. She's been having contractions."

I set the water bottle down. "Is she okay?"

"She's fine. But I might need to fly down to Florida sooner than I thought. Maybe in a week or two." She hesitates. "And I'm not sure how long I'll need to stay. First grandchild, you know. She's nervous, and her husband works long hours, and..."

"Of course." I hear myself saying the words, calm and reasonable, while my brain short-circuits, running through every possible scenario. "Family comes first. You should be there."

"I hate to leave you in a lurch. I know the season is—"

"We'll figure it out," I say again.

Mrs. Hendricks nods, but her expression tells me she hears what I'm not saying. *We'll figure it out* isn't a plan. It's a prayer.

I have no backup childcare. My mom lives in Quebec and can fly down for emergencies, but she can't stay indefinitely—she's got her own life, her own job. Sienna is... not an option. Even if I wanted to ask her, which I don't, she made it clear a long time ago that she's not interested in being a mother more than once or twice a year when it's convenient for her Instagram aesthetic.

"I can ask around," Mrs. Hendricks offers. "I know a few women from church who do childcare. Good people."

"That would be great. Thank you."

She pats my arm, maternal and kind, and goes back to the mac and cheese. I stand there for a minute, staring at nothing, trying to figure out how I'm supposed to hold all of this together.

Injured shoulder. Playoff push. Six-year-old who needs stability more than anything. And now the one reliable thing in our routine is about to disappear.

We'll figure it out.

Right.

Bedtime takes an hour.

Bath, pajamas, teeth brushing, three books (because Maisie negotiates like a tiny lawyer and I'm too tired to fight her down to two), and finally lights out. I sit on the edge of her bed while she burrows under the covers, stuffed elephant tucked under her chin.

"Daddy?"

"Yeah, Maze?"

"If Mrs. Hendricks leaves, who's going to watch me when you're gone?"

My heart clenches. "I don't know yet. But I'll figure something out, okay? You don't have to worry about it."

"But what if you have a game?"

"Then Grandma will come, or I'll find someone else. Someone nice."

She's quiet for a long moment. Then she asks, "What if they leave too?"

I don't have an answer for that. Not one that won't be a lie.

So I just lean down, press a kiss to her forehead, and say the only thing I can, "I'm not going anywhere, Maze. You're stuck with me."

"Promise?"

"I promise."

She nods, seemingly satisfied, and closes her eyes. I wait until her breathing evens out before I slip out of the room, leaving the door cracked and the hallway light on, the way she likes it.

The townhome is quiet once she's asleep. Too quiet.

I ice my shoulder on the couch, twenty minutes on, twenty minutes off, like Tori instructed. I'm a good boy, following her rules.

The TV is on, some hockey recap show I'm not really watching. I should be reviewing game tape, meal prepping, or answering the twelve emails from my agent that have been sitting in my inbox for three days. Instead, I'm just sitting here, ice pack melting against my skin, thinking about a woman who told me I wasn't allowed to lie to her.

I can't fix what you won't admit is broken.

She was talking about my shoulder. I know she

was talking about my shoulder.

But the words keep echoing anyway, bouncing around my skull, finding all the places I don't let anyone see.

I think about Maisie's family tree. The empty circle. The way she said, *it's supposed to be parents*, like she already knows she got cheated.

I think about Mrs. Hendricks, leaving for Florida, and how the ground keeps shifting under my feet no matter how hard I try to hold it still.

I think about Sienna, who decided Maisie and I weren't worth staying for. Who walked out when Maze was six months old and never came back.

I think about my shoulder, and the six to eight weeks I don't have, and the career that's the only reason I can give my kid the life she deserves.

And I think about Tori, with sharp eyes and a sharper tongue, who smiled at me over tacos and didn't flinch when I tried to push her away.

I can't fix what you won't admit is broken.

Maybe she wasn't just talking about my shoulder.

Maybe that's the problem.

3

THE EX FILES

Tori

One week into Zayden Bishop's rehab protocol, and I've learned three things.

One: he's not an easy patient. He pushes back on everything—rest days, ice baths, the number of reps I assign. He argues like it's a sport, negotiating his way through every session like he's trying to find the loophole that lets him skip ahead to being healed.

Two: he's not the arrogant ass I expected. There's no entitlement in the way he pushes. No *do you know who I am* energy.

Three: I look forward to our sessions more than I should.

"You skipped your cooldown again."

It's 3 PM on a Thursday, and Zayden is on my treatment table, his shoulder already showing signs of the inflammation I specifically told him to manage. He's got dark circles under his eyes that he's doing a bad job of hiding, and his jaw is tight in that way I'm starting to recognize as his default setting.

"I had somewhere to be," he says.

"Your daughter's recital isn't for another two hours."

His head snaps toward me. "How do you know about the recital?"

"I know everything, Bishop. It's my job."

He stares at me for a beat, and I watch the corner of his mouth twitch. Not quite a smile, but close. "You're kind of scary, you know that?"

"I prefer 'thorough.'"

"Sure." He leans back on the table, letting me work on his shoulder. "We'll go with *thorough*. If it helps you sleep at night."

I press into a knot near his scapula, maybe a little harder than necessary. He hisses.

"Damn, Tori. At least buy me dinner first before the kinks come out."

I freeze for a second, then roll my eyes so hard I'm surprised they don't get stuck. "That's what you get for skipping cooldowns."

"Noted. Seriously though, you're supposed to wine and dine a guy before you torture him."

"Sorry to disappoint. I don't date players."

He glances back at me, eyebrow raised. "No?"

"Never."

"Probably a good rule." He settles back onto the table, and I get an eyeful of his back—and I work to maintain clinical detachment while staring at a body that should come with a warning label.

His eyes flick to mine—warm and brown—and I can tell he's not done. "So who do you date?"

"Why do you care?"

"I'm injured and bored. Humor me."

I dig my thumb into another knot, and he grunts.

"Lately? No one. My track record is... not great."

"How *not great* are we talking?"

I shouldn't answer. This is personal territory, the kind of conversation that blurs lines I need to keep sharp. But something about the way he asked—curious, not flirty—makes me say, "My last date spent forty minutes talking about CrossFit and then tried to explain why I should let him manage my crypto portfolio."

Zayden snorts. "On a first date?"

"He had a pie chart. On his phone. Ready to go."

"Please tell me you walked out."

"I finished my drink first. I was raised with manners." I move to his rotator cuff, working through the tension there. "Before that, there was a guy who showed up twenty minutes late, complained about the restaurant I picked, and then asked me to Venmo him for my half of the appetizer we shared."

"The appetizer."

"Spinach dip. It was like eight dollars."

He's quiet for a second, and when I glance at his face, he looks genuinely offended on my behalf. "What's wrong with people?"

"If I knew that, I'd be a lot richer and a lot less single."

"So CrossFit guy and Venmo guy. Anyone else in the lineup?"

"There was a radiologist who talked about himself in the third person. And a financial advisor who told me I had 'good birthing hips.'"

Zayden chokes. "He said *what*?" He turns to look at me fully now, disbelief written all over his face. "You're making this up."

"I wish I was."

He shakes his head slowly. "How is that possible? You're—" He stops. Clears his throat. "I mean, those guys sound like idiots."

I catch the stumble. File it away. Pretend I didn't notice.

"Yeah, well." I gesture for him to lie back down. "That's dating in New York. It's a wasteland out there."

"What about before? College, whatever?"

My hands still on his shoulder for just a second. "That's a story for another session. Maybe after you actually complete a full cooldown."

"Bribery. Nice." He settles back onto the table with a half-smile.

"What about you?" I ask, moving to his lower traps. "Since we're sharing."

"What about me?"

"Dating. Relationships. Any Venmo-requesting nightmares in your past?"

He's quiet for a second. "No."

"No nightmares, or no dating?"

"Both." He shifts slightly under my hands. "Haven't really... there hasn't been anyone. Since Maisie's mom."

My hands slow. "Maisie's your daughter?"

"Yeah. Maze is six now." Something in his voice changes when he says her name. Softer. Like the word itself is precious. "She's, uh... she's my whole world, basically."

I process this information while working a knot out of his trapezius. My hands slow. "Wait. You said she's six?"

"Yeah."

"So you haven't dated anyone in six years?" My eyebrows shoot up.

"Haven't had time. Between hockey and Maze, there's not a lot left over." He says it like it's nothing. Like six years of being alone is just a scheduling issue.

I try to do the math. Six years of no—

Okay, no. He's a professional athlete, not a monk. He probably just handles things casually, scratches the itch when he needs to. No strings, no complications, no one who sticks around long enough to meet his kid.

Not that I should be thinking about Zayden Bishop scratching any itches.

But now that I've started, I can't stop. My brain unhelpfully supplies images of what that might look like—those broad shoulders over me, those big hands pinning my wrists, all that controlled intensity unleashed on someone who—

My face goes hot, and my heart kicks up, pounding against my ribs like it's trying to escape.

I'm suddenly very aware of the warmth of his skin under my palms. The way his muscles flex when he breathes. The sheer size of him on my table, how he makes the room feel smaller just by existing in it.

Stop. Stop it right now.

I clear my throat and focus on a knot near his spine, pressing harder than necessary.

"*Câlice*," he mutters under his breath, then catches himself. "Sorry. That one's deep."

"Was that French?"

"Quebecois. It's... not polite."

I smile. "I figured from the tone." I continue pressing, working up my courage. "So, six years is a long time," I say, and thank God my voice comes out steady.

"Tell me about it."

"But you're—" I stop myself, but not fast enough.

"I'm what?"

Ugh. Fine. "A hot single dad, and an NHL star. You must have women lining up."

He's quiet for a beat, and I keep my eyes fixed on his shoulder blade so I don't have to see his reaction to me calling him hot.

"Sure. They line up." His voice is flatter now. "Then they hear I have a kid, and realize I'm not interested in anyone who sees her as an obstacle. That weeds out most of them pretty quick."

We fall into a rhythm—me working through the tension in his muscles, him pretending it doesn't hurt as much as it does. It's become our thing over the past week, this back-and-forth. I push, he resists, I push harder, he eventually gives in. Rinse and repeat.

I shouldn't like it as much as I do.

"How's the pain been?" I ask, moving to his rotator cuff. "Scale of one to ten. Real answer."

"Four."

"Zayden."

He sighs. "Five. Maybe six in the mornings."

"That's almost honest. I'm impressed."

His lips twitch. "I'm a work in progress."

I snort before I can stop myself, and he glances back at me with something that looks dangerously close to satisfaction. Like making me laugh was the goal.

Stop it, I tell myself. *He's a patient. This is professional.*

But it doesn't feel professional. It feels like something else, something I don't have a name for yet, and that's exactly the problem.

Halfway through the session, his phone starts buzzing.

It's on the bench near his gear bag, screen lighting up every thirty seconds with texts and calls he's very deliberately not answering. I watch his jaw tighten each time it goes off, his focus fracturing even as he tries to hold it together.

"You need to take that?"

"It's handled."

It's clearly not handled. The phone buzzes again—a call this time—and I see the name flash on the screen before he reaches over and flips it face-down.

Mrs. Hendricks.

The nanny. I remember her name from his file, from the emergency contacts section I reviewed when I took over his case.

"Bishop."

"I said it's handled."

His voice is sharper than I've heard it, edged with something that sounds like barely controlled panic. I hold up my hands, backing off.

"Okay. Just checking."

He exhales slowly, rolling his shoulder, and the

tension in the room shifts. He's somewhere else now, his head clearly not in the session, and I make a note to cut things short if he can't focus.

"Sorry," he mutters after a minute. "Didn't mean to snap."

"It's fine."

"It's not, but thanks for pretending."

I don't push. Whatever's going on with him, it's not my business. I'm his physical therapist, not his counselor, and the line between those two things is one I need to keep very, very clear.

But I notice things. It's my job to notice things.

I notice the way he checks his phone the second I turn my back, thumbs flying over the screen before he shoves it in his pocket. The way he looks like he's running on fumes, held together by caffeine and sheer stubborn will.

By the time we wrap up, he's distracted enough that he doesn't even argue when I tell him to ice for twenty minutes before he leaves.

Friday afternoon, Coach Reynolds corners me in the hallway.

Donovan Reynolds is old-school hockey—salt-and-pepper hair, a permanent scowl, the kind of guy who's seen everything and is impressed by nothing. He's been coaching for twenty years and probably hasn't smiled since the Obama administration.

"Wells."

"Coach."

He falls into step beside me, which is never a good sign. "Whatever you're doing with Bishop, keep doing it."

I blink. "Sorry?"

"He showed up to cooldown yesterday. First time in months." Reynolds shakes his head, almost disbelieving. "I've been on his ass about it all season. Nothing. You've had him for a week and suddenly he's following protocol like a goddamn choirboy."

I don't know what to say to that. "I just... told him to do it."

"Yeah, well, it's working. Don't screw it up."

He walks off before I can respond, leaving me standing in the hallway trying to figure out if that was a compliment or a threat.

Probably both.

I head back to my office, turning his words over in my head. *Whatever you're doing with Bishop, keep doing it.*

The problem is, I don't know what I'm doing. I'm treating him like I treat any patient—firm boundaries, clear expectations, no tolerance for bullshit. That's it. That's the whole strategy.

But somewhere along the way, it became something else. The banter. The discussions when he's on my table. The way he looks at me sometimes, like I'm a puzzle he's trying to solve.

The way I catch myself looking forward to his sessions.

I sink into my desk chair and stare at the ceiling.

Coach is right. Whatever I'm doing, it's working. Zayden is showing up. He's following proto-col, and making progress.

I should feel proud.

Instead, I just feel worried.

Because I'm starting to care about whether he's okay. Not his shoulder—*him*. The guy who shows up on four hours of sleep because he doesn't know how to let people down. The guy who teases me about my spotty dating history.

The guy I absolutely cannot afford to care about.

I close my eyes, take a breath, and remind my-self of the rules.

4

BEST LAID PLANS

Zayden

The kitchen is warm, the radiator clicking softly in the corner when I enter. And Mrs. Hendricks is crying.

Not dramatic, heaving sobs—just quiet tears streaming down her face as she sits across from me at the kitchen table, twisting a tissue in her hands. She's been with us for two years. She knows Maisie's favorite cereal, her bedtime routine, and which stuffed animal she needs when she's sick. She's the closest thing to stability my daughter has besides me.

And she's leaving.

"The baby came two weeks early," she says, dabbing at her eyes. "A little girl. Six pounds, two ounces. They're both healthy, but my daughter— she's overwhelmed. She needs me."

"Of course she does." I keep my voice steady even as my stomach drops. "Family comes first."

"I'm so sorry. I know the timing is terrible, and Maisie—" Her voice cracks. "I love that little girl."

"She loves you too." I reach across and squeeze

her hand. "When do you need to leave?"

"Saturday. I already booked the flight." She winces. "I know that's only a week; I'm sorry."

"It's okay." It's not okay. Saturday is the day before the road trip starts. "We'll figure it out."

She gives me a watery smile. We both know "figure it out" isn't a plan. And this is an absolute disaster.

Through the doorway, I can hear Maisie in the living room, the soft murmur of her cartoon. She doesn't know yet. Doesn't know that the woman who braids her hair and makes her favorite mac and cheese and knows exactly how she likes her sandwiches cut is about to disappear from her life.

Another person leaving. Another hole to fill.

That night, after Maisie's asleep, I lie in bed and stare at the ceiling.

One week. Mrs. Hendricks leaves Saturday. Road trip starts Sunday—Chicago, Detroit, then Boston. Which means I need someone to watch Maisie from Sunday through Wednesday while I'm gone.

Four days. I need to find coverage for four days.

I rub my hands over my face and try to breathe.

This is the part no one tells you about single parenting. It's not the tantrums or the sleepless nights—it's the logistics. The constant math of making a life work when you're the only adult in the equation. Every road trip is a puzzle. Every person I depend on is one emergency away from leaving me stranded.

I roll onto my side, then onto my back again. The pillow is too flat. The room is too quiet. I can hear my own heartbeat, steady and insistent, reminding me that I'm awake when I should be sleeping.

Tomorrow I have practice, a PT session, and somehow I need to find time to interview nanny candidates. The schedule is a Tetris game I'm losing.

My mind drifts to Tori. It keeps doing that lately.

I think about our session yesterday. The way she dug her thumb into that knot near my spine while I told her about my nonexistent dating life. *Six years. No one since Maisie's mom.*

Her hands had slowed on my back.

No one in six years?

I'd played it off. *Haven't had time. Between hockey and Maze, there's not a lot left over.*

And she'd told me about her disasters. Cross-Fit guy with the crypto pie charts. Venmo guy who made her pay for spinach dip. A radiologist who talked about himself in the third person.

I remember lying on that table thinking—*What is wrong with men?*

Because Tori Wells? She's sharp. Quick. Doesn't miss anything and doesn't let you get away with anything either. She's got this dry humor that catches me off guard, and when she smiles—really smiles—it changes her whole face.

And yeah. She's gorgeous.

Dark hair she wears pulled back, and I keep

wondering what it looks like down. Brown eyes that see way more than I want them to. Soft lips that are usually telling me I'm doing something wrong, which shouldn't be as attractive as it is. She's got curves she tries to hide under scrubs and athletic wear. It doesn't work. I've noticed. Tried not to, but I've noticed.

Any guy with a functioning brain would see Tori and count himself lucky. Instead, she's stuck with finance bros and men who can't cough up eight dollars.

Makes no sense.

I roll onto my side and try to stop thinking about my physical therapist.

It doesn't work.

The nanny interviews are a disaster.

Candidate one shows up that afternoon. Twenty-two, blonde, spends the first ten minutes looking around my townhouse like she's mentally redecorating.

"So," she says, leaning forward, "do the other players ever come over? Like, for team dinners?"

"Sometimes."

"That's so cool. I saw Logan Palmer at a club once. He's even hotter in person." She giggles. "Is he single?"

"I'm looking for someone to watch my daughter. Not set up my teammates."

She blinks like this hadn't occurred to her. "Oh, totally. I'm great with kids. I love babysitting my cousin."

"Thanks for coming in," I say, standing. "I'll be in touch."

I won't.

Candidate two is better. Mid-forties, experienced, and she has good references. She also asks the right questions about Maisie's routine. I'm starting to feel hopeful until—

"I should mention, I'm not available on weekends. Saturdays are date night with my husband, and Sundays are church."

I blink at her. This was all spelled out in the job posting she applied for. "Most of my games are on weekends."

"Oh." She frowns. "I assumed you'd have those covered."

"If I did, I wouldn't need full-time help."

She leaves looking offended.

Candidate three doesn't show up at all. I wait forty-five minutes before accepting she's not coming.

Three interviews. Zero options.

I'm running out of time.

Wednesday night. I'm making spaghetti—one of four things I can cook without burning—when Maisie wanders into the kitchen.

She's already in pajamas even though bedtime isn't for another hour. Stuffed elephant tucked under her arm. She looks small and serious, the way she does when she's working up to something.

"Daddy?"

"Yeah, shadow?"

"Is Mrs. Hendricks really leaving?"

I set down the wooden spoon and crouch to her level. "Yeah, baby. Her daughter had a baby, remember? She needs to go help."

"Like a grandma."

"Exactly like a grandma."

Maisie's forehead wrinkles. "Will the new nanny be nice?"

"I'm going to find someone great." The words come out automatically. "I promise."

But she doesn't nod and accept it like she usually does. She looks at me with those dark eyes—my eyes, everyone says—and her expression goes careful. Guarded.

"You always promise," she says.

It's not an accusation. That's what kills me. She's not angry, not hurt—she's just stating a fact. A statement of how the world works according to Maisie Bishop, age six.

People promise things. Sometimes they keep them. Sometimes they don't.

Best not to expect too much.

My chest squeezes so tight I can barely breathe.

"Hey." I put my hands on her shoulders. "Look at me."

She does.

"I know things have been hard. Your mom not being around, me traveling, people coming and going. I know that's confusing."

She watches me with that too-old expression.

"But I'm going to find someone good. Someone nice who's going to take care of you when I can't be here. And if the first person doesn't work out, I'll keep looking."

"What if there isn't a right person?"

The question hits like a cross-check.

She's not asking about nannies. She's asking about people. Whether anyone besides me is ever going to show up for her and stay.

I don't have a good answer. Can't promise everyone will be reliable. Can't undo the damage Sienna did by walking out, or the parade of caregivers who've come and gone.

All I can do is be here.

"There's always a right person," I say. "Sometimes it just takes a while to find them."

She considers this. "Okay."

I pull her into a hug. She smells like strawberry shampoo and the grape popsicle she had after school.

She's so small. I forget sometimes, because her personality is so big, her observations so sharp. But wrapped in my arms, she's still just a little girl. All knobby elbows and baby-fine hair and a heartbeat I can feel fluttering against my chest.

I want to protect her from everything. Every disappointment, every letdown, every person who might promise something and fail to deliver.

I can't. I know I can't.

But God, I want to.

"I love you, Maisie girl."

"Love you too, Daddy."

She squirms away after a few seconds and wanders to the living room. A minute later, the TV clicks on and I hear *Bluey* in the background.

I stay hunched over the stove and try to focus on pasta sauce.

I hate this. Hate that she hedges her expectations. That she's six and already knows promises don't always mean anything. I'd give anything to unlearn that for her. To show her that some promises actually hold. The problem is, I'm not sure if I believe it myself anymore.

I finish making dinner and pretend I'm fine.

Later, after she's asleep, I grab my phone and do what I should've done three days ago.

I text Bree Lockwood—my teammate Archer's wife.

> Hey, huge favor. My nanny is leaving for Florida to watch her grandbaby. And the road trip starts Sunday. Any chance you could take Maze until we're back Wednesday?

The three dots appear almost immediately. Bree's a night owl, thank God.

> Of course. She can stay here with the twins. They'll love it.

Relief floods through me so hard my hands shake.

> You're a lifesaver. I owe you.

> You owe me nothing. Hockey families stick together. But Zay—you need a full-time nanny. What's your long-term plan?

I stare at the screen.

I don't have a long-term plan. I have duct tape and prayers and a list of agencies that can't find anyone who meets my "scheduling requirements."

I set the phone down and tip my head back against the couch.

This time, I got lucky. Bree came through. But she's got her own kids, her own life. I can't keep asking her to bail me out every time something falls apart.

And something always falls apart.

My phone buzzes again with a different number.

Tori:

I picture her on the other end—probably in her own apartment, maybe curled up on a couch of her own, phone in hand. Does she text all her patients reminders? Probably. She seems like the type to be thorough.

But it's nine-thirty at night. She's thinking about my shoulder at nine-thirty at night.

I shouldn't read into that. I read into it anyway.

Three dots. Then:

I set the phone down.

Crisis averted. For now. But I'm one emergency away from total disaster, and I know it.

And somehow, a text from Tori is the first thing that's made me smile all week.

I'm in trouble.

5

TURBULENCE

Tori

The team charter is already buzzing by the time I board. Someone's playlist is competing with a poker argument in the back, and there's a catering spread that could feed a small army.

It's... a lot.

The plane is sleek and spacious, leather seats arranged in clusters of four with tables between them. I grab a window seat near the front and try to look like I belong here.

"First time on the bird?"

I look up. Logan Palmer is grinning down at me, all golden retriever energy and floppy hair. He's twenty-three, a rookie forward, and possibly the most cheerful person I've ever met. The guys call him "Cupcake" because he's too pretty for hockey—all blue eyes, dimples, and a jawline that belongs in a skincare commercial.

"That obvious?"

"You're sitting up straight, and you haven't touched the snacks." He drops into the seat across from me. "Rookie mistake. Always hit the snacks before Woody gets here. Guy's a bottomless pit."

"Woody?"

"Archer Lockwood. Aka Woody." He shrugs. "We're not that creative with nicknames."

I smile. "Yours is Cupcake, right?"

He grins. "Yeah. I've embraced it. Gotta lean into your brand, you know?" He waggles his eyebrows. "Also, the puck bunnies love it."

I snort. "Of course they do."

He leans back, propping his feet on the seat next to me. "So you're Bish's shadow now, huh? How's that going?"

"Bish?"

"Bishop. Bish. Zay. Daddy. Daddy Z." He ticks them off on his fingers. "The man has endless nicknames because he's too easy to mess with."

My face goes hot at *Daddy*, and my brain takes a sharp left turn into territory it has no business visiting.

"You okay?" Logan's watching me with a curious expression. "You look kind of flushed."

"Fine. Just, um, it's warm on the plane." I fan myself like an idiot. "So. You were saying. About Bishop."

"Right. He giving you trouble?" Logan grins. "He gives everyone trouble."

"He's... a work in progress."

Logan laughs, the dimple in his left cheek appearing. "That's diplomatic. Banks just calls him a stubborn asshole."

"Banks isn't wrong."

The voice comes from behind me, deep and dry.

I turn to find Banks Callahan settling into the seat behind Logan. He's huge—six-four, built like a brick wall, with a permanent scowl that makes him look like he's contemplating murder at all times. Defenseman. Twenty-nine. The guys call him "The Wall" for obvious reasons.

"Don't scare the new girl, Walls," Logan says.

"I'm not new," I point out. "I've been here two months."

"You're new until you've survived a road trip." Banks pulls out a book and doesn't look up again. "Good luck."

More players file on. Archer Lockwood—Woody—drops into a seat near the back and immediately passes out, hat pulled low over his eyes. I remember he's got two-year-old twins at home. The man probably hasn't slept in two years.

Grayson Reed swaggers past with two other guys I don't know well, laughing too loud at something on his phone. He catches my eye and winks.

I don't wink back.

"Reed's a tool," Logan says, following my gaze. "Ignore him."

"Noted."

"I mean it. He's got a thing for—" Logan stops abruptly, looking past me. "Hey, Bish."

I turn. Zayden is standing in the aisle, duffel over his shoulder, looking at Logan's feet propped on the seat next to me.

"Palmer," he greets Logan with a cool tone.

"What's up?"

"You're in my seat."

Logan blinks. "Since when do you sit in the

front?"

"Since now."

There's a beat of silence. Something passes between them—some kind of guy telepathy I'm not fluent in—and then Logan grins, pulling his feet down.

"All yours, man." He stands, shooting me a look I can't quite read. "Catch you later, Tori."

He ambles toward the back of the plane, leaving me alone with Zayden, who slides into the seat Logan just vacated.

"You didn't have to do that," I say.

"Do what?"

"Kick him out."

"I didn't kick him out." Zayden stows his bag under the seat. "I just wanted this seat."

"You said yourself you don't usually sit up front."

He shrugs, not meeting my eyes. "Maybe I like the view."

I don't know what to do with that, so I do what I always do when Zayden throws me off-balance—I deflect.

"How's the shoulder?"

Dark eyes assess me. "We're not working right now."

"I'm always working. Scale of one to ten."

He finally lets his guard drop, and there's something tired in his expression. More than tired. Heavy.

"Four," he says.

"Zayden."

"Fine. Five." He leans his head back against

the seat. "Can we not do this right now? I just need to..."

He trails off. Closes his eyes.

I should push. It's my job to push. But something about the way he looks—worn thin, like he's holding himself together through sheer stubbornness—makes me say, "Okay."

He opens one eye. "Okay?"

"We can do it later. Get some sleep."

He stares at me for a long moment, like he's waiting for the catch. Then he closes his eyes again, and something in his posture loosens. Just a fraction.

"Thanks," he murmurs.

I pull out my tablet and pretend to review his file while he rests. But I'm not really reading. I'm too aware of him—the warmth of his body in the confined space, the steady rhythm of his breathing, the way his face looks softer when he's not bracing for a fight.

Stop it, I tell myself. *He's a patient.*

I'm getting really tired of that reminder.

An hour into the flight, I get up to use the restroom.

The back of the plane is a whole different world. Banks is still reading, somehow making a paperback look intimidating. Archer hasn't moved, dead to the world. A group of guys is playing cards at one of the tables—I recognize the backup goalie, Martinez, and a couple of defensemen whose names I haven't learned yet.

"Hey, Doc!" one of them calls. "You play poker?"

"She's not a doctor, dumbass," another one says. "She's a PT."

"Same thing."

"It's literally not."

"I'm good," I say, sidestepping toward the bathroom. "Thanks, though."

"Come on, we need a fourth. Arch's useless, and Banks won't play."

"Because you cheat," Banks says without looking up from his book.

"I don't *cheat*, I *strategize*—"

I slip into the bathroom before I get pulled into whatever that argument is becoming.

When I come out, I take my time getting back to my seat, stretching my legs. That's when I see Zayden.

He's not sleeping anymore. He has his phone in his hand, and he's FaceTiming someone. A small face fills the screen—dark hair, dark eyes, the same stubborn set to her jaw that I recognize from her father.

This must be his daughter.

I slow down without meaning to.

"I'll be back Wednesday night, Maze," Zayden is saying, his voice so soft I barely hear it over the plane noise. "That's only three sleeps."

"I know." Her voice is small, tiny through the phone speaker. "But that's a lot of sleeps."

"I know it is. But Lily and Luke's mom is taking good care of you, right?"

"I guess." A pause. "She makes weird mac and

cheese. It has green stuff in it."

Zayden's mouth twitches. "Green stuff?"

"I think it's broccoli? I didn't eat it."

"Maze, you have to eat what she makes."

"But it was *green*, Daddy."

"I hear you. But you still have to be polite, okay? She's doing us a big favor."

Maisie's quiet for a second. Then, softer, "I don't want Lily and Luke's mom. I want *you*."

My chest tightens. I should keep walking. This is private—a moment I have no business witnessing. But my feet won't move.

Zayden's whole face changes. The exhaustion is still there, but underneath it is something raw. Tender. The kind of love that doesn't need words.

"I know, shadow," he says. "I want to be there too. But I have to work, and—"

"I know." She sounds resigned. Six years old and already resigned. "It's okay, Daddy. I'm okay."

"You sure?"

"Yeah." A pause. "Can you bring me something? From the trip?"

"What do you want?"

"Something good. You pick."

"Deal." He presses his hand against the screen, and she does the same on her end—their version of a goodbye hug, I realize. "I love you, Maze. Be good."

"Love you too. Bye, Daddy."

The screen goes dark.

Zayden sits there for a second, staring at his phone, and I see him take a slow breath. Composing himself. Putting the armor back on.

I slide back into my seat and stare out the window at the clouds below, trying to get my heart rate under control.

I don't want Lily and Luke's mom. I want you.

That was sweet.

I think about what Zayden told me in our session—six years of single parenting, no help, no partner, just him and a little girl who's learned too young that people leave. I think about the way his voice went soft when he talked to her, the way his expression softened for her.

He's not what I expected.

When I first saw his file, I thought I knew the type. Pro athlete, famous, probably the kind of guy who thinks the rules don't apply to him, who's never heard "no" from a woman and wouldn't know what to do with it if he did.

But that's not Zayden. Not even close.

He's stubborn, sure. He pushes back on everything I tell him. But it's not entitlement—it's desperation. He can't afford to be injured because he can't afford to stop. There's no safety net. No backup plan. Just him, holding everything together through sheer force of will.

And I'm starting to—

"Deep thoughts?"

I jump. Zayden tucked his phone back into his pocket and is looking at me.

"Just reviewing files."

"Liar. The screen's been dark for ten minutes."

Damn. He caught me.

"Fine. I was thinking about... work stuff."

"Work stuff." He raises an eyebrow. "Compelling."

"It's very compelling. Lots of spreadsheets."

"Uh huh." He doesn't look convinced. "You always this bad at lying?"

"I'm an excellent liar."

"You're really not."

I narrow my eyes at him. "How would you know? Maybe I've been lying to you this whole time. Maybe your shoulder is fine, and I just like torturing you."

"I knew it." His mouth quirks. "So it is a BDSM thing, this kink of yours."

"Oh my God, are you ever going to let that go?"

"Probably not."

I shake my head, but I'm fighting a smile. This is dangerous—the banter, the ease of it. Every time I'm with him, my walls get a little lower. My rules get a little blurrier.

"How's Maisie?" I ask, and immediately regret it.

His expression flickers. "You saw that?"

"I wasn't eavesdropping. I just—I walked past."

"It's fine." He runs a hand through his hair. "She's... she's having a hard time. New place, new people. She doesn't do well with change."

"Most kids don't."

"Most kids don't have a revolving door of caregivers." He says it flatly, like it's just a fact. "Mrs. Hendricks was with us for two years. That's the longest anyone's lasted besides me."

"What about her mom?"

The question slips out before I can stop it. I

know she's not really in the picture, but I don't know the details.

Zayden's jaw tightens. "What about her?"

"Sorry. That's none of my business."

"No, it's—" He stops. Starts again. "Sienna left when Maze was six months old. Decided motherhood wasn't for her. She shows up maybe twice a year, makes a big fuss that she's back, takes some photos for Instagram, and disappears again."

"That's..." I don't have words for what that is. *Shitty*.

"It is what it is. We're fine." He doesn't sound fine. "Maisie's better off without someone who doesn't want to be there. I just wish—"

He stops himself.

"What?"

"Nothing." He shakes his head. "Forget it."

I should let it go. This is way past professional territory. But something about the way he's looking at me—tired and unguarded in a way I've never seen him—makes me push.

"You can tell me. If you want."

He's quiet for a long moment. When he speaks, his voice is rough. "I just wish she didn't have to learn these hard life lessons so young. That people can hurt you, that people leave. She's *six*. She should believe in... I don't know. Happy endings. Instead, she looks at me like she's waiting for me to disappear too."

The ache in his voice hits me somewhere deep. His accent is thicker when he's tired, I've noticed. The hard consonants soften, certain words tilting toward French—which shouldn't be as attractive as it is.

"You're not going to disappear," I say softly.

"I know that. But she doesn't. Not really." He looks at me, and there's something raw in his eyes. "How do you teach a kid to trust when the world keeps proving to her that people don't stay even when they say they're going to?"

I wish I could fix it, but I can't. So I just sit with him in the silence, thirty thousand feet above the ground, and let him not be okay for a minute.

It feels like the least I can do.

The hotel in Chicago is nice—team money nice, which means I have a room bigger than my apartment with a view of the lake that probably goes for five hundred a night.

I should sleep. It's almost ten, and Zayden has an early morning session before the game. But my brain won't shut off, so I end up in the hotel bar, nursing a glass of wine and staring at nothing.

"Can't sleep either?"

I look up. It's Zayden.

He slides onto the stool next to me, signaling the bartender. "Sparkling water. Lime."

"Sparkling water?" I raise an eyebrow. "Wild night."

"Game day tomorrow." He shrugs. "Gotta stay sharp."

"And yet you're in a bar at ten instead of resting."

"Could say the same about you." He nods at

my wine glass. "What's your excuse?"

"Brain won't shut off."

"Yeah." He scrubs a hand over his face. "I know that feeling."

The bartender sets down his water, and he takes a long sip, staring at nothing. Up close, under the low bar lighting, I take him in. The defined jaw, the dark stubble, lips that I'm absolutely not staring at. The way his throat moves when he swallows.

I take a sip of wine and look away before I do something stupid, like keep looking. "Rough night?" I ask.

"Rough week. Rough month." He rolls the glass between his palms. "Rough year, if I'm being honest."

"Want to talk about it?"

"Not really." He glances at me sideways. "But I probably will anyway because apparently I have no filter around you."

"Must be my trustworthy face."

"Must be." He's quiet for a second, staring into his glass. "The agency called today. Still no candidates who meet my 'scheduling requirements.'" He makes air quotes. "Which is code for 'you're a single dad with a hockey schedule, and no one wants to deal with that.'"

"What about family?"

"My mom's in Quebec. She offered to come down for a few weeks, but she's got her own life. I can't ask her to put everything on hold." He takes another sip. "And Sienna's family..."

"Not an option?"

"Her parents think I ruined her life by getting

her pregnant. So no, not an option. Plus they also work full-time."

"That's..." I search for the right word. "Unfair."

"Life usually is." He says it without self-pity, just stating a fact. "I'll figure it out. I always do."

"You will," I say, taking a sip of my wine.

He glances my way with an apologetic half-smile. "Sorry for venting about my mess."

"Maybe I don't mind your mess."

The words hang between us. I didn't mean them to sound like... that. But now they're out there, and Zayden is looking at me with an expression I can't quite read.

"Careful," he says quietly. "That almost sounded like you care."

"I'm your physical therapist. Caring about my patients is literally my job."

"Is that what this is? Professional concern?"

No. It's not. And we both know it.

"I should go," I say, reaching for my wallet. "Early morning."

"Tori."

I stop.

"Thank you," he says. "For listening. For... I don't know. Being here."

"You don't have to thank me."

"I know. That's why I'm doing it." He holds my gaze for a beat too long. "Goodnight."

"Goodnight, Bishop."

I walk away before I can do something stupid, like stay.

In my hotel room, I lie in bed and stare at the ceiling.

I keep thinking about him taking that seat across from me on the plane. I keep thinking about the bar. The way he said *apparently I have no filter around you* like it surprised him as much as it surprised me.

I keep thinking about the way he looked at me when I said *maybe I don't mind your mess.*

Like he wanted to believe me but couldn't let himself.

This is a problem. A big, complicated, career-ending problem. Because somewhere between the easy banter and the late-night confessions, I'm starting to see him as more than a patient.

I see a man I want to do deeply unprofessional things to. A six-foot-two French-Canadian snack I'd like to ride into the sunset, and wow, okay, I really need to get laid if this is where my brain goes after one late-night conversation.

...which is a thought I'm going to blame on the wine and never revisit again.

The problem is, I want to help him. Not because it's my job, but because it's *him*.

That's terrifying.

I roll over, punch my pillow into shape, and try to sleep.

It doesn't work.

6

TOUCH-STARVED

Zayden

Iwake up thinking about her.

Not in a dirty way—although, let's be honest, my brain went there around midnight and I had to take a cold shower like some kind of horny teenager. No, this is worse. I'm lying in a hotel bed in Chicago, staring at the ceiling, replaying the way she said *maybe I don't mind your mess* like it meant something.

It didn't mean anything. She's my PT. She's paid to care about my well-being. That's literally her job description.

I scrub a hand over my face and try to get my head on straight.

Here's the thing, it's been a long time since I've been with anyone. And I don't mean dating—I already told Tori about that wasteland. I mean *with* someone. Physically. The last time was... I don't even want to do the math. Let's just say Maisie was a lot younger and I was a lot more willing to make questionable decisions.

So maybe that's the problem. I'm touch-starved

and projecting. Tori puts her hands on me every single day, works out the knots in my shoulders, presses her fingers into my muscles, and my body is confusing clinical contact for something else.

I just need to get laid. That's all this is. Find someone fun, blow off some steam, and stop obsessing over a woman who calls me "Mr. Bishop" when she's annoyed and looks at me like I'm a puzzle she's not sure she wants to solve.

Simple.

Except even as I think it, I know it's bullshit. Because it's not just the physical stuff. It's the way she laughs, unguarded and real. The way she calls me out. The way she sat with me at that bar last night and just... listened. Like what I had to say actually mattered.

When's the last time someone did that?

I roll out of bed and hit the shower, turning the water as cold as I can stand. Game day. I need to focus. Chicago's been playing well this season, and my shoulder needs to hold up for three periods of hockey.

Everything else can wait.

My pre-game session with Tori is at ten.

She's already set up in the training room they've given us at the arena—portable table, her kit laid out with military precision, tablet open to what I assume is my file. She's wearing team athletic wear today, a Knights T-shirt that stretches across her chest and a pair of black leggings. Her hair is pulled back, and she looks up when I walk in with an expression that's pure business.

"Bishop. On the table."

"Good morning to you too."

"It'll be a good morning when I confirm your shoulder isn't going to fall apart during the game." She pats the table. "Shirt off. You know the drill."

I do know the drill. That's the problem.

I pull my shirt over my head and settle onto the table, trying to think about literally anything other than the fact that her hands are about to be on me. Hockey. I'll think about hockey. Defensive strategies. Forechecking patterns. The way Chicago's goalie tends to cheat left on breakaways.

Tori's hands press into my shoulder, and my brain goes blank.

"How'd you sleep?" she asks, working along my trapezius.

"Fine."

"Liar. You've got tension knots that say otherwise."

I smirk. "Maybe I just have a stressful job."

"Mm-hmm." She digs into a particularly tight spot, and I bite back a groan. "What were you stressed about?"

You. At the bar last night. The way you looked at me like I was more than a shoulder to fix.

"Just game stuff," I say. "Chicago's been hot lately."

"Their offense is ranked third in the league right now." She moves to my rotator cuff. "But their defense has been shaky. If you can get pucks on net, you'll have chances."

I twist to look at her. "You've been studying their stats?"

"I study everyone's stats." She pushes me back down. "Stay still. And don't look so surprised. I'm good at my job."

"Never said you weren't."

"You were thinking it. That face you made—" She mimics an expression of exaggerated shock. "Very flattering."

"I was not making that face."

"You absolutely were."

I'm smiling now, and I don't even know when that happened. She has this way of pulling it out of me, even when I'm trying to be serious.

Her hands move lower, working along my spine, and I have to close my eyes. Focus. Hockey. Chicago's penalty kill. Their power play setup. Anything except the warmth of her palms and the way her fingers find every spot that needs attention like she's got a map of my body memorized.

"You're distracted today," she says.

Understatement. "I'm fine."

"You keep tensing up. More than usual." She pauses. "Is this about last night? The bar?"

Yes. "No."

"Because if I said something that made things weird—"

"You didn't." I open my eyes and meet hers. "It wasn't weird. It was... nice. Talking to you."

Something shifts in her expression. Just for a second. Then she looks away, clearing her throat.

"Well. Good." She steps back. "You're cleared. Shoulder's holding up. Don't do anything stupid out there, and ice between periods."

"Yes, ma'am."

"I mean it, Bishop. I'll be watching."

"I know you will."

Our eyes meet again, and there's a moment—just a beat—where neither of us looks away. The air feels heavier. Charged.

She breaks first, turning to her tablet, and I grab my shirt and get the hell out of there before I say something I can't take back.

Game time.

There's nothing like it. The roar of the crowd, the cold bite of the ice, the way everything else just... stops. When I'm on the ice, I'm not a single dad with a failing childcare situation and a woman I can't stop thinking about. I'm just a hockey player. Pure instinct. Pure focus.

The first period is a grind. Chicago comes out hard, testing our defense, and I spend most of my shifts battling along the boards. My shoulder holds—it's tight, but functional. Tori's protocol is working.

In the second period, we start finding our rhythm. Banks breaks up a two-on-one and sends the puck up the ice to Logan, who dekes past a defender before feeding it to Archer at the point. Archer one-times it, and I'm already moving toward the net, stick ready.

The rebound comes right to me.

I don't think. I just shoot.

Top corner. Glove side.

The goal light goes red, and the guys swarm me, knocking their helmets into mine, gloves pounding my back. Logan's yelling something I can't hear over the crowd, and Banks gives me a nod—which, from him, is basically a standing ovation.

And then, without meaning to, I look toward the bench.

She's there. Standing behind the medical staff area, tablet in hand, and she's—

Smiling. Actually smiling. At me.

My chest does something stupid, and I have to force myself to focus on the faceoff.

Get your head in the game, Bishop. She's just doing her job.

In the third period, I get an assist on Logan's game-winner. We take it 3-2, and the locker room after is loud and chaotic, the way it always is after a road win. Coach gives us a brief speech—"Good start, don't get comfortable, Detroit's next"—and then it's showers and postgame routines.

I take my time, letting the hot water work out the soreness in my muscles. By the time I'm dressed, most of the guys are lounging around, half in their suits, riding the high of the win.

"Hell of a shot, Bish." Logan drops onto the bench next to me, hair still wet. "That release was filthy."

"Got lucky."

"Lucky my ass. That was pure skill, and you know it."

Grayson Reed wanders over, towel around his waist, smirking at something on his phone. I tense automatically. Reed's got this way of making everything feel like a transaction—like he's always calculating what he can get out of any situation.

"Did you see that hot PT during warm-ups? Standing by the boards?" Grayson grins. "I'm telling you, she was into it. Couldn't take her eyes off the ice."

"She's paid to watch us," Banks says flatly, not looking up from his book. "It's her job."

"Nah, man, this was different. She was *watching*." Grayson makes a crude gesture that makes my jaw clench. "I'm gonna shoot my shot. Girl like that, legs for days, ass that won't quit—"

"Reed." My voice comes out harder than I intended.

He looks at me, eyebrows raised. "What?"

"She's staff. Show some respect."

"Whoa, easy, Daddy Z." He holds up his hands, grinning. "Didn't realize you'd already called dibs."

"I didn't call—" I stop myself. Take a breath. "Just keep it professional. She doesn't need that crap from us."

Logan shoots me a look I can't read. Banks definitely notices—I see his eyes flick up for a half-second before going back down. Archer's inhaling a protein bar in the corner, headphones in, checked out from the conversation entirely.

Grayson shrugs, unbothered. "Whatever, man. Your loss."

He saunters off toward the showers, and I have to physically unclench my fists.

"You good?" Logan asks quietly.

"Fine."

"Because that seemed like—"

"I said I'm fine."

He holds up his hands in surrender. "Chill, Zay. Just asking."

I finish getting dressed in silence, trying to shake off the anger coiling in my chest. It's not even about Grayson. Not really. It's about the fact that he said out loud what I've been trying not to think, and hearing someone else talk about Tori like that made me want to put my fist through his face.

That's not a normal reaction to have about your physical therapist.

That's a problem.

I find her in the training room for my post-game check.

She's got resistance bands laid out, her tablet open, all business as usual. But when I walk in, she looks up, and there's something warmer in her expression than I'm used to seeing.

"Nice game," she says. "That goal was impressive."

"You saw it?"

"I told you I'd be watching." She gestures to the table. "Let's see how the shoulder held up."

I settle onto the table, still in my suit pants and white undershirt. She moves closer, and I catch a whiff of her shampoo—something floral, subtle—and then her hands are on my shoulder, and I'm right back where I started this morning.

Except now she's close enough that I can see the small freckle on her jaw. The way her lashes cast shadows on her cheeks when she looks down.

"Movement looks good," she murmurs, rotating my arm slowly. "Any pain during the game?"

"Nothing major. Tightness in the third, but it loosened up."

"That's normal. We'll ice tonight and reassess in the morning before Detroit."

She leans in to check my range of motion, and I notice her pause. Just for a second. Her eyes flick to my neck, then away.

"What?" I ask.

"Nothing. You just—" She steps back, cheeks going pink. "You smell good. Whatever that body wash is."

I chuckle softly while Tori turns pink.

"Ignore me. Sorry. That was weird." She steps back, suddenly very interested in her tablet. "I mean—compared to some of the guys who come in here post-game, you're practically a breath of fresh air. Martinez nearly knocked me out last week."

"High praise."

"Don't let it go to your head."

But I'm grinning now, and she's fighting a smile. This is what I like about being around her, the ease of it, the way she makes me feel like I can just... be.

"You're all set," she says, still not quite meeting my eyes. "Ice for twenty, then get some sleep. We travel early tomorrow."

"Yes, ma'am."

I hop off the table, and our hands brush as I

reach for my jacket on the chair behind her. Just the barest contact—her fingers against mine—and it shouldn't mean anything.

But we both freeze.

She looks up at me. I look down at her. And for a second, neither of us moves.

"Tori..."

"You should go," she says quietly. "Get some rest."

She's right. I know she's right.

I nod once and depart.

Back in my hotel room, I ice my shoulder and stare at the ceiling.

I keep replaying it flashes from tonight. The way she smiled when I scored, the way she said *you smell good* like it slipped out before she could stop it, the way her breath caught when our hands touched.

That wasn't nothing. I don't care what my rational brain says—that wasn't nothing.

And here's the thing I keep coming back to— this isn't about being touch-starved. It's not about needing to blow off steam or find someone to scratch an itch.

It's about *her*.

I think about Grayson's comment, and my hands curl into fists again.

Legs for days. Ass that won't quit.

He's not wrong. She's gorgeous. But that's not what this is about, and the fact that he reduced her to body parts makes me want to break something—preferably his face.

Tori Wells is smart and sharp and funny as hell. She's the first person in years who's made me feel like maybe I don't have to carry everything alone. And I'm lying in this hotel room at midnight, icing my shoulder, coming to terms with a realization I've been dodging for days.

I'm falling for her.

And I have absolutely no idea what to do about it.

7

WHAT HAPPENS IN DETROIT

Tori

We win in Detroit.

Not just win—we demolish the Kings, 5-1, with Zayden getting two assists and Logan scoring his first career hat trick. The entire team is buzzing with the kind of energy that only comes from a road trip going better than expected.

I watched from my spot near the bench, tracking Zayden's shoulder mechanics every shift, telling myself that's the only reason I couldn't take my eyes off him.

It wasn't. But it's the lie I'm going with.

By the time I'm halfway back to the hotel, my phone buzzes.

Logan

Team drinks. Hotel bar then somewhere else. You're coming.

Me

I don't remember agreeing to that.

I stare at my phone and smirk. He sent me cupcake emojis. Cute. Logan's cute. But he's not the hockey player who's been occupying my thoughts lately. That would be a different one entirely—one with a trim waist and broad shoulders I want to climb. I reapply my mascara and add lip gloss. Just because.

One drink. That's all.

The bar is loud and crowded, a local spot the guys found that has good reviews and an impressive beer selection. We commandeer a back corner—Logan, Archer, Banks, a couple of the younger guys whose names I keep mixing up, Zayden, and me.

I'm on my second vodka soda, which is already one more than I planned, and I'm feeling... good. Loose. The tension I've been carrying for days is finally starting to ease, helped by Logan's ridiculous play-by-play commentary and Archer's dry observations.

"—and then Grayson just stood there," Logan

says, gesturing wildly. "Like a statue. I'm screaming at him to move, and he's just—"

"I was screening the goalie," Grayson protests. "It's called strategy."

"It's called being in my way."

"Your shot went in!"

"Because I'm talented. Not because of your so-called strategy."

I laugh, and Zayden catches my eye from across the table. He's nursing a beer—just one, I've noticed—and there's a softness to his expression I don't usually see. Relaxed. Happy. It's nice to see this side of him.

"Having fun?" he asks, leaning closer so I can hear him over the noise.

"Maybe."

"That's practically a ringing endorsement coming from you."

"What's that supposed to mean?"

"It means you're usually so..." He searches for the word. "Controlled. It's nice to see you let loose."

"I'm always loose."

He raises an eyebrow.

"Okay, fine. I'm occasionally loose. In specific circumstances. With adequate preparation."

He laughs—actually laughs, head tipped back, throat exposed—and the sound makes my stomach flip. "There she is. The woman who needs a flowchart to have fun."

"I don't need a flowchart. I just like to be prepared."

"For fun?"

"For everything."

He shakes his head, still smiling. "You're something else, Tori Wells."

I don't know what to say to that, so I take another sip of my drink and try to ignore the warmth spreading through me that has nothing to do with vodka.

An hour later, I'm exiting the restroom when someone stops right in front of me, blocking my path.

"Hey there."

I glance up at a guy in his thirties, decent-looking, wearing a button-down that's trying too hard. He's got that confident smile that suggests he's used to women responding well to him.

"Hi," I say, trying to edge around him.

"I'm Ryan."

"Okay."

He laughs like I've said something charming instead of dismissive. "Feisty. I like it. Can I buy you a drink?"

"I'm good, thanks."

"Come on. One drink. You look like you could use some company."

"I have company." I nod toward the table where the guys are still deep in conversation. "I'm with them."

Ryan follows my gaze, then turns back with a knowing smirk. "The hockey players? What are you, a puck bunny?"

I bristle. "I'm a physical therapist."

"Even better." He leans closer, and I catch a whiff of cologne that's way too strong. "So you're good with your hands?"

Oh, for the love of—

"Look, Ryan, I appreciate the offer, but I'm not interested."

"You don't even know me yet."

"I know enough."

His smile falters, then hardens. "What, you think you're too good for me? I'm just trying to be nice."

"And I'm just trying to get back to my table. Alone."

He doesn't move. If anything, he shifts closer, leaning into my space. "You know, most women would be grateful for the attention."

His hand lands on my waist, and I go rigid, anger and discomfort warring in my chest.

"Touch her again." Zayden's voice dropped to something low and lethal. He didn't raise it—didn't need to. He just moved into Ryan's space, all six-foot-two of barely leashed violence, and the temperature in the hallway plummeted. "And we're going to have a problem you won't walk away from."

Ryan goes still, then drops his hand.

I turn and see Zayden. His eyes are fixed on Ryan with an expression I've never seen before—cold, focused, deadly.

"We're just talking, man," Ryan says, but he pulls back.

"No. You were leaving."

"Excuse me?"

"She told you she wasn't interested. Twice." Zayden's hand comes to rest on my lower back—

warm, steady, grounding. "So now you're going to walk away, find someone else to bother, and forget this conversation happened."

Ryan looks between us, calculation flickering behind his eyes. He's sizing Zayden up—the height, the build, the fact that he's clearly not someone to mess with—and whatever math he's doing, the answer comes up in our favor.

"Relax, dude." He moves away, straightening his shirt.

Zayden takes a step forward, and Ryan practically trips over himself backing away, disappearing into the crowd.

For a moment, neither of us moves. Zayden's hand is still on my lower back, and I can feel every point of contact like a brand.

"You okay?" His voice is softer now.

"I'm fine. I had it handled."

"I know you did." He doesn't move his hand. "But I wanted to help anyway."

I turn to face him, and he's closer than I realized. Close enough that I can see the flecks of gold in his dark eyes, the tension in his jaw, the way he's looking at me like he's barely holding himself back from something.

"Thank you," I say quietly.

"Anytime."

I push the strap of my purse onto my shoulder with hands that aren't quite steady. "I think I'm done for the night," I manage.

"Yeah." He's still watching me with that intense expression. "I'll walk you back."

"You don't have to—"

"I know. I want to."

The night air hits me as we step outside, cold and sharp. January in Detroit isn't any friendlier than January in New York—the wind cuts through my jacket, and I shiver before I can stop myself.

Without a word, Zayden shrugs off his jacket and drapes it over my shoulders.

"I'm fine," I protest, even as I pull it tighter. It smells like him—that body wash, plus something warm and distinctly *Zayden*.

"You were shivering."

"It's cold."

"Hence the jacket."

I don't argue. Partly because I'm tired, partly because wearing his jacket feels good in a way I refuse to examine.

We walk in silence, footsteps echoing on the empty sidewalk. The hotel isn't far—maybe ten minutes—but the distance feels both endless and not nearly long enough.

"That guy was an asshole," Zayden says.

"Yeah."

"Does that happen a lot? Guys not taking no for an answer?"

I shrug. "Sometimes. It's an occupational hazard of existing while female."

His jaw tightens. "That's not okay."

"No. But it's reality."

We walk another half block in silence. I'm hyperaware of everything—the brush of his sleeve against mine, the fog of our breath in the cold air, and the electricity humming between us.

"Tori."

There's something about the way he says my name. The slight softening of the 'T', the way it sounds almost like "Toh-ree" when he's not paying attention. Quebec bleeding through the edges of his accent.

I look up. He's stopped walking, and we're almost at the hotel—the entrance maybe fifty feet away, light spilling from the lobby onto the sidewalk.

"Yeah?"

He doesn't answer. Just looks at me with an expression I can't quite read—intense and searching, like he's working something out.

"What?" I ask, suddenly nervous.

"Nothing. I just..." He takes a breath. "I should get you back."

"Okay," I breathe.

Neither of us moves.

The moment stretches, thick with something unspoken. He's looking at my mouth—I know because I'm looking at his, cataloging the shape of his lips, wondering what they'd feel like against mine.

I should step back. Say goodnight. Walk inside and put distance between us before I do something I can't undo.

I don't move.

He lifts his hand slowly, giving me time to pull away, and brushes a strand of hair from my face. His fingers graze my cheek, feather-light, and I forget how to breathe.

"Tori," he says again, and my name sounds like a confession.

"Yeah?"

His thumb traces along my jaw, tilting my face up. We're inches apart. I can feel the warmth of his breath, see the way his pupils have gone dark.

This is a bad idea. I have rules. I have—

His eyes search mine, asking a question I don't know how to answer.

Then he steps back.

Cold rushes in where his warmth used to be, and I have to stop myself from swaying toward him.

"I should let you get some sleep." His voice is rough, strained. "Early flight."

I nod, not trusting myself to speak.

He gestures toward the entrance. "After you."

We walk the last fifty feet in charged silence. The elevator ride is worse—we stand on opposite sides of the small space like we're afraid of what might happen if we get too close. The air feels thick, electric, and I can barely breathe around the tension. I have never in my life wanted to kiss someone this badly. Every nerve in my body is tuned to him, cataloging the rise and fall of his chest, the clench of his jaw, the way his hands are shoved in his pockets like he doesn't trust them to behave. I dig my nails into my palms and watch the floor numbers climb.

My floor comes first. I step out and turn.

"Goodnight, Zayden."

"Goodnight, Tori." His eyes hold mine as the doors slide closed. "Sleep well."

I stand in the hallway for a long moment, hand pressed to my chest, heart hammering against my ribs.

Then I walk to my room on unsteady legs, let myself in, and lean back against the door.

I can still feel his fingers on my jaw, the warmth of his jacket around my shoulders, the way he looked at me like I was something precious he wanted but wouldn't let himself take.

I need a cold shower to wash away the feeling of *almost*—almost kissing him, almost giving in to something I know I shouldn't want but absolutely do.

Zayden Bishop almost kissed me tonight.

And I would have let him.

8

LITTLE SHADOW

Zayden

Maisie launches herself at me the moment Bree opens the door.

"Daddy!"

I catch her, swinging her up into my arms, and the tightness I've been carrying in my chest for the past few days finally loosens. She smells like strawberry shampoo and maple syrup, and she's wearing a glitter crown that's shedding sparkles everywhere.

"Hey, shadow. Nice crown."

"Lily made it for me. We're princesses."

"I can see that."

Bree leans against the doorframe, looking exhausted but amused. She's got a twin on each hip—Luke is half-asleep, and Lily is waving a glitter-covered wand that explains a lot about the state of my daughter's hair.

"She was an angel," Bree says. "Honestly, the easiest kid I've ever watched. Unlike these two monsters."

"I no monster!" Lily protests. "I'm fairy godmother."

"My mistake."

I shift Maisie to my other arm. "Thanks again, Bree. Seriously. I owe you."

"You don't owe me anything." But her eyes are knowing when they meet mine. "How was the trip?"

Three wins. Two assists. A hat trick for Logan. And yet somehow, none of that is what replays in my head when I think about the trip. No, my brain is stuck on a sidewalk in Detroit, Tori's face tilted up toward mine, her breath catching when I touched her jaw, waiting for a kiss I didn't let myself take.

"Good," I say. "We swept all three."

"I saw." She's still watching me with that look—the one that says she sees more than I'm saying. Archer probably tells her everything. "Well. Let me know if you need anything else."

"Actually, the agency's sending someone tomorrow. Another interview."

"That's great. Fingers crossed."

"Yeah." I'm not holding my breath, but I don't say that. "Thanks again."

Maisie waves goodbye to the twins as I carry her to the car, chattering the whole way about princesses, glitter, and how Luke tried to eat a crayon while Lily told on him.

Maisie. Home. Real life.

This should feel like enough. It's always been enough.

I don't know why it suddenly feels like I'm missing something I never had in the first place.

The gym at the practice facility is nearly empty when I get there the next morning. Just Banks on the bench press and Logan doing something with a resistance band that looks vaguely obscene.

"Bish!" Logan grins when he sees me. "You're alive!"

"Why wouldn't I be alive?"

"I don't know. You disappeared pretty quick from the bar the other night." He waggles his eyebrows. "Walk Tori back to the hotel?"

I grab a set of dumbbells and don't look at him. "She was tired."

"Uh-huh." He grins at me, waiting.

"It was late."

"Sure." His smile grows.

"Drop it, Cupcake."

Banks racks his bar and sits up, wiping his face with a towel. He doesn't say anything, but I can feel him watching me.

"What?" I ask.

"Nothing."

"You're staring."

He shrugs and picks up his water bottle. "You seem tense."

"I'm not tense."

"You're doing bicep curls like the dumbbells insulted your mother."

I look down. My grip is white-knuckled, and I'm moving way too fast. I force myself to slow down, but my jaw is still tight.

"I'm fine," I say.

Banks nods like he doesn't believe me for a second. "Cool."

We lift in silence for a while. Logan eventually gets bored and wanders off to bother Archer, leaving me alone with Banks—who's never been one for unnecessary conversation. It's one of the things I like most about him. He doesn't push.

Except today.

"The PT," he says, not looking at me. "Tori."

My hands tighten on the dumbbells again. "What about her?"

"Nothing." He starts loading plates for his next set. "Just noticed you two have been spending a lot of time together."

"She's my PT. That's literally her job."

"Right."

"It is."

"I said right." He's built like a tank and about as expressive as one. But I've known him long enough to read the micro-expressions other people miss. And right now, he's fishing.

I set the dumbbells down harder than necessary, muttering something in French that would make my grandmother cross herself. "Is there something you want to say?"

Banks finally looks at me. His expression is unreadable—it always is—but there's something almost sympathetic in his eyes.

"Just be careful," he says. "That's all."

"There's nothing to be careful about."

He doesn't argue. Just turns back to the bench press and starts his next set.

I grab heavier dumbbells and try to burn off the

restless energy crawling under my skin. It doesn't work.

The nanny candidate shows up at two o'clock.

Her name is Hannah Torres. She's in her late forties with a warm smile, and a practical bun. She's got fifteen years of experience, glowing references, and a calm energy that reminds me of Mrs. Hendricks.

"I understand your schedule is unpredictable," she says, sitting across from me at the kitchen table. Maisie's at school, so we've got the place to ourselves. "That's not a problem. I raised two kids while working full-time. Flexibility is my middle name."

"Weekends?"

"Available."

"Road trips? Sometimes I'm gone five or six days at a time."

"Also fine." She folds her hands on the table. "Mr. Bishop, I'll be honest with you. I'm at a stage in my life where I want work that matters. Helping a single father raise his daughter? That matters."

I study her, waiting for the catch. The red flag. The thing that's going to disqualify her like all the others.

"My daughter's been through a lot of changes," I say slowly. "People coming and going. She takes a while to warm up."

"That's understandable. Trust is earned, not given."

"She's got a routine. Specific foods, a stuffed elephant she can't sleep without, a nightlight that stays on. I'm not interested in someone who's going to come in and try to start changing—"

"Mr. Bishop." Her voice is gentle but firm. "I've worked with kids who had far more complicated needs than a favorite stuffed animal. Your daughter sounds lovely."

I let out a breath. "When can you start?"

She hesitates, and my stomach drops. Here it comes.

"I have a vacation planned. A non-refundable trip to see my sister in California—I booked it months ago, before I knew I'd be interviewing." She looks genuinely apologetic. "I leave tomorrow and will be back in five days. I could start the Monday after?"

Five days. I can figure out five days.

"That works," I say, and we shake hands.

It's not perfect. But it's close. I just need to survive five more days of duct tape and prayers.

How hard can that be?

It's midnight. Maisie's asleep and the townhouse is quiet.

I'm lying in bed, staring at the ceiling, replaying the same moment on a loop. Tori's face in the streetlight. The way her breath caught when I touched her. The way she looked at me like she was waiting—hoping—for me to close the distance.

I should've kissed her.

I grab my phone off the nightstand and do something stupid.

The app downloads in seconds. Red icon, little flame. I've never used it before—never needed to—but Banks mentioned it once, saying it's what guys use when they just want something casual. No strings. No complications.

That's what I need. Something casual to get this out of my system. Tori cannot and will never be my hookup buddy. No matter how hot she is. She has rules. I have a daughter. This thing between us—whatever it is—can't go anywhere.

So I'll find someone else. Burn off the tension. Move on.

I start scrolling.

Blonde, twenty-six, likes hiking and mimosas. Pretty. But I'm not interested.

Brunette, thirty-one, marketing executive. Great smile. Doesn't do anything for me.

Redhead, twenty-eight, "looking for fun." Objectively attractive. I feel nothing.

I keep scrolling. Face after face, profile after profile. Some of them are beautiful. Some of them seem interesting. A few of them are exactly the type I would've gone for, before Maisie, before everything got complicated.

None of them are her.

I stop on a brunette with a sharp jaw and dark eyes. She's pretty—really pretty—and something about her reminds me of...

No.

I close the app and stare at the ceiling.

This is pathetic. I'm a grown man lying in bed

at midnight, swiping through strangers, trying to convince myself that any of them could make me forget the way Tori looked at me in Detroit.

They can't. I know they can't.

My mother would have opinions about this. She'd tell me—in rapid-fire Quebecois French that I'd pretend not to fully understand—that I'm too stubborn, too closed off, too much like my father. She'd also tell me that when I find the right woman, I'll know.

I'm starting to think she might be right.

I delete the app.

The icon disappears, and I drop my phone on the mattress, pressing the heels of my hands into my eyes.

The thing is, even if I was willing to risk it—even if she was—I've got Maisie. My daughter has watched enough people walk in and out of her life. I'm not going to introduce someone new unless I'm sure, absolutely sure, that they're going to stay.

Tori's not a sure thing. She can't be. We work together. This thing between us might just be proximity and tension and two people who've been alone too long.

It might be nothing.

Except it doesn't feel like nothing.

I lie there in the dark for a long time, not sleeping, not doing anything except accepting the truth I can't outrun anymore.

I'm falling for someone I can't have.

And I have absolutely no idea what to do about it.

9

WINE AND CONFESSIONS

Tori

"**O**kay, spill."

Winnie doesn't even wait for the wine to arrive. We're barely settled into our corner booth at Rosario's—yes, the tourist trap, sue me—and she's already got her elbows on the table, chin in her hands, staring at me like I'm a puzzle she's about to crack.

"Spill what?"

"Don't play dumb with me, Victoria. You texted me 'I need wine and carbs immediately' at 3 PM. That's code for something happened."

"Maybe I was just hungry."

"At 3 PM. After a road trip with a bunch of hockey players." She narrows her eyes. "Try again."

The waiter appears with our wine—a pinot grigio for me, a malbec for Winnie—and I take a very long sip before answering.

"How's Derek?" I ask, deflecting.

"Derek is Derek." She waves a hand dismissively. "But we're not talking about Derek. We're talking about whatever has you looking like you haven't slept in three days and maybe got hit by a truck. A hot truck. A truck you want to get hit by again."

I quirk an eyebrow in her direction. "That metaphor got away from you."

"I know. I'm workshopping it." She leans forward. "Seriously, Tor. What happened?"

I open my mouth. Close it. Take another sip of wine.

The thing is, I've been holding this in for days. The whole flight back from Detroit, I sat three rows behind Zayden and pretended to be fascinated by the in-flight magazine while my brain replayed the almost-kiss on a loop. Then I spent two days at work carefully avoiding being alone with him, which is hard when you're literally assigned to touch him every morning.

I need to talk about this. I'm going to explode if I don't.

"I almost kissed Zayden Bishop," I blurt out.

Winnie's eyes go wide. "I'm sorry, you what?"

"Or he almost kissed me. I don't know. We almost kissed each other. On a sidewalk. In Detroit."

"Oh my God." She's grinning now, that delighted grin she gets when gossip exceeds her expectations. "Start from the beginning. Don't skip anything."

So I tell her.

I tell her about the plane, how he kicked Logan out of the seat so he could sit by me and said, *maybe I like the view*. I tell her about overhearing his FaceTime with Maisie, how cute he is with her. I tell her about running into him at the hotel bar that first night, the way he said, *apparently I have no filter around you*, like he couldn't help but be honest.

"Wait, wait." Winnie holds up a hand. "And then what?"

"Then I said something stupid about not minding his mess, and he looked at me like..." I trail off, not sure how to describe it. "Like he wanted to believe me but was afraid to."

"Tori." She clutches her chest dramatically. "This is the most romantic thing you've ever told me, and you once dated a guy who wrote you a poem."

"That poem was terrible."

"It really was. Keep going. What happened in Detroit?"

I tell her about the game, watching from the bench, and how I ended up at a bar with the team even though I knew it was a bad idea.

"A bar with hockey players." Winnie shakes her head. "Living dangerously."

"It gets worse."

I tell her about that douchey guy who stopped me in the back hallway of the bar. The way Zayden appeared out of nowhere and said, *touch her again and we're going to have a problem*, in a voice that made the guy practically trip over himself backing away.

"I think I'm attracted to your hockey player," Winnie says. "Is that weird? That's probably weird."

"He's not *my* hockey player."

"Sure, Jan. Continue."

I tell her about the walk back to the hotel. His jacket around my shoulders. The way he stopped under the streetlight and looked at me like I was something he wanted but couldn't have.

"He touched my face," I say, and my voice comes out quieter than I intended. "Brushed my hair back and just... let his fingers linger on my jaw. And I thought he was going to kiss me. I wanted him to kiss me. I tipped my face up toward his, but then he stepped back and said he should get me back to the hotel, and we rode the elevator in total silence. I've been losing my mind ever since."

Winnie is quiet for a long moment, which is alarming because Winnie is never quiet.

"Okay," she finally says. "I have questions."

"Of course you do."

"Question one: what's he like?"

I smile, thinking how in the world to explain Zayden. Bish. Daddy Z.

"Well, he's French-Canadian, which means he swears in two languages and has opinions about hockey that border on religious."

Winnie's already got her phone out, thumbs flying. "Zayden Bishop, right? Let me see what we're working with here."

"Win, you don't need to—"

"Oh." She stops scrolling. Tilts her head. "Oh, Tori."

"What?"

She turns the screen toward me. It's a team photo from some charity event—Zayden in a fitted suit, jaw sharp enough to cut glass, dark eyes smoldering.

"This is your patient?" Winnie zooms in. "This man right here? With the whole... brooding lumberjack meets Calvin Klein model thing going on?"

"He doesn't look like that in real life."

"Liar." She swipes to another photo. Him on the ice this time, helmet off, hair damp with sweat, jersey stretched across shoulders that suddenly seem way broader than I remembered. "God, look at his hands. Those are dad hands. I bet he builds furniture on the weekends."

"I wouldn't know."

"And that jawline? That's genetic unfairness, is what that is." She sighs dramatically. "No wonder you have a crush."

"I don't have a crush."

She gives me a look that says she's known me too long for this. "Sure you don't. Question two: on a scale of one to ten, how badly do you want to sleep with this man?"

"Winnie."

"It's a valid question! I need to assess the situation."

I drain the rest of my wine and signal the waiter for another. "Eleven. Maybe twelve."

"Noted." She grins like this news delights her. "Question three: is there an actual rule against this? Like, in the employee handbook?"

I've thought about this. A lot. "Not... explicitly. There's stuff about professional conduct and not engaging in relationships that could create conflicts of interest. But it's vague. It's not like there's a line that says 'no banging the hockey players.'"

"So you wouldn't get fired."

"I honestly don't know. Maybe not fired, but..." I sigh. "It's complicated. I've worked really hard to be taken seriously in this field. If people found out I was sleeping with a player, that's all anyone would see. I'd be 'the PT who slept with Zayden Bishop,' not 'the PT who's good at her job.'"

Winnie's expression softens. "Like what happened to that woman you told me about."

"Carla Drake." Even saying her name makes my stomach twist. "She was brilliant, Win. Like, genuinely brilliant. I interned with her my junior year—she was the head PT for the basketball program, and everyone knew she was going places. NBA, Olympics, whatever she wanted."

"What happened?"

"She fell for one of the players. He was a senior, projected first-round draft pick, charming as hell." I trace the rim of my wine glass, remembering. "They thought they were being careful. Secret relationship; no one at work knew. Except someone always knows, right? His ex-girlfriend found out and went all scorched earth on social media. Screenshots of texts, photos, the whole thing."

Winnie winces. "Oh no."

"Yeah, it was a nightmare. The university launched an investigation. Carla maintained nothing happened until after she was no longer his PT, which might have even been true—she'd transferred him to another therapist. But it didn't matter. The optics were bad, and the athletic department needed someone to blame."

"Let me guess. Not the star basketball player."

"He got a stern talking-to and a reminder to

'be more discreet.' That's it. He got drafted that spring, signed a multi-million dollar contract, and last I checked, he's starting for the Celtics." I take a long sip of wine. "Carla got fired. Quietly, so they could avoid a lawsuit, but fired. And word travels fast in sports medicine. Every time she applied somewhere, they'd already heard the rumors. She couldn't get hired anywhere near a professional team again."

"That's... that's so unfair."

"Last I heard, she's doing physical therapy at a retirement home in Ohio. Which is fine; it's good work, but—" I shake my head. "She was supposed to be working with Olympians. She was that good. And one relationship ended all of it."

Winnie is quiet for a moment. "But that was her situation. Different circumstances, different—"

"Different how? She was a woman in sports medicine who got involved with an athlete. I'm a woman in sports medicine who's..." I trail off.

Winnie reaches across the table and squeezes my hand. "Tori." She sets down her wine glass, her expression softening. "I love you. You know I do. But I've heard of Zayden Bishop. Everyone's heard of Zayden Bishop."

My stomach tightens. "What's that supposed to mean?"

"It means he's got a reputation. The guy used to be tabloid fodder—women, club photos, all of it. Just because he's got a cute kid doesn't mean he's suddenly a saint."

"That was years ago. Before Maisie was born, mostly."

"Mostly." She raises an eyebrow. "And you know this how? Because he told you? Of course he's going to seem like a good guy when he's trying to get into your pants."

"He's not trying to get into my pants."

She meets my eyes with a knowing look. "He almost kissed you on a sidewalk in Detroit."

"And then he walked away."

"Which could mean he's a gentleman, or it could mean he's playing the long game." She sighs. "Look, I'm not saying he's definitely a player. I'm saying you don't actually know him. You know the version of him he shows you during your sessions and team trips. That's not the same thing."

I want to argue, but the words stick in my throat. Because she's not wrong. I don't know him—not really. I know he loves his daughter. I know he's funny when he lets his guard down. I know the way his jaw tightens when he's holding something back.

But do I know what he does when I'm not around? Who he texts at midnight? Whether there's a rotation of puck bunnies waiting for him after every home game?

The idea of it makes my skin crawl.

"I've seen how these guys operate," Winnie continues, gentler now. "Different girl in every city, the whole thing." She gives me a sad smile. "I just don't want you to get hurt."

I stare into my wine glass, my chest tight.

The thing is, she's right to be cautious. I know she's right. Zayden Bishop does have a past—a documented, photographed, tabloid-covered past.

And the fact that he's been sweet to me doesn't erase any of that.

"I'm not going to do anything stupid," I finally say. "I have rules, remember?"

"I know you do." Winnie reaches across the table and squeezes my hand. "Just... keep them. Okay? At least until you know for sure what kind of guy he really is." My chest does something complicated at her words.

"I will." But even as I say it, I'm not sure I believe it.

"So what are you going to do?"

"Nothing." I say it firmly, as if saying it out loud will make it true. "I'm going to do my job, maintain my boundaries, and get through the rest of this season without doing anything stupid."

"And if he tries to almost-kiss you again?"

I don't have an answer for that.

Because the truth is, if Zayden Bishop looks at me the way he looked at me in Detroit, I'm not sure I'll be strong enough to walk away.

"Let's order food," I say instead. "I need something to absorb this wine before I start making confessions I can't take back."

Winnie lets me change the subject, but her expression says this conversation isn't over.

It's probably not.

But for now, I'm going to eat my weight in tacos and pretend that my carefully constructed life isn't on the verge of falling apart.

I get to the training facility early.

Not because I spent half the night staring at my ceiling, replaying Winnie's warning on a loop. And definitely not because I need time to compose myself before a certain French-Canadian hockey player shows up for his 8 AM session.

I'm just... punctual. That's all.

The hallways are quiet this early—just the hum of the HVAC and the distant sound of someone in the equipment room. I drop my bag in my office, pull my hair back into a ponytail, and head toward the training room to set up.

That's when I hear his voice.

Low, tense, coming from around the corner near the vending machines. I slow down without meaning to.

"She's not a prop for your Instagram, Sienna." Zayden's voice is barely controlled, like he's fighting to keep it level. "You can't just show up when it's convenient—"

Silence. He's listening to whatever she's saying on the other end.

I should keep walking. This is private. None of my business.

Too bad my feet won't move.

"Fine." The word comes out flat. Resigned. "Sunday. Two hours. Supervised. I'll be there the whole time."

More silence. Then he laughs, but there's no humor in it.

"Yeah, Sienna. I know you're her mother. You remind me every time you want something." A pause. "I'll text you the details."

The silence stretches, and I realize the conversation is over. I'm about to get caught eavesdropping like some kind of creep. I start walking again, rounding the corner at what I hope looks like a natural pace.

Zayden's leaning against the wall next to the vending machine, phone still in his hand, head tipped back, eyes closed. He looks... wrecked. There's no other word for it. The mask he usually wears—the stoic, untouchable thing—is gone, and what's underneath is raw.

Then he opens his eyes and sees me.

For a second, neither of us moves. I watch him pull himself together in real time, watch the walls go back up brick by brick. It's impressive, honestly. And also a little heartbreaking.

"Everything okay?" I keep my voice neutral. Casual. Like I didn't just hear his entire conversation.

"Maisie's mom." He pushes off the wall, shoving his phone in his pocket. "She wants a visit."

I nod. Don't push.

"She does this," he says, and I can tell he didn't mean to keep talking but can't seem to stop. "Shows up every few months, plays mom for an afternoon, takes some photos for her followers. And Maze gets her hopes up every single time, and then Sienna leaves, and I'm the one picking up the pieces."

"I'm sorry," I murmur, truly unsure what I can say that would help.

"I'm just not sure what else I can do."

"You just be there to support your daughter." I

hold his gaze. "That's what you do."

He stares at me for a long moment. "You make it sound simple."

"It's not. But you're good at it."

His guard dropped for half a second—surprise flickering through those dark eyes, maybe gratitude—and I felt the pull between us. Dangerous. Undeniable. It would be so easy to close the distance. To reach out and touch his arm, his face, to offer comfort that has nothing to do with being his PT.

I don't.

"I'll see you at eight," I say instead, and continue down the hallway before I do something I can't take back.

I spend the next twenty minutes setting up equipment I don't need and reorganizing supplies that are already organized. Anything to keep my hands busy and my brain from spiraling.

Winnie's voice keeps echoing in my head. *I've heard of Zayden Bishop. Everyone's heard of Zayden Bishop.*

But the man I just saw in that hallway—the one who looked gutted at the thought of his daughter getting hurt again—that's not the guy from the tabloids. That's not a player running game or working an angle.

That's just a dad trying to protect his kid.

Unless that's exactly what he wants me to think.

Ugh, I'm exhausting myself.

I check the clock. 7:45. Fifteen minutes until Zayden's session. I need to get out of my own head.

The weight room is just down the hall, and I can hear music thumping through the door—something with heavy bass that probably violates several noise ordinances. When I push inside, I find Logan Knight doing bicep curls in front of the mirror, mouthing along to what sounds like a Taylor Swift remix.

He catches my eye in the reflection and grins, not even slightly embarrassed.

"Tori! Just who I wanted to see!"

"Why does that sound ominous?"

He racks the weights and grabs his water bottle. "What brings you to my domain?"

"Your domain?"

"I'm here more than anyone else. That makes it mine. I've claimed it." He gestures grandly at the rows of equipment. "Welcome to Casa de Cupcake."

I snort. "That's not a thing."

"It's absolutely a thing. I'm making it a thing." He drops onto a bench and pats the space next to him. "Sit. Chat. Tell me all your secrets."

"I don't have secrets."

"Everyone has secrets. Mine is that I actually hate cardio but I do it anyway because Coach will kill me if I don't." He takes a long swig of water. "See? Sharing is caring."

I sit down, shaking my head. Logan is ridiculous, but he's also weirdly easy to be around. No subtext, no hidden agenda—just golden retriever energy and a complete lack of filter.

"How's the knee feeling?" I ask, because I should at least pretend I'm here for professional reasons.

"Good. Great. Ready to score a million goals." He flexes dramatically. "I'm basically superhuman at this point."

"Uh-huh. And the stretching protocol I gave you?"

"I'm doing it. Mostly. Sometimes." He catches my look. "Okay, I did it once and then forgot. But I'll do it today! Right after this. Scout's honor."

"Were you ever actually a scout?"

"No, but I feel like I have the vibe, you know?"

I laugh despite myself. "You're impossible."

"Impossibly charming, you mean." He grins, then tilts his head, studying me. "You okay? You seem... I don't know. Tense."

"I'm fine."

"That's what Bish says when he's not fine. You two are spending too much time together." He says it casually, but there's something sharper underneath—curiosity, maybe. "Speaking of which, how's his shoulder? He gonna be good for the playoffs?"

"He's progressing. Ahead of schedule, actually."

"That's because you're a genius." Logan points at me with his water bottle. "Seriously. Whatever you're doing, keep doing it. I've never seen him actually follow a protocol before. Usually, he just grunts at whoever's treating him and does whatever he wants."

"He grunts at me plenty."

"Yeah, but he also listens. That's new." Logan's grin turns sly. "Maybe he just likes you."

My face heats before I can stop it. "He's my patient."

"Didn't say he wasn't." But he's watching me now with an expression that's a little too knowing for comfort. "Relax, Tori. I'm just messing with you. Bish is... he's a good guy, under all the grumpy. He's just been through a lot."

"I know."

"Do you?" Logan's voice softens slightly. "Because a lot of people don't bother to find out. They see the reputation, buy into the rumors, and they think they know the whole story. But that's not him. That's never been him."

I think about Winnie's warnings. About all the reasons I have to be careful.

Then I think about Zayden in the hallway, looking wrecked over a phone call about his daughter.

"I know it's not," I say quietly.

Logan nods, seemingly satisfied. "Good. Then we're cool." He stands up, stretching his arms over his head. "Now if you'll excuse me, I have to go pretend to do cardio for thirty minutes so Coach doesn't murder me."

"Good luck with that."

"Thanks. I'll need it." He heads for the door, then pauses, looking back. "Hey, Tori?"

"Yeah?"

"For what it's worth? I think you're good for him. Whatever this is." He waves vaguely between us—meaning me and the absent Zayden, I assume. "I've known Bish for two years. He doesn't let people in. Like, ever. But with you..." He shrugs. "I don't know. He seems lighter or something. Less like he's carrying the whole world."

He's gone before I can respond, leaving me alone in the weight room with Taylor Swift still thumping through the speakers and my heart doing something complicated in my chest.

He seems lighter.

I check the clock. 7:58.

Time to go put my hands on a man I definitely don't have feelings for and pretend everything is normal.

This should be fun.

10

PURPLE DRESS

Zayden

Sienna is late.

Not by much—fifteen minutes—but Maisie has been standing by the window for the past hour, watching every car that passes as if it might be the one. She's wearing the purple dress she picked out herself, the one with the sparkles on the sleeves, and she brushed her hair herself this morning, even though it took her twenty minutes and the part is crooked.

She wanted to look pretty for her mom.

I wanted to cancel this whole thing. I'm pretending to read the newspaper at the kitchen table, but the words blur together. I haven't turned a page in twenty minutes.

"She's here!" Maisie's voice is bright and hopeful, and it hits me right in the chest. She's already running for the door before I can say anything, and I follow, bracing myself for whatever version of Sienna is about to walk into our lives.

The answer: Instagram Sienna.

She steps out of an Uber looking like she's

about to walk a red carpet. Hair perfectly styled, makeup flawless, outfit probably straight from her latest haul video—looking like she spent more time getting ready than she will spend here with Maisie today. She's holding her phone in one hand—already filming, I realize—and she crouches down as Maisie runs toward her.

"There's my baby girl!"

The hug looks good. It'll look great on camera, actually—the loving mother reuniting with her daughter, sunlight catching the tears in her eyes. Except I know those aren't real tears. And I know that Maisie's arms around her neck are stiff and uncertain, like she's not quite sure this is allowed.

"Say hi to the camera, Maze!" Sienna angles the phone so they're both in frame. "We're having a girls' day!"

"Put it away." I'm already moving, stepping between the phone and my daughter. "No cameras."

"God, you're so—"

"No. Cameras." I hold her gaze until she huffs and shoves the phone in her pocket.

Behind me, I feel Maisie's hand slip into mine. A silent thank you. She squeezes once, and I squeeze back.

"Relax, I'm not posting it. It's just for me." She gives me that look, the one that dares me to argue. We've had this fight before. I've threatened lawyers, she's called me controlling, and somehow she always finds a way to post anyway, with Maisie's face conveniently angled away or covered with a sticker.

I let it go. Pick my battles. But my jaw aches

from clenching.

"Okay!" Sienna pockets the phone and stands, finally looking at me. "Zayden. You look... tired."

"Long season."

"Mm." She doesn't ask about the season. Doesn't inquire about anything, really. "So, the park? I thought we could do the park."

"Yeah, that's what Maisie wanted."

"Perfect. Let me just—" She pulls out her phone again, typing something. "Sorry, one sec. Work thing."

Maisie looks up at me, and I see the hope in her eyes dim just a little. I put my hand on her shoulder and squeeze.

This is going to be a long two hours.

Thankfully it's not that cold today. The park is three blocks away. Maisie walks between us, holding my hand but not Sienna's—though Sienna doesn't seem to notice. Probably because she chatters the whole walk—about her apartment, her brand deals, some drama with a friend Maisie's never met. She's not ignoring Maisie on purpose. She just doesn't know how to talk to a six-year-old.

"And then Chloe had the audacity to—" She stops, glancing down. "You okay, baby?"

Maisie nods.

"Good." Sienna pats her head like she's a puppy and keeps talking.

Sienna asks about school, about her friends, about what she's been up to. The questions are right. The tone is right. But her eyes keep drifting to her phone buzzing in her pocket.

"That's great, baby," she says when Maisie mentions her art project. "I'd love to see it sometime."

She won't. We both know she won't. But at least she's saying the words.

We make it to the playground eventually. Maisie runs for the slide—her favorite—while Sienna settles onto a bench and immediately starts editing photos. I stand near the bottom of the slide, close enough to catch Maisie if she needs me.

"Daddy! Watch!"

"I'm watching."

She climbs to the top, waves at me, and slides down with a shriek of joy that makes something in my chest loosen. This is what matters. This moment right here—my kid being happy, being a kid.

"Sienna." I don't turn around. "You should watch her."

"I am watching."

"You're looking at your phone."

"I can multitask."

I bite back the response I want to give and focus on Maisie, who's already climbing back up for another go.

For a few minutes, things are almost okay. Maisie plays, I watch, Sienna does whatever Sienna does. It's not ideal, but it's manageable.

Then Maisie falls.

It happens fast—her foot slips on the ladder, and she tumbles sideways, landing hard on the wood chips. I'm moving before she even starts crying, but I hear it—that sharp wail that means she's actually hurt, not just surprised.

"Hey, hey, I've got you." I scoop her up, checking the damage. Skinned knee, not deep, but bleeding enough to scare her. "You're okay, it's just a scrape."

"It hurts, Daddy."

"I know. Let me see." I sit down on the edge of the playground structure, settling her in my lap so I can get a better look. The cut isn't bad—a little antiseptic and a bandage and she'll be fine. But she's crying now, big heaving sobs, and I pull her against my chest and let her get it out.

Sienna appears next to us, phone in hand. "What happened?"

"She fell. Skinned her knee."

"Oh." She looks at Maisie—crying, bleeding, clinging to me—and her expression shifts into something I can only describe as inconvenienced. "Baby, you're okay. It's just a little cut."

Maisie cries harder.

"Come here." Sienna reaches for her, and for a second, I think maybe I've misjudged. Maybe she's going to actually comfort her daughter, actually be a mother for five minutes.

But Maisie doesn't reach back. She burrows deeper into my chest, and Sienna's hands drop.

"She's so dramatic," she mutters, rolling her eyes. "It's barely even bleeding."

I bite my tongue so hard I taste copper.

"I've got her," I manage. "Why don't you see if you have some tissues in your purse?"

"Fine." She turns and walks away, already back

on her phone before she's taken three steps.

I hold Maisie until the sobs slow to hiccups. "You're okay," I murmur against her hair. "I've got you. You're okay."

"Mommy didn't even care."

The words are so quiet I almost miss them. But I don't. And they carve something out of my chest that I'm not sure I'll ever get back.

"She cares," I lie. "She just doesn't know how to show it sometimes."

Maisie doesn't respond. Just presses her face harder into my shirt and holds on.

Sienna leaves an hour early.

"Something came up with work," she says, not quite meeting my eyes. "A brand thing. I have to take a call."

On a Sunday. Sure. I guess it's possible, but not very likely.

"Say bye to Mommy, Maze."

Maisie is sitting on the couch, bandaged knee visible beneath the hem of her purple dress. She doesn't get up. Doesn't run to hug her mom goodbye.

"Bye, Mommy."

"Bye, baby girl!" Sienna blows a kiss from the doorway. "I'll see you soon, okay? We'll do this again!"

She won't. We both know she won't. But I don't say that.

"Thanks for coming," I say instead, because I

was raised with manners even when I don't want to use them.

"Of course. She's my daughter too, Zayden."

I take a deep breath and let it out slowly.

The door closes behind her, and I stand there for a second, fists clenched at my sides, breathing through the anger that's threatening to swallow me whole.

Then I turn around, and Maisie is just... sitting there. Not crying. Not angry. Just quiet, staring at her hands like they hold the answers to questions she's too young to be asking.

"Hey, shadow." I cross to the couch and sit down next to her. "You hungry? We could make mac and cheese. The good kind, with the bread-crumbs."

"I'm not hungry."

"Okay. What about a movie? We could watch *Encanto* again."

"I don't want to."

I don't push. Just sit there with her, shoulder to shoulder, and let the silence stretch.

After a long moment, she says, "She didn't even look at my dress."

My heart cracks clean in half.

"I saw it," I tell her. "You look beautiful, Maze. The most beautiful girl in the whole park."

"But she didn't see."

"I know." I put my arm around her, and she leans into me—small and warm and so much stronger than any kid should have to be. "I'm sorry."

"It's okay."

It's not. It's so far from okay I don't even know

how to begin fixing it. But I don't say that either. I just hold my daughter and wish, not for the first time, that I could be enough to fill the hole her mother keeps leaving.

Bedtime is quiet.

We go through the routine—bath, pajamas, teeth brushing, two books instead of three because she's tired in a way that has nothing to do with sleep.

The bath water turned gray from the playground dirt, swirling down the drain like the day washing away. She didn't splash like she usually does. Didn't make her rubber ducks talk to each other in silly voices. Just sat there, quiet, while I washed her hair and tried to pretend everything was normal.

Her pajamas are the ones with the unicorns—her favorites—and I made sure to pick them specifically. Small comfort. Better than nothing.

I tuck her in, make sure Ellie the elephant is in position, and click on the nightlight.

Then I lie down next to her, because some nights she needs that. Tonight is definitely one of those nights.

"Daddy?"

"Yeah, shadow?"

"Is she coming back?"

I stare at the glow-in-the-dark stars we stuck on her ceiling last summer, searching for an answer that isn't a lie but also won't break her heart.

"I don't know," I finally say. "But I'm always here. Yeah?"

"Yeah."

She's quiet for a long moment, and I think maybe she's fallen asleep. Then I feel her hand—small, warm—fist in the fabric of my shirt. Holding on tight, like she's afraid I might disappear if she lets go.

"I'm not going anywhere, Maze." I press a kiss to the top of her head. "You're stuck with me, remember?"

"I remember."

Her breathing slows, evens out, and eventually, she sleeps. But her hand stays fisted in my shirt, and I don't move. Don't even try to untangle myself and go to my own bed.

I just lie there in the dark, my daughter holding onto me like I'm the only solid thing in her world, and I make a promise I have no idea how to keep.

I'm going to fix this.

I don't know how. I don't know when. But someday, she's going to know what it feels like to have someone choose her first. To be loved without conditions, without cameras, without having to perform for an audience.

She deserves that.

She deserves everything.

And I'm going to spend the rest of my life trying to give it to her.

11

IN THE QUIET

Tori

The training facility is quiet at five o'clock on a Monday.

Most of the guys cleared out after practice, heading home, to dinner, or wherever hockey players go when they're not practicing or being poked and prodded by medical staff. The hallways have an empty echo, with lights dimmed in the sections no one is using.

I should've gone home too. But Zayden texted, asking if we could push his session to late afternoon—something about Maisie's school pickup— and I said yes without thinking.

I'm trying not to think about what that means. The fact that I rearranged my entire schedule for him. The fact that I'm still here, alone, waiting.

He walks in at 5:07, and I immediately know something's wrong.

It's not obvious. He's dressed for a session— athletic shorts and a fitted black T-shirt that does things I'm not going to acknowledge—and he nods at me like everything's normal. But there's a tension radiating from him.

"Hey," I say. "How's the shoulder feeling?"

"Fine."

One word. Clipped. No banter, no jokes, no almost-smile.

Okay then.

"Let's start with mobility work," I say, keeping my voice neutral. "Then we'll move to the resistance exercises."

He nods and gets on the table without argument, which somehow feels more alarming than if he'd pushed back. Zayden Bishop always pushes back. It's our thing.

I work through his shoulder in silence, feeling the knots beneath my fingers. He's tight everywhere—traps, deltoids, the muscles along his spine. Like he's been clenching his entire body for hours.

"You're holding a lot of tension," I say.

"I'm aware."

Still nothing. No smartass comment about my hands, no raised eyebrow, no heat simmering beneath the surface. Just... flatness.

We move to the weights. I hand him a resistance band and talk him through the first set of exercises, watching his form. It's good—it's always good—but he's rushing. Pushing through the reps like he's trying to outrun something.

"Slow down," I tell him. "You're going to strain something."

He doesn't slow down. If anything, he goes faster, jaw clenched, eyes fixed on a point somewhere over my shoulder.

"Zayden."

Nothing.

"Zayden, stop."

He finishes the rep and reaches for a heavier band. I step forward and put my hand on his arm.

"Hey." I wait until he looks at me. His eyes are dark, distant, like he's here but not really here at all. "Where are you right now?"

"I'm here."

"Your body's here. Your head's in another zip code."

He stares at me for a long moment. Then he sets down the band and runs a hand through his hair, exhaling hard.

"Maze had a rough night."

The visit. Sienna. I don't say it out loud, but I don't have to.

"Yeah," he says, reading my face. "It was... well, it wasn't great."

I wait but don't push. I just stand there with my hand still on his arm, feeling the warmth of his skin, the tension humming beneath the surface.

"She didn't cry when Sienna left." His voice is rough. "That's the thing. She didn't cry, she didn't throw a fit, she just... went quiet. Like she was expecting it. Like she's learned not to hope for anything."

My chest aches.

"She's six years old, Tori. She shouldn't know how to protect herself like that. She shouldn't have to."

"No," I agree softly. "She shouldn't."

He's looking at the floor now, shoulders

hunched, and I've never seen him like this. Cracked open. Vulnerable. It makes me want to wrap my arms around him and not let go.

I don't do that. But I want to.

"I couldn't fix it," he says. "I just had to lie there while she fell asleep holding onto my shirt like she was afraid I'd disappear too. And I couldn't do anything."

"You were there. That's not nothing."

"It's not enough."

"It's everything." I step closer, close enough that he has to look at me. "You're a great dad, Zayden."

He goes still and gazes up at me with a soft expression.

The silence stretches between us, heavy with something I can't name.

"How do you do that?" he asks quietly.

"Do what?"

"Say exactly what I need to hear."

I don't have an answer for that. Or maybe I do, but it's not one I'm ready to give.

The training room feels smaller suddenly. The hum of the fluorescent lights, the distant sound of someone vacuuming in another part of the building—it all fades to background noise. There's just him, and me, and the three feet of charged air between us.

"Take a breath," I say, and my voice comes out softer than I intended. "We can finish the session, or we can call it for today. Your choice."

He doesn't answer right away. Just stands there, looking at me with those dark eyes, and I feel the weight of his attention like something physical. Like a touch.

"Tori..."

The way he says my name—low, rough—makes my heart stutter.

"Yeah?"

He opens his mouth. Closes it. And I watch him make a decision, pulling back from whatever edge he was about to step over.

"Let's finish," he says. "I'll slow down."

I nod, ignoring the strange twist of disappointment in my chest. "Okay. From the top. And this time, actually listen to me."

The corner of his mouth twitches. Not quite a smile, but close. "Yes, ma'am."

We get back to work.

But something has shifted between us.

I hand him the resistance band and pretend my hands aren't shaking.

12

JUST US

Zayden

The building is empty—the parking lot was nearly deserted, and the hallways were dim. It's just us now. Me and Tori and the hum of the HVAC, and whatever this thing is that keeps pulling us together.

She's working on my shoulder, her hands firm and focused. I've done this a hundred times with a dozen different trainers. Pressure, release. Find the knot, work it out. Clinical. Routine.

Except there's nothing clinical about the way my pulse kicks up when she touches me. Nothing routine about the way I track her every movement—the rustle of her clothes when she shifts position, the soft exhale of her breath, the faint scent of something floral that cuts through the antiseptic smell of the training room.

Lavender, maybe. Or vanilla. Something soft and warm that makes me want to lean closer and breathe her in.

I don't. I grip the edge of the treatment table and stare at the wall and pretend I'm not hyperaware of every single place her body is near mine.

It's never felt like this.

Every point of contact burns. Her fingers rest on my bicep, and I have to concentrate on breathing, on not reacting, on keeping my body from doing something stupid.

She hits a tight spot near my neck, and I hiss before I can stop myself.

Her hands still. "Too much?"

"No." My voice comes out rougher than I intended. "Keep going."

She does. I have to close my eyes because if I look at her right now—if I see her face, her lips, the way she's biting her bottom lip in concentration—she's going to see everything. Every thought I've been trying to bury. Every want I've been pretending doesn't exist.

She shifts to work from a different angle, moving around the table, and her body presses closer. The warmth of her radiates through the thin fabric of her polo, and I can feel the soft curve of her hip brush against my arm as she reaches across me.

Then—her breast grazes my bicep. Soft. Brief. Probably accidental.

Every rational thought exits my brain.

The contact lasts maybe half a second, but it brands itself into my memory. The softness of her. The way my entire body went rigid. I stare at the far wall like it contains the secrets of the universe and try to remember how to breathe.

She doesn't seem to notice. Or maybe she does and she's pretending she doesn't. Either way, I stop breathing for a solid five seconds, just sitting there like an idiot while my blood rushes south and my hands grip the edge of the table hard enough to leave marks.

Her hands slow as she finishes, smoothing over my shoulder. She doesn't pull back. Her palm stays pressed against my skin, warm and steady, longer than it needs to.

"You're making good progress," she says, her voice slightly hoarse. "The inflammation is way down. Another few weeks and you should be back to full capacity."

"Thanks to you."

I turn to face her, swinging my legs over the side of the table. She doesn't step back. Doesn't give herself room. Just stands there, close enough that when I part my knees, she's right there be-tween them.

She's looking at my shoulder. At least, that's what she's pretending to do. But I see the way her gaze drifts—down my chest, across my abs, back up to my face. I see her swallow.

I'm shirtless. She's in athletic leggings that hug every curve and a fitted team polo, her pony-tail loose from hours of work. A strand of hair falls across her cheek. My fingers itch to brush it back.

Her lips are slightly parted. She's not wearing lipstick—she never does at work—but they're pink anyway, full and soft-looking.

I shouldn't be noticing her lips. I definitely shouldn't be thinking about what they'd feel like under mine.

"Zay—"

"I know." I don't move. Can't. "I know the

rules."

"Then why are you looking at me like that?"

Because I can't help it. Because you're the first person in years who makes me feel like I'm more than a jersey number and a custody agreement. Because when I'm with you, I remember what it feels like to want something for myself.

I don't say any of that. But I think she hears it anyway.

"Tell me to back off," I say quietly. "And I will."

She's supposed to say it. She's supposed to remind me about professional boundaries and her career and all the reasons this is a terrible idea. She's supposed to tell me no.

"I can't."

Two words. Barely a whisper. But they hit me like a puck to the chest.

She's still standing between my thighs, close enough that I can feel the warmth radiating off her.

I lift my hand slowly, giving her time to pull away. My knuckles brush along the side of her face, tucking that loose strand of hair behind her ear, then tracing the line of her jaw. She leans into the touch before she seems to catch herself. Her eyes flutter closed. My thumb strokes the soft skin of her cheek.

"This is a bad idea," she whispers.

"Probably."

Her eyes open—dark and wanting. She's so close now I can see the rapid pulse fluttering at the base of her throat.

I don't make her close the distance. That's on

me. After another heartbeat, I lean in and press my mouth to hers.

The kiss is soft at first. Careful. Testing. Like we're both waiting for the other to come to their senses and pull away.

She doesn't.

Her hands land on my chest, and a quiet noise escapes her throat—half gasp, half sigh—and it undoes something in me. I slide my hand to the nape of her neck, angling her head, and the kiss deepens into something hungrier.

Her lips part under mine, and I take the invitation, my tongue sliding against hers, and the sound she makes sends heat barreling through me.

I've been starving for this. For her. She melts against me like she's been waiting too, like this has been building since that first day.

My other hand finds her hip, pulling her closer, and she comes willingly, stepping between my legs where I'm sitting on the treatment table. Her hands slide up my chest, over my shoulders, into my hair, and I groan against her mouth because this is—

Her phone buzzes on the table.

Loud. Jarring. Obnoxious.

We break apart like we've been shocked.

Reality crashes back in like a bucket of ice water.

We freeze—her hands still fisted in my hair, mine still gripping her hip, our mouths hovering an inch apart. Our breath mingles, ragged and hot. I can see my own shock reflected in her eyes.

What the hell were we doing?

She's breathing hard, lips swollen, eyes wide.

I'm not much better—chest heaving, heart pounding, every nerve ending in my body screaming at me to pull her back.

The phone buzzes again.

"I should—" She grabs it, not looking at the screen. "I have to go."

"Tori—"

But she's already moving. Grabbing her bag, shoving her phone in her pocket, avoiding my eyes like if she looks at me again she'll do something she regrets.

"We can't—" She stops at the door, hand on the frame. "I need to think."

"Okay."

She finally looks at me, and what I see there makes my chest ache: want, fear, and confusion, all tangled together.

"Okay," she repeats, like she's trying to convince herself. "I'll... I'll see you tomorrow."

And then she's gone.

The door swings shut behind her, and I sit there in the empty training room, heart still racing, the taste of her still on my lips.

I should regret that. I should be thinking about all the ways this complicates everything—her career, the fact that we work together, and I have a daughter who can't afford for me to screw up another relationship.

But all I can think about is the sound she made when I kissed her. The way her fingers slid over my chest.

The way she kissed me back like she'd been waiting for it just as long as I had.

I run a hand through my hair and let out a long breath.

I'm in so much trouble.

And I don't even care.

13

SPIRALING

Tori

I don't sleep. Every time I close my eyes, I'm back in that training room—his hand on the back of my neck, the warmth of his mouth, the way he looked at me before he leaned in. I kissed him back like my life depended on it.

I roll over and stare at the ceiling.

And God, can he kiss. That's what I can't stop thinking about. I've kissed my share of guys. Some were fine, some forgettable, and some made me wonder if they'd ever actually kissed a woman before.

Zayden Bishop kissed like he was an expert on the subject. The way his mouth moved against mine showed he knew exactly what he was doing—confident, patient, completely in control ... until he wasn't.

My phone sits on the nightstand, dark and silent. He hasn't texted. I don't know if that makes it better or worse.

I'd consider calling Winnie—spilling everything, letting her talk me down, talk me up, or just talk until I'm too exhausted to feel anything. But I already know what she'd say.

I told you so.

She'd be right.

I press my palms against my eyes and try to think. I'm good at thinking, at making plans and protocols, at keeping my head when everything else is chaos. That's who I am. That's who I've always been.

So why did I let him kiss me?

Why did I kiss him back?

Why am I lying here at three in the morning, replaying the sound he made when I put my hands on his chest—that low groan that vibrated through my entire body—instead of figuring out how to fix this?

Because you wanted it, a voice whispers. You've wanted it for weeks.

I roll over again, burying my face in my pillow.

This is fine. I can fix this. One kiss doesn't have to mean anything. People make mistakes all the time. They acknowledge them, move on, and pretend they never happened.

That's what I'll do—acknowledge it and move on.

Simple.

I don't fall asleep until after four, and when I do, I dream about his hands.

I get to the facility an hour early.

Partly because I couldn't stand lying in bed

anymore, and partly because I needed time to prepare myself—to build the walls back up, brick by brick, before he walks through that door and I have to look him in the eye.

I set up the training room with mechanical precision. Resistance bands, ice packs. I arrange everything twice, then rearrange it again, because my hands need something to do that isn't shaking.

7:52 AM. Eight minutes until his session.

I can do this. I'm a professional. I've handled difficult situations before. One ill-advised kiss with a patient doesn't have to derail my entire career.

It was just a kiss.

A really, really good kiss.

No. Stop it. I'm reviewing his file on my tablet—staring at it without actually reading anything—when the door opens.

Zayden walks in, and the air immediately changes.

He looks like he didn't sleep either. Dark shadows under his eyes, jaw tight, shoulders tense. He's wearing a black T-shirt and gray joggers, his hair still damp from a shower, and I hate that I notice. I hate that I'm cataloging every detail like my brain is trying to memorize him.

Our eyes meet.

For a second, neither of us speaks. The silence is suffocating—thick with everything we're not saying, everything that happened yesterday, everything that can never happen again.

"We should talk about last night," he says.

My stomach drops even as I lift my chin. "There's nothing to talk about."

"Tori—"

"It was a mistake." I keep my voice clinical. Professional. The tone I use with difficult patients, the one that leaves no room for argument. "We were tired. Boundaries got blurred. It happens."

His jaw tightens, a muscle ticking near his temple.

"Right," he says slowly. "A mistake."

"It won't happen again."

He's quiet for a long moment, studying me with those dark eyes. I can't read his expression—it's shuttered now, closed off—nothing like last night. Last night, he looked at me like I was something precious. Now he looks at me like I'm a stranger.

Good. That's what I want. That's what I need.

"If that's what you want," he finally says.

It's not. That's the problem. What I want is to cross the room and kiss him again, to feel his hands in my hair and his mouth on my neck, and forget about every rule I've ever made for myself.

But wanting something doesn't make it right.

"It is," I lie. "Now get on the table. We have work to do."

He holds my gaze for one more second. Then he nods, pulls off his shirt, and settles onto the treatment table without another word.

I put my hands on his shoulder and pretend I don't feel him flinch.

The week that follows is brutal.

Gone is the easy banter, the teasing, the way

he'd catch my eye across the room and smile.

In its place? Clinical instructions. Minimal eye contact. A careful, calculated distance that feels like a chasm.

"Fifteen reps," I tell him on Tuesday. "Slow and controlled."

"Got it."

No pushback. No smartass comment about my bossy streak. Just compliance.

I hate it.

"Your mobility is improving," I say on Wednesday, not looking at him as I write notes on my tablet. "Another two weeks and we can increase resistance."

"Sounds good."

That's all I get. Two words and a nod, and the specific kind of politeness that's worse than rudeness because at least rudeness would be honest.

My mom calls Wednesday night, right when I'm stress-eating leftover pad Thai and watching a home renovation show I'm not really seeing.

"Hi, honey! How's my favorite daughter?"

"I'm your only daughter, Mom."

"Which makes you my favorite by default." I can hear her smile through the phone. "How's work? How's the shoulder guy? The grumpy one?"

I close my eyes. Of course she remembers me mentioning him. I made the mistake of calling her after that first session, back when he was just an annoying patient and not... whatever he is now.

"He's fine. Recovery's on track."

"Mm-hmm." She's using her I-know-you're-not-telling-me-something voice. "And how are *you*?"

"Fine."

"Victoria."

"Mom."

She sighs, the kind of sigh that says she knows I'm full of it. "You sound tired," she says, gentler now. "Are you sleeping?"

"Enough."

"Are you eating?"

"I'm literally eating right now."

"Real food or takeout?"

I look at the pad Thai container. "...Real-adjacent."

"Tori."

"It has vegetables in it!"

She laughs, and something in my chest loosens. My mom has a way of making everything feel manageable, even when it's not. She did it when I was nineteen, lying in a hospital bed, realizing I'd never play competitive soccer again. She did it when I called her sobbing about my hardest break-up. She's doing it now, even though she doesn't know what's wrong.

"Your father wants to know if you're coming for Easter," she says. "Danny's bringing his girlfriend. We're all very curious about her."

"Danny has a girlfriend?"

"Apparently. He's been very secretive about it, which means she's either wonderful or has a criminal record."

"Knowing Danny, it could be both."

She laughs again. "So? Easter?"

"I'll try, Mom. The season's crazy right now."

"I know, honey. I just miss you." A pause. "You know, your father and I were talking the other day about when you used to play. Remember that game against Duke? When you scored in the last thirty seconds?"

My throat tightens. "Yeah. I remember."

"You were so happy. I don't think I've ever seen you that happy." Another pause, more careful this time. "I want you to be that happy again, Tori. Not about soccer—I know that door closed. But about something. Someone."

"Mom..."

"I'm not pushing. I'm just saying." Her voice is soft. "You deserve good things. Don't forget that."

I think about Zayden. About the kiss. About the way he looked at me this morning when I called it a mistake—like I'd ripped something out of his chest.

"I won't forget," I lie.

We talk for another ten minutes about nothing important—Danny's new apartment, Dad's golf game, the neighbor's dog who keeps digging up Mom's garden. Normal stuff.

When we hang up, I sit in the silence of my apartment and think about what she said.

You were so happy.

I was. Soccer was everything to me—the team, the competition, the feeling of my body doing exactly what I asked it to do. Then one bad tackle, one torn ligament, and it was over. Four surgeries.

Eighteen months of rehab. I pursued a career in sports therapy because if I couldn't play, at least I could help those who still could.

I'm good at my job. I know I'm good at my job. But Mom's right—I haven't been happy in a long time.

Not until recently.

Not until a grumpy French-Canadian hockey player burst into my life. I shove the thought away and turn up the volume on my renovation show.

By Thursday, I want to scream.

He shows up exactly on time, does exactly what I tell him, and leaves exactly when we're done. No lingering, no banter, no heat simmering beneath the surface. He treats me like I'm furniture—necessary but unremarkable. A tool to fix his shoulder and nothing more.

It's exactly what I asked for.

I hate it.

The only crack in his armor comes a few hours after our session, when he appears in the doorway of my office and sets a takeout bag on the edge of my desk.

"What's this?" I ask.

"Tacos. From Tito's." He still won't meet my eyes. "You mentioned once that you skip lunch when you're stressed."

Then he's gone, the door clicking shut behind him. I'm left with a bag of tacos from the place he mentioned liking weeks ago, trying not to cry in the middle of my office.

He's giving me space. He's respecting my boundaries. And he's still showing up for me in the only way I'm letting him.

I eat the tacos alone at my desk, hating myself a little more with every bite. And he wasn't wrong, it's delicious.

After I finish the tacos, I do something stupid.

I pull up the employee handbook on my laptop—the same PDF I downloaded during orientation, the same one I've specifically avoided looking at again. Like maybe if I don't acknowledge the rules, they don't exist. Idiotic, I know.

I scroll to Section 7.3: Employee Conduct and Professional Relationships.

Romantic or sexual relationships between players and staff members are prohibited due to potential conflicts of interest, favoritism concerns, and the maintenance of professional standards. Violations may result in reassignment, termination, or other disciplinary action at the organization's discretion.

I read it three times, letting the words sink in like stones.

Conflicts of interest. Like wanting his recovery to succeed, not because it's my job, but because watching him hurt makes me physically ache.

Favoritism concerns. Like the way I rearranged my entire schedule last week just to ensure that I was the one treating him instead of James.

Maintenance of professional standards. Like professionalism means anything when I can still feel the ghost of his mouth on mine every time I close my eyes.

I shut the laptop harder than necessary and push it away from me like the policy itself is contagious.

I worked too hard to get here. One man is not worth blowing up my entire career. I don't care how unfairly attractive he is or how great that kiss was.

On Friday afternoon, I'm in my office pretending to review patient files when Dana appears in my doorway.

"You okay?"

I look up, schooling my expression into something neutral. "Fine. Why?"

"You seem... off this week. Distracted." She tilts her head, studying me. "Everything good with Bishop?"

My heart stutters at his name. "His recovery is progressing well. Ahead of schedule, actually."

"That's not what I asked."

I meet her eyes and lie through my teeth. "Everything's fine."

She doesn't look convinced, but she doesn't push either. "Okay. Let me know if you need anything."

She leaves, and I slump back in my chair, pressing my fingers against my temples.

Everything is not fine. Everything is the opposite of fine. I kissed my patient and then told him it was a mistake, and now I have to see him every day and pretend I don't want him.

My phone buzzes with a text from Winnie.

Winnie

How's Operation Pretend Nothing Happened going?

I stare at the screen for a long moment before typing back.

Me

Terrible. I hate everything.

Winnie

Want to talk about it?

Me

No.

Winnie

Want wine?

Me

Yes.

Winnie

My place. 7 PM. Bring your feelings.

I almost smile. Almost.

Then I think about Zayden's face this morning—blank, polite, distant—and the almost-smile dies a fiery death.

I made the right call. I know I made the right call. Kissing him was reckless. Getting involved with him would be career suicide. Every rational part of my brain knows this.

But there's another part. A smaller, quieter part

that whispers, *What if you're wrong? What if this is the one thing you're not supposed to walk away from?*

I tell that part to shut up.

Winnie's apartment smells like lavender when I enter. There's no sign of Derek, thank God. Winnie's boyfriend has the emotional depth of a puddle, and tonight I don't have the bandwidth to pretend otherwise. He wasn't always this annoying—when they first started dating, he was actually kind of sweet. Attentive. The type who remembered her coffee order and texted good morning every day. But somewhere along the way, he turned into the kind of guy who talks over women at dinner parties and thinks his fantasy football opinions count as conversation. Winnie swears the old Derek is still in there somewhere. I'm less convinced.

She already has two glasses of wine poured when I walk in, and she takes one look at my face before pushing the fuller glass toward me.

"That bad?" she asks, curling up on the opposite end of the couch.

She tucks her legs beneath her, looking like a golden retriever in human form—all warmth and good intentions and the kind of effortless beauty that makes men walk into lampposts. She's beautiful in a way that makes other women want to hate her, except she's so genuinely nice that you can't. She also teaches yoga for a living and radiates the sort of calm energy I've never once possessed.

"Worse." I drop onto her couch and take a long sip. Then another. "I kissed him."

"You—" Winnie's eyes go wide. "Wait. You kissed him? Like, you initiated?"

"Well, technically he kissed me. But I didn't stop him. And then I..." I close my eyes, remembering. "I pulled him closer. By his shoulders. Because he wasn't wearing a shirt."

"I'm sorry, he was shirtless?"

"It was a PT session. He's always shirtless."

"Right, right." She waves her hand, as if fanning herself. "Continue. Shirtless hockey player, you pulled him closer—"

"And then we made out. In the training room. And it was..." I trail off, searching for words that don't exist.

"Good?"

"The best kiss of my life." I take another gulp of wine. "And I've been kissed before. A lot. But this was... he kissed me like he'd been thinking about it for weeks. Like I was something he wanted to take his time with."

Winnie fans herself again. "Okay, I need details. Tongue? Hands? Where were his hands?"

"My hip. The back of my neck." I can still feel the ghost of his fingers threading through my hair. "Affirmative on the tongue. And then my phone buzzed, and we broke apart, and I panicked and ran away."

"You ran away."

"I literally grabbed my bag and left. Didn't even say goodbye properly."

Winnie stares at me. "Tori."

"I know."

"That poor man."

"I know."

She refills my glass even though it's not empty. "Okay. So what happened after? Today?"

"I told him it was a mistake. That it won't happen again." The words taste bitter even now. "He just... accepted it. Didn't argue, didn't push back. And now he's being perfectly professional and polite, and I hate it."

"You hate that he's respecting your boundaries?" Her eyes widen.

"I hate that I set boundaries I don't actually want." I lean my head back against the couch cushions. "What is wrong with me?"

Winnie is quiet for a moment, tucking her legs underneath her. "Can I say something? And you promise not to bite my head off?"

"No promises."

"Fair." She takes a breath. "Last week, I warned you about him. His reputation, the tabloid stuff, all of it. And I stand by that—you should be careful."

"But?"

"But." She swirls her wine. "The way you're talking about this kiss? That's not how you talk about a mistake. That's how you talk about something that matters."

My chest tightens. "It can't matter. I won't let it."

She sets down her glass and turns to face me fully. "Look, I'm not saying to throw caution to the wind and ride off into the sunset with him. I'm just saying maybe don't slam the door completely shut just because you're scared."

"I'm not scared."

She simply looks at me.

"Okay, fine. I'm terrified." I take another gulp of wine and stare at the ceiling. "I re-read the employee handbook today, like a crazy person. And it was pretty dang clear."

"Okay, but—"

"And he's got a kid." The words tumble out before she can finish. "A six-year-old who's already been abandoned by her mom. If I start something with him and it falls apart, it's not just me who gets hurt."

"That's actually a really good point."

"I know. That's why I'm freaking out."

We sit in silence for a moment. Somewhere in the apartment, Winnie's cat knocks something over. Neither of us moves to check.

"What does your gut say?" Winnie finally asks.

I think about Zayden in the hallway, wrecked after a phone call with his ex.

"My gut says he's different," I admit quietly. "My gut says this could be real."

"And your head?"

"My head says I'm an idiot who's about to ruin everything."

Winnie reaches over and squeezes my hand. "For what it's worth, I think your gut might be onto something. But you're the only one who can decide if it's worth the risk."

"That's very wise and unhelpful."

"I know. It's my specialty." She grabs the wine bottle. "More?"

"Please."

We drink until the bottle is empty, and I'm tipsy enough to almost forget the look on Zayden's face when I called it a mistake.

Almost.

Saturday morning, I go for a run.

It's freezing—late January in New York, the kind of cold that burns your lungs—but I need it. I need the physical exhaustion, the clarity that comes from pushing my body until my brain finally shuts up.

It doesn't work.

I run four miles and think about him the entire time.

His hands. His mouth. The way he said, *tell me to back off,* like he would have walked away if I'd asked, even though it would have killed him.

The way he looked at me after I called it a mistake—like I had taken something fragile and crushed it.

I stop at a crosswalk, breathing hard, as a family passes in front of me. Dad, mom, and a little girl in a pink coat. The dad is carrying the girl on his shoulders, and she's laughing, tugging at his ears.

I think about Maisie. About Zayden lying next to his daughter at bedtime, letting her hold onto his shirt so she knows he won't disappear.

And I pushed him away.

The light changes. I start running again.

Maybe I made a mistake.

Not the kiss—the kiss was inevitable, a collision we had been hurtling toward since the first taco debate.

The mistake was pretending it didn't mean anything.

Because it did. It does.

And I have no idea what to do about it.

14

SUIT AND TIE TORTURE

I hate these things. Team banquets, sponsor schmoozing, whatever you want to call it—it's all the same. Uncomfortable suit, forced small talk, and rich people eager to shake your hand so they can brag to their golf buddies that they met a hockey player.

My collar is too tight. I've loosened my tie twice already, but it still feels like it's strangling me. I'd rather be home with Maisie, watching *Bluey* for the nine hundredth time and eating chicken strips off paper plates.

Instead, I'm standing in a ballroom at the Waldorf, nursing a sparkling water and trying to look like I want to be here. Coach made it clear that attendance is mandatory—something about "building relationships with key partners" and "representing the organization."

So here I am. Representing.

The room is packed—players in suits, wives and girlfriends in cocktail dresses, sponsors in expensive watches checking their phones. Logan is working the crowd like he was born for it, dimples on full display as he charms a group of older women who are probably donors. Banks is lurking near the bar, looking like he'd rather be literally anywhere else, which makes two of us.

And Tori...

Tori is across the room, talking to Coach Reynolds.

She's wearing a black dress that shouldn't be affecting me the way it is. It's not even that revealing—high neck, sleeves to her elbows—but it fits her perfectly, hugging every curve and I can't stop looking. Her hair is down for once, dark waves falling past her shoulders, and I keep thinking about what it felt like threaded through my fingers.

Stop it. She made herself clear.

It was a mistake.

I drain the rest of my sparkling water. The bubbles burn my throat, sharp and cold. Not cold enough to put out the fire she started.

I force my eyes somewhere else. Anywhere else. It's been ten days since the kiss. Ten days of clinical sessions and professional distance, her treating me like I'm just another patient with a shoulder problem. Ten days of giving her exactly what she asked for.

It's killing me.

"You look like someone ran over your dog."

I glance sideways. Banks has materialized next to me, drink in hand, his face as unreadable as ever.

"I don't have a dog."

"Hence the metaphor." He follows my gaze across the room—to where Tori is now laughing at something Coach said—and makes a low sound in his throat. "Ah."

"Don't."

"I didn't say anything."

"You were about to."

"I was going to ask how your shoulder's doing." He takes a sip of his drink. "But sure. Let's talk about the PT you've been moping over."

"I'm not moping."

"You're standing in a corner glaring at everyone who talks to her. That's textbook moping." He shrugs. "No judgment. She's hot. I get it."

I shoot him a look that would make most people back off. Banks just raises an eyebrow, unimpressed. The man has the emotional range of a glacier and apparently the observational skills of a hawk. It's an annoying combination.

Banks claps me on the shoulder—the good one—and heads toward the buffet line, leaving me alone with my sparkling water and my bad decisions.

The universe, apparently, has a sense of humor.

Because ten seconds later, Tori appears at the bar next to me.

"Hey."

My whole body goes tight. "Hey."

She's not looking at me. She's looking at the bartender, ordering a glass of white wine with the kind of casualness that tells me she's just as aware of me as I am of her.

The bartender hands her the glass. She doesn't leave.

Silence, the kind that's so thick you could

choke on it.

"So," she says finally, still not looking at me. "Hannah started, right?"

Right. The nanny. Normal small talk. I can do normal small talk.

"Yeah. Last Monday." I take a sip of my water, needing something to do with my hands. "Maisie likes her. She makes a good grilled cheese, apparently. That's Maze's metric for trustworthiness."

Tori's lips twitch. Almost a smile. "Smart kid. Grilled cheese is important."

"She ranked the last three nannies by their grilled cheese quality. Hannah's currently in second place, behind Mrs. Hendricks."

"What about you? Where do you rank?"

"Dead last. My grilled cheese is, and I quote, 'too crunchy and kind of sad.'"

She laughs. It's quiet, barely there, but it's real—and hearing it after ten days of nothing feels like stepping into sunlight after a long winter.

Then the laughter fades, and we're back to silence.

She's close enough that I can smell her perfume. Something warm, a little sweet. I want to bury my face in her neck and inhale.

"This is ridiculous," she says quietly.

"What is?"

"This. Us." She finally looks at me, her eyes bright with something I can't name. "The way we're acting like strangers when we're not. I hate it."

My jaw tightens. "You said it was a mistake."

"I know what I said."

"So what do you want me to do, Tori? You set the rules. I'm following them."

She flinches slightly, and I hate that I'm the one who put that look on her face. But I'm also tired—tired of pretending I don't think about her constantly, tired of acting like that kiss didn't matter.

"I don't know," she admits. "I don't know what I want. But I know this—" she gestures between us, small and frustrated— "isn't it."

I set down my drink.

"Come with me."

She blinks. "What? Where?"

I don't answer. I just take her hand—her fingers are cold, trembling slightly in mine—and lead her through the crowd. Past the donors, past the sponsors, past Logan, who raises an eyebrow but has the good sense not to say anything.

Just drink your beer, Cupcake.

There's a side door near the back. I push through it, pulling her with me, and suddenly we're in a hallway. It's empty and quiet, the noise of the party fading to a dull murmur behind us.

"Zay—"

I kiss her.

Not soft this time. Not careful. I kiss her like I've been starving for it—which I have—backing her against the wall, one hand on her hip, the other cupping her jaw. She makes a sound against my mouth, surprised and wanting, and then she's kissing me back, fingers twisting in my lapels, pulling me closer.

"Câlice." I breath against her mouth. "Do you have any idea what you do to me?"

She tastes like wine and want and everything I've been trying not to think about for ten days. I angle her head, deepening the kiss, and she responds by arching into me, her tongue stroking mine. Rational thoughts vanish.

My hand slides from her hip to her lower back, pulling her flush against me, and she gasps into my mouth. I swallow the sound, greedy for it, greedy for her. Her fingers find my hair, tugging slightly, and I groan—low and rough and completely beyond my control.

"Zayden." My name comes out broken, breathless, and hearing it like that does something to me.

I'm already hard, straining against my suit pants, and when her body presses into mine, she makes this soft sound of surprise that turns into something hungrier. I'm hard—instantly, embarrassingly hard—and there's no way she doesn't feel it.

I should be embarrassed. Should pull back, apologize, give her space.

I don't.

Because her hips roll forward—a tiny, instinctive movement—and the friction makes us both gasp. Her head falls back against the wall, exposing the long line of her throat, and I can't resist. I drag my mouth down her jaw, her neck, finding that spot beneath her ear that makes her shiver.

"Zay—" Her voice is wrecked. Broken. The most beautiful sound I've ever heard.

I groan against her mouth, something low and desperate, and I think I say her name but the rest comes out French, the accent I usually hide slipping loose because I can't control anything right now, least of all myself.

My erection presses into her stomach, but she doesn't retreat. She grinds against me, slow, just enough to make me groan.

"Tor." I pull back just enough to look at her. Her lips are swollen, her eyes dark, her chest heaving. She looks wrecked in the best possible way. "That wasn't a mistake," I say.

She swallows hard. "No. It wasn't."

"I need—" I can't finish. I press my forehead to hers, breath ragged, hands flexing on her hips. "Six years, Tori. Six years of nothing, and now I can't think straight. Can't sleep. Can't look at you without wanting—" My voice breaks off. "Tell me this isn't just me. Tell me I'm not losing my mind."

Her hand comes up to rest against my chest, right over my heart. "It's not just you," she breathes.

I lean my forehead against hers, breathing her in. "You're killing me, you know that?"

"I know." Her hand comes up to rest against my chest, right over my heart. "Believe me, it's killing me too."

We stay like that for a long moment. Foreheads touching, breath mingling, the muffled sound of the party filtering through the walls. I want to stay here forever. I want to take her home. I want to do a lot of things that aren't appropriate for a hallway at a team banquet.

Instead, I wait for my body to chill the hell out.

"We should go back," she says finally.

"Yeah."

Neither of us moves.

"Separately," she adds.

"Yeah."

Still not moving.

She laughs—quiet, shaky—and pulls back, straightening her dress, touching her hair like she can smooth away the evidence of what just happened.

"Five minutes," she says. "You wait here. I'll go first."

"Tori."

She pauses, hand on the door.

"This isn't going away," I tell her. "Whatever this is between us. Pretending it doesn't exist isn't working."

"I know." She meets my eyes, and there's something raw in her expression.

Then she's gone, slipping back through the door, leaving me alone in the hallway with a racing heart and the taste of her still on my lips.

I give her ten minutes instead of five. Partly to be safe. Partly because I need the time to get myself under control.

When I walk back into the ballroom, I don't look for her. I make myself talk to sponsors, shake hands, and do the schmoozing thing Coach wanted. I laugh at jokes that aren't funny and nod along to conversations I don't care about.

But I feel her.

Every time I turn, I know exactly where she is in the room. Near the dessert table. Talking to

Dana. Laughing with Logan about something.

And every now and then, our eyes meet.

Just for a second. Just long enough for my pulse to spike and my skin to heat and the memory of her mouth to flash through my brain like lightning.

She looks away first. Every time.

But she always looks back.

Banks appears at my elbow again near the end of the night. "You seem less like someone ran over your dog."

I smirk. "Told you. I don't have a dog."

"And yet." He studies me with those sharp eyes that see too much. "Something changed."

"Nothing changed."

"Liar." But he doesn't push. Just lifts his glass in a silent toast and walks away.

I watch Tori say goodbye to Dana, gather her coat, and head for the exit. She doesn't look at me as she leaves.

This is going to get complicated. I know it is. She's my PT. She has rules. I have a daughter who can't handle another person walking in and out of her life.

There are a hundred reasons why this is a terrible idea.

But for the first time in years, I'm not sure I care.

15

BABYSITTING

My phone buzzes while I'm elbow-deep in laundry.

I almost ignore it. It's Sunday afternoon, and my day has consisted of laundry, leftover Chinese food, and a true crime documentary I'm only half paying attention to.

Then I see the name on the screen.

Zayden.

My stomach flips. We haven't talked since the banquet two nights ago. Since the hallway. Since he kissed me like he was trying to prove a point—and he succeeded spectacularly.

I stare at the phone for three full rings before answering.

"Hello?"

"Hey." His voice is tight, stressed. "I'm sorry to call like this, but I need a favor. A big one."

"What's wrong?"

"Hannah's mom fell. She's at the hospital—broken hip, they think. Hannah had to leave, and I have a team meeting in forty minutes that I can't miss, and my mom's flight doesn't land until to-morrow, and—" He stops and takes a breath. "I don't have anyone else to call."

I sink onto the edge of my bed, my heart hammering. "You need me to watch Maisie."

"Just for a few hours. Three, maybe four. I know it's a lot to ask, and if you can't—"

"I'll be there."

Silence. Then, "Yeah?"

"Text me your address."

"Tori..." He sounds like he wants to say more. Thank you, maybe. Or something bigger.

"Just send the address, Zayden. I'll be there."

I hang up before I can second-guess myself.

His townhouse is in a quiet neighborhood in Brooklyn.

I don't know what I expected—something sleek and modern, maybe, all glass and angles like you see in those athlete home tours online or on MTV Cribs. But this is... warm. A brick rowhouse with a blue door and window boxes that probably hold flowers in the spring.

I stand on the sidewalk for a full thirty seconds, trying to remember how to breathe.

This is his life. His real life—not the arena, the training room, or stolen moments in hallways. This is where he makes breakfast, reads bedtime stories, and exists as something other than a hockey player. Where he's someone's dad.

I'm about to step inside it.

The door swings open before I can knock.

Zayden's standing there in jeans and a gray henley, looking harried, grateful, and unfairly attractive. His hair is messy, like he's been running his hands through it, and there's something on his sleeve that might be peanut butter.

"Hey." He steps back to let me in. "Thank you. Seriously. I owe you."

"You can repay me in tacos. The good kind, not Tito's."

He almost smiles. "Deal."

The inside of the house is exactly what the outside promised. Cozy. Lived-in. There's a toy bin in the corner of the living room overflowing with stuffed animals, a stack of picture books on the coffee table, and crayon drawings taped to the refrigerator that I can see through the kitchen doorway.

It smells like laundry detergent and something baking. Cookies, maybe.

"Hannah put cookies in before she left," Zayden says, following my gaze. "The timer should go off in about ten minutes. Maze knows she's only allowed two."

"She'll try for three?"

"She'll try for six. Don't fall for the face." He grabs his jacket from a hook by the door. "She's in her room. I told her you were coming."

"What did you tell her about me?"

He pauses, jacket half-on. "That you're the person who's helping Daddy's shoulder get better. And that you're nice."

"Am I nice?"

"Sometimes." His eyes meet mine, and there's

a flicker of heat beneath the stress. "When you want to be."

Before I can respond, a small voice calls from upstairs. "Daddy? Is she here?"

"Yeah, shadow. Come say hi."

Footsteps on the stairs—quick, a little clumsy—and then Maisie Bishop appears.

She's smaller than I expected, with dark hair in two slightly uneven braids, wearing leggings adorned with dinosaurs and a purple sweater that says GIRLS RULE. She has Zayden's big, dark, serious eyes, and she's currently studying me with an intensity that makes me feel like I'm being interviewed for a very important position.

"Hi," she says carefully. "I'm Maisie. But you can call me Maze if you want."

"Hi, Maze." I crouch down to her eye level. "I'm Tori."

"I know. Daddy told me." She tilts her head. "You fix people's shoulders?"

"I do. Arms and legs too, sometimes."

"Did you fix Daddy's shoulder?"

"I'm working on it. He's not always a very good listener."

Maisie nods solemnly, like this confirms something she already suspected. "He doesn't listen about vegetables either."

Behind her, Zayden makes an indignant sound. "I eat vegetables."

"Not the green ones."

"Broccoli is a scam, Maze. We've discussed this."

I press my lips together to keep from laughing,

but Maisie catches it anyway and gives me a tiny, conspiratorial smile.

"The cookies are almost ready," she tells me. "I'm only allowed two, but sometimes I can have three if I ask nicely."

"Maisie." Zayden's voice is warning but fond.

"I'm just telling her the rules, Daddy."

"Uh-huh." He checks his watch and winces. "I have to go. Tori, her bedtime is eight. She can have screen time until seven, then it's bath, books, bed. Ellie—that's her elephant—has to be in the exact right spot or she can't sleep."

"Which spot?"

"Under her left arm, trunk facing out. She'll tell you if it's wrong."

"Trunk facing out. Got it."

He hesitates, looking between me and Maisie, unsure if he should leave. Like he's entrusting me with something precious, fragile, and irreplaceable.

Which he is.

"Go," I tell him gently. "We'll be fine."

"Yeah, Daddy." Maisie grabs my hand—just like that, easy as breathing—and starts tugging me toward the kitchen. "We're gonna be fine. Go do your meeting."

Zayden watches us for another moment. Then he meets my eyes, and something passes between us—gratitude, yes, but also something deeper. Trust.

"I'll text you when I'm on my way back," he says.

"Take your time."

He leaves, and I'm alone with his daughter in

his house, holding her small hand in mine.

No pressure.

The cookies are chocolate chip, and they're incredible.

Maisie eats her two—she doesn't even attempt a third, which makes me think Zayden oversold the negotiation tactics—and then gives me a tour of the house. Her room is upstairs, painted lavender, with glow-in-the-dark stars on the ceiling and a small bookshelf overflowing with picture books.

"This is Ellie." She holds up a well-loved stuffed elephant, gray and slightly balding in places. "She's been my best friend since I was a baby."

"She's beautiful."

"She's a little old," Maisie admits. "But Daddy says that just means she's extra loved."

My chest tightens.

We color for a while—Maisie is very particular about staying within the lines and even more particular about which colors go where—and then we watch an episode of *Bluey*, which I've never seen before but is apparently the greatest show ever created, according to Maisie.

"This one's about when Bluey doesn't want to go to sleep," she explains very seriously. "It's a good one."

"Is that a problem you have? Not wanting to go to sleep?"

She considers this. "Sometimes. When Daddy's not home, it's harder."

"Why?"

"Because..." She picks at a thread on the couch cushion. "What if he doesn't come back?"

The question hits me like a punch to the sternum. I have inadvertently wandered into territory I have no business being in. Eating cookies and coloring and watching cartoons was my sweet spot. Not… this. But Maisie's still looking at me.

"He always comes back," I say carefully. "Doesn't he?"

"Yeah. But my mom didn't." She says it matter-of-factly, as if she's explaining that the sky is blue. "She was supposed to come back, and then she didn't. So sometimes I worry."

I don't know what to say. I'm not equipped for this—for the casual devastation of a six-year-old who's learned that people leave.

"Your dad loves you very much," I finally manage. "I can tell."

"I know." She looks up at me with those dark, serious eyes. "He says I'm stuck with him forever."

"That sounds like something he'd say."

"Daddy talks about you," she says, her eyes still on the TV.

I blink. "He does?"

"Mm-hmm. He says your name funny." She scrunches her nose, thinking. "Like it's special or something."

I don't know how to respond to that. I've always liked the way he says my name. I thought it was just me. My face feels warm.

"Do you like my daddy?" she asks next.

The question is so casual, so matter-of-fact, that it takes me a second to process.

"I… yes. He's my friend."

"Good." She nods, satisfied, and turns back to

Bluey.

I sit there with my heart in my throat, wondering how a six-year-old just saw straight through me.

Bedtime goes smoother than I expected.

Bath, pajamas, teeth brushing. Maisie insists on picking three books instead of two, and I don't have the heart to argue. We read about a hungry caterpillar, a runaway bunny, and a little girl who tames a wild thing.

Ellie goes under her left arm, trunk facing out. Maisie adjusts her twice before declaring it acceptable.

She's asleep within minutes, her breathing slow and even. I sit there longer than I need to, thinking. She's so small. So brave. So determined to be okay, even when the world keeps giving her reasons not to be.

Something dangerous unfurls in my chest. Not just affection, but want. The kind I've been pushing down for years, telling myself there's time, telling myself career first. But sitting here in this lavender room filled with books and stuffed animals and a unicorn nightlight? I want this, and that persistent little ache I push down grows a little.

I carefully extract my hand and slip out of the room, leaving the door cracked and the hallway light on.

Then I go downstairs and try to remember how to breathe normally.

Zayden gets home at nine.

I'm on the couch, pretending to watch TV when I hear his key in the lock. My whole body goes alert, pulse spiking, and I hate how much I've been waiting for this. For him.

He steps inside and immediately looks for me. When our eyes meet, something in his expression softens.

"Hey."

"Hey yourself." I stand, smoothing my hands over my jeans. "She went down easy. Three books instead of two, but I figured that was an acceptable bribe."

"She suckered you."

A soft laugh escapes my lips. "Completely. I had no defenses against those eyes."

He smiles—a real one, tired but genuine—and shrugs off his jacket. "Thank you. For doing this. I know it was a lot to ask."

"It wasn't." I mean it. "She's a great kid, Zayden."

"Yeah." He moves into the living room, close enough that I can smell his cologne and see the shadow of stubble on his jaw. "She is."

We stand there, the space between us charged with everything we're not saying. The banquet. The hallway. The kiss I've been trying not to think about for two days.

"She told me you talk about me," I blurt out.

His eyebrows rise. "She did?"

"Apparently, you say my name funny." I make

air quotes. "Like it's special or something."

Something flickers across his face—surprise, maybe. Or embarrassment. "She's six. She doesn't know what she's talking about."

"Doesn't she?"

He holds my gaze, and the air between us thickens.

"Do you want something to drink?" he asks, his voice lower now. "I have wine, beer, or sparkling water if you want to stay hydrated and boring."

"I should probably go."

"Probably."

Neither of us moves.

"One drink," he says. "To thank you. For everything."

I know what I should do. I should say no, grab my coat, and walk out the door before this goes somewhere we can't come back from.

"One drink," I hear myself say instead.

We end up in his kitchen, leaning against opposite counters, glasses of red wine in hand. I try not to stare, but it's hard.

The kitchen is stunning—herringbone hardwood floors, a marble backsplash that catches the under-cabinet lighting, and an island big enough to seat four, complete with a built-in wine cooler beneath. It has professional-grade everything—a kitchen you'd see on Pinterest and assume no one actually owns. But there's a step stool by the sink so Maisie can reach the faucet, and a cookie jar shaped like a dinosaur sits on the counter. A bowl of clementines rests nearby, and a chore chart on the wall features Maisie's name in glitter letters. A permission slip for a field trip clings to the fridge with a magnet shaped like a hockey puck. It's not a showroom; luxury meets real life, and somehow, that makes it even more attractive.

"She showed me around her room," I say. "Very strong opinions about bookshelf organization."

"Let me guess—arranged by height?"

"Tallest to shortest. She made me fix one I accidentally bumped."

"That's my girl." He takes a sip of wine, and I watch his throat move as he swallows. "What else did you two talk about?"

"*Bluey*, Ellie the elephant, and the fact that you don't eat green vegetables."

"She lies."

"She also mentioned her mom."

His expression shifts—not exactly closing off, but becoming careful. "What did she say?"

"Just that her mom left and didn't come back." I set my wine glass down. "And that she worries about you not coming back too.'"

Zayden is quiet for a moment. "I know. I'm trying to show her I'm not going anywhere. But it's hard to undo that kind of damage."

"You're doing a good job. She knows you love her."

He smiles, soft and tired. "Yeah."

The silence stretches, warm, comfortable, and dangerous. I should go. I really should go.

"I should go," I say aloud, but I don't move.

"Yeah." He doesn't move either. "You probably should."

"Maisie's upstairs."

"She is."

"And we're... whatever we are."

"Whatever we are," he repeats, a hint of a smile curling at the corner of his mouth. "What are we, exactly?"

"I have no idea." I pick up my wine glass and take a long sip. "But I know we shouldn't be doing what we're doing with your daughter twenty feet away."

"Probably not." He pushes off from the counter, moving closer. "Even though what we're doing is just drinking wine."

"Is that all we're doing?"

"At the moment."

He's close now—close enough that I can see the gold flecks in his dark eyes and the slight curve of his lips.

"You're trouble," I murmur.

"So I've been told." He reaches out, tucking a strand of hair behind my ear. His fingers linger on my jaw, feather-light. "But you like trouble."

"I really don't."

His thumb strokes my cheek. "Then why are you still here?"

I don't have an answer. Or I do, but it's not one I'm ready to say out loud.

His thumb moves across my cheekbone, and I lean into the touch without meaning to. It would be so easy to close the distance, to let him kiss me again and lose myself in the heat and desire coursing through my veins.

But Maisie is upstairs. This is his home, his real life, and if I cross this line, there's no going back.

"I should go," I say again.

This time, I step back, putting space between us. I cross the room and pick up my coat from the couch.

He doesn't stop me, just watches with those dark eyes, hands shoved in his pockets.

"Thank you," he says quietly. "For tonight. For watching Maze."

"Anytime." I mean it more than I should.

I'm at the door when he speaks again.

"Tori."

I turn.

"She liked you." There's something vulnerable in his voice. "Maze doesn't warm up to people easily. I can tell she liked you."

My throat tightens. "I liked her too."

"That means something. To me."

I hold his gaze for a long moment, then nod, open the door, and step out into the frigid night air.

I'm halfway to my car before I let myself exhale.

I just spent the evening with his daughter. I read her bedtime stories, tucked her in, and let her hold my hand while she fell asleep.

This isn't just a kiss in a hallway anymore. This isn't just tension, attraction, and stolen moments.

This is starting to feel like something real.

And I'm terrified.

16

EARLY BIRD GETS THE GIRL

Zayden

The facility's quiet this early. Most of the guys won't roll in for another twenty minutes, which is exactly why I like getting here first. Fewer people. Less noise. More time to get my head right before practice.

"Morning, Mr. Bishop." Eddie, the security guard who's been here longer than most of the roster, looks up from his crossword puzzle.

"Eddie. How's the knee?"

"Better since I started those exercises you told me about." He grins. "Physical therapy works. Who knew?"

"Crazy concept." I tap the desk twice as I pass. "Take it easy."

I'm halfway down the hall toward the locker room when I see them.

Grayson Reed, leaning against the wall outside the training room, arms crossed, that smug smile on his face. He's talking to Tori—or rather, talking *at* her while she tries to organize equipment. His body language is all wrong. Too close. Too confident. Like he's already decided how this is going to end.

Tori's expression is polite but closed off. Professional. The same face she gives difficult patients, the one that says *I'm tolerating you because it's my job*.

I know that face. I used to get that face.

Now I get something different. Softer. Warmer. A look I'm trying very hard not to think about.

Grayson says something, and Tori shakes her head, stepping back to create distance. He follows. Of course he follows. Guys like Grayson don't understand the word no—they hear it as *try harder*.

My hands curl into fists at my sides.

"Easy." Banks appears next to me, gear bag over his shoulder. "You're staring."

"I'm not staring."

"You're about to bore holes through Reed's skull with your eyes."

I force myself to look away. To breathe. To remember that I have no claim on Tori Wells, no right to act like a jealous boyfriend when we're not even—

What are we?

Two kisses. One night in my kitchen where she met my daughter and didn't run screaming. A thousand moments that felt like something but might be nothing.

I don't know what we are. But I know what we're not: public. Official.

So I can't do anything about Grayson Reed except watch and hate every second of it.

Practice is brutal, as usual.

Coach has us running drills until my legs burn, then run them again because Woody missed a pass and someone has to suffer. By the time we hit the locker room, I'm exhausted, but it has nothing to do with hockey.

I shower fast, wanting to get out of here before I have to make small talk with anyone. My shoulder aches—not bad, just enough to remind me it's there—and I'm thinking about Tori. About last night. About the way she looked in my kitchen, holding a glass of wine like she belonged there, all cozy and domestic.

I'm mid-thought when I hear Grayson's voice.

"—been working on her for weeks, man. She's playing hard to get, but they all give in eventually."

I freeze, shirt half-over my head.

"The PT?" someone asks. I think it's one of the rookies. "That Tori chick?"

"Who else?" Grayson laughs. "Ten bucks says I get her number by the end of the road trip. Maybe more than her number, if you know what I mean."

The rookie snickers. "She doesn't seem interested, dude."

"That's the game. They act like they're not interested, you push a little harder, and eventually…" He makes a sound that turns my vision red. "Trust me. I've got a system."

My feet are moving before my brain catches up.

Banks intercepts me three steps from Grayson's locker, hand clamping down on my arm hard enough to bruise.

"Don't."

"He's talking about her like she's—" I can't even finish the sentence. Like she's a conquest. A game. A thing to be won instead of a person who deserves respect.

"I know." Banks' voice is low, steady. "But you throw a punch, you prove every headline they've ever written about you. The temper. The instability. All of it."

"I don't care."

"You should. You've got a kid, Zay. You've got a career. You really want to blow that up because Reed's a piece of shit?" He tightens his grip. "Everyone already knows he's trash. Don't give him the satisfaction."

I'm shaking. Actually shaking, with the effort of not crossing this room and putting my fist through Grayson Reed's perfect teeth.

Câlice.

The Quebecois curse words pop into my head when I'm too angry for English. My mother would still smack me for them, even now. But it gives the rage somewhere to go that isn't my fists.

"Let it go," Banks says again.

I breathe. In through my nose, out through my mouth. The way Tori taught me when my shoulder pain was at its worst and I wanted to punch a wall instead of doing my stretches.

Tori. Who doesn't deserve to be talked about like that. Who's probably dealt with guys like Grayson her entire career—guys who see a woman in sports medicine and assume she's there for their entertainment. It pisses me off.

She's been so careful. So protective of herself.

And assholes like Grayson are exactly why.

"Zay." Banks again, quieter now. "You good?"

I unclench my fists. Roll my shoulders. Force my face into something neutral.

"Yeah," I lie. "I'm good."

He doesn't believe me—I can tell by the way he's watching me—but he lets go of my arm anyway.

I finish getting dressed without looking in Grayson's direction. Without acknowledging the conversation I wasn't supposed to hear. Without giving any indication that I'm two seconds away from committing aggravated assault.

But I'm filing it away. Every word, every laugh, every casual assumption that Tori is something to be won.

Grayson Reed is going to learn otherwise.

I'll make sure of it.

I find Tori in the training room after everyone else has cleared out.

She's wiping down one of the tables, hair pulled back, clearly lost in thought. When she sees me in the doorway, her expression shifts—guarded at first, then softer when she realizes it's me.

"Hey. I thought you'd left."

"I wanted to check in about my shoulder." It's not entirely a lie. "It's a little tight."

"Come here. Let me look."

I cross the room and sit on the table, letting her prod at the joint with those competent hands. She's close enough that I can smell her shampoo—something citrusy—and see the faint freckles across her nose that you'd miss if you weren't paying attention.

I'm always paying attention.

"It feels okay," she says. "Maybe ice tonight, just to be safe. Are you sleeping on it weird?"

"Probably."

"Try to stay on your back. I know it's not comfortable, but—"

"Has Grayson been bothering you?"

She goes still. "What?"

"I saw him earlier. Outside the training room. He was…" I search for a word that isn't going to make me sound as angry as I feel. "Persistent."

"He's harmless." She says it too quickly, the way you do when you've been telling yourself something long enough that you almost believe it.

"Is he?"

"Zayden—"

"Because if he's making you uncomfortable, you should tell Dana. Or Coach. Or—"

"I can handle Grayson Reed." Her voice is firm now, a little sharp. "I've been handling guys like him my entire career. I don't need you to fight my battles."

"I know you don't." I catch her hand, stopping her from prodding at my shoulder. "But you shouldn't have to."

She looks at me, and something in her expression cracks. Just for a second. Just enough for me to see the exhaustion underneath.

"It's fine," she says quietly. "Really. He's annoying, but he's not… he's not a threat."

Ten bucks says I get her number by the end of the road trip.

I don't tell her what I heard. It would only make her feel worse—like she's being talked about, evaluated, reduced to a bet between bored athletes. She already knows how this industry works. She doesn't need the specifics.

"If that changes," I say instead, "you tell me. Yeah?"

Her lips twitch. Almost a smile. "Are you going to beat him up?"

With pleasure. "Do you want me to?"

"No." But she doesn't pull her hand away from mine. "Violence isn't the answer."

"What if it's a really satisfying answer?"

Now she does smile, small and reluctant. "Still no."

"Fine." I squeeze her fingers gently before letting go. "But the offer stands."

She shakes her head, but the tension in her shoulders has eased slightly. That's something.

"Ice your shoulder," she says, stepping back into professional mode. "And try not to start any fights on the road trip."

"No promises."

"Zayden."

"Fine. I promise to *try*."

She rolls her eyes, but she's still smiling when I leave.

I meant what I said. I won't throw a punch—not unless Grayson gives me a reason that even Banks can't argue with.

But I'll be watching.

And if he so much as looks at her wrong, all bets are off.

17

DOWNWARD DOG

Tori

Winnie's yoga classes should come with a warning label.

Something like: *May cause excessive sweating, public embarrassment, and the uncomfortable realization that you have zero core strength despite telling yourself you're "pretty fit."*

I'm rolling up my mat in the back of the studio, still catching my breath from what she cheerfully called a "gentle flow" but was actually forty-five minutes of controlled torture. My thighs are shaking, my arms feel like noodles, and Winnie is up front looking like she just took a leisurely stroll through a meadow, not a single hair out of place in her perfect ponytail.

"You coming?" She bounces over, yoga mat tucked under one toned arm. "I'm dying for a smoothie."

"I'm dying, period."

"Drama queen." She rolls her eyes. "You did great."

"I fell out of tree pose. Twice."

"Everyone falls out of tree pose."

"You didn't."

She waves a hand dismissively. "I've been doing this for years. You've been doing it for—"

"Three classes."

"Exactly. Baby steps." She links her arm through mine and steers me toward the door. "Smoothies. My treat. You can tell me about the latest with your hockey player."

My face heats immediately. "He's not *my* hockey player."

"Mm-hmm. Sure he's not."

The smoothie shop is two blocks from the studio, one of those places with too many options and a line out the door because everyone in Brooklyn apparently needs acai and spirulina at eleven on a Saturday morning.

We grab a spot in line, and I watch the familiar phenomenon unfold.

Three guys at the counter turn to look when we walk in. The one making smoothies nearly drops a blender cup. A dad with a stroller does an actual double-take, then immediately looks guilty about it.

Winnie doesn't notice any of it. She's studying the menu board with genuine concentration, like choosing between mango and passion fruit is a life-altering decision.

This is what it's like being friends with Winnie Garrett.

She's five-foot-six with the kind of effortless beauty that makes people walk into doors. Long, shiny hair, big blue eyes, a body that somehow manages to be both athletic and soft in all the right places.

And the thing is, she genuinely has no idea. I've known her for years, and I've never once seen her use her looks to get anything. She just... exists, being absurdly gorgeous while remaining completely oblivious to the trail of slack-jawed men she leaves in her wake.

"I think I want the green goddess," she says, turning to me. "What about you?"

"Whatever has the most sugar and the least vegetables."

"So the tropical sunrise." She nods approvingly. "Good choice."

"My reward for surviving yoga." I grin.

The guy at the register gives us a thirty percent discount for no apparent reason. Winnie thanks him sweetly and doesn't seem to register that he's blushing so hard he might actually combust.

We grab a table by the window, and she settles across from me, tucking one leg underneath her in that effortlessly flexible way that makes me feel like a wooden board in comparison.

"Okay." She props her chin on her hand. "Spill. What's happening with Grumpy Hockey Dad?"

"Don't call him that."

"Would you prefer Daddy Z? I believe that's one of the official team nicknames."

I choke on air. "How do you know that?"

"You told me. Last week. After your second glass of wine." She grins.

I drop my forehead to the table. "I hate you."

"You love me. Now talk. What's the update?"

I lift my head and take a long sip of my smoothie, stalling. Because the truth is, I don't even know where to start. The last two weeks have been a blur of stolen moments, lingering glances, and the constant, low-grade hum of want that I can't seem to shake no matter how hard I try.

"I met his daughter," I finally say.

Winnie's eyebrows shoot up. "You what?"

"His nanny had an emergency. He needed someone to watch her. I was..." I trail off. "Available."

"Available." She repeats the word slowly, like she's testing it for hidden meaning. "So you babysat for him."

I shrug. "I was just... helping out."

"For how long?"

"A few hours."

"And?"

I stare into my smoothie. "And she's great. She's six, and she's funny and sweet and way too smart for her own good. She made me rank her stuffed animals by importance and quizzed me on dinosaur facts, and she—" My throat tightens unexpectedly. "She fell asleep holding my hand."

Winnie is quiet for a moment. When I look up, her expression has shifted into something softer, more serious. "Tori."

"I know."

"You met his kid. You were in his house. You tucked his daughter into bed."

"I know, okay? I know." I press my palms against my eyes. "And then he came home, and we had wine in his kitchen, and he was looking at me like—"

"Like what?"

Like I was something he wanted to keep. I don't say that out loud. It sounds too big. Too real.

"Like he wanted to kiss me again," I say instead.

"Again?" Winnie leans forward. "Wait. Back up. You kissed again?"

I nod. "In the training room and then at a team banquet, and I—" I'm rambling now, words tumbling out faster than I can organize them. "The second one was in a hallway, and he had me against the wall, and I could feel—I mean, he was—"

"Hard?"

"Winnie."

"What? I'm just clarifying." She's grinning now, enjoying this way too much. "So you've made out with your hockey player multiple times, you've met his daughter, you've been in his home, and you're sitting here acting like this is still somehow professional?"

"It is still professional. Technically. We haven't actually..." I make a vague gesture.

"Haven't actually what? Jumped his bones? Let him score?"

"Please stop."

"Let him put the puck in the net? Taken a ride on his hockey stick?"

"I will throw this smoothie at you."

She laughs, bright and delighted, and a guy two tables over literally turns around to stare at her.

"Okay, okay." She holds up her hands in surrender. "I'll behave. But Tori, seriously." Her expression sobers. "You know what's happening here, right?"

"Nothing is happening."

"Something is definitely happening. You're falling for this guy."

The words land in my chest like a stone dropped into still water, ripples spreading outward and disturbing everything.

"I can't fall for him," I say quietly. "I have rules. Rules that exist for a reason. You're the one who warned me about his reputation, remember?"

"I know. And I stand by being cautious." She reaches across the table and takes my hand. "But I've also been watching you for the past few weeks, and you know what I see?"

"What?"

"Someone who's actually happy." She squeezes my fingers. "When's the last time you felt like this about anyone?"

I think about my nonexistent dating life.

"It's been a while," I admit.

"Exactly." She releases my hand and sits back. "Look, I'm not saying throw caution to the wind. I'm just saying... maybe don't let fear make your decisions for you."

"I'm not—"

"I know you, Tori. You use logic like a shield."

That lands a little too close to home. I take another sip of my smoothie just to have something to do.

"He's got a kid," I say finally. "Anyone he dates isn't just dating him—they're auditioning for stepmom. That's... a lot."

"So?"

"So am I even ready for that? I'm twenty-six. I still forget to water my plants. I ate cereal for dinner three times last week." I drain half my glass. "And Maisie's already been abandoned by her mom. She doesn't need some random woman waltzing in and then disappearing when things get hard."

Winnie tilts her head, studying me. "Do you think that's what you'd do? Waltz in and disappear?"

"No. I don't know. Maybe."

"Tori." She sets down her wine. "You've wanted kids for as long as I've known you. You used to babysit three families on our street at the same time and loved every second of it. You cried at that diaper commercial last month."

"It was emotional. The dad learned to braid hair."

"My point is, you're not some flight risk. You're the most loyal person I know." She pulls her smoothie closer. "And yeah, dating a guy with a kid is serious. But you're not some random woman. You're you. And from everything you've told me, that little girl already likes you."

I think about Maisie looking up at me with those trusting eyes, telling me her daddy talked about me.

My throat tightens.

"What if I mess it up?"

"What if you don't?"

I drop my head onto the table with a groan and Winnie pats it.

"Not every relationship ends in disaster. Some

of them actually work out."

I look up. "Says the woman who's been with Derek for two years."

Something flickers across her face. There and gone, so fast I almost miss it.

"How is Derek?" I ask, suddenly realizing I haven't asked in weeks. I've been so wrapped up in my own drama. "Is everything okay with you guys?"

"Fine." She says it too quickly, the same way I say "fine" when things are definitely not fine.

"Win."

"It's fine, Tori. We're just... going through a thing." She waves a hand vaguely. "Every couple goes through things."

"What kind of thing?"

She's quiet for a moment, stirring her smoothie with the paper straw. "The kind where I'm starting to wonder if we want the same things. Or if we ever did."

My chest tightens. Winnie and Derek have never made sense to me, but I thought she was happy. They're not the most obviously compatible couple—he's kind of a dudebro with strong opinions about protein intake, the "right" way to grill a steak, and why everyone should be doing cold plunges. And she's... well, Winnie, the sweetest, kindest, most genuine soul—but I always assumed they were solid.

"Do you want to talk about it?"

"Not really. Not today." She looks up and gives me a smile that doesn't quite reach her eyes. "Today is about your love life drama. Mine can wait."

"Win—"

"I mean it. I'm fine." She reaches over and pats my hand. "Besides, we were in the middle of something important. You were telling me about your hockey player's impressive... attributes."

"I was not telling you that."

"You were about to. I could see it in your eyes."

I laugh despite myself. "You're impossible."

"I'm delightful. There's a difference." She grins, and it's almost her normal grin. Almost. "Now. Back to the important stuff. You've kissed him twice. Met his daughter. So, what's the plan?"

"There is no plan. I'm just... taking it day by day."

"That's not a plan. That's avoidance."

"It's called being cautious."

She takes a breath. "I think you're going to sleep with him."

I nearly spit out my smoothie. "Winnie."

"No, I mean it. You're going to sleep with him, and it's going to be amazing, and then you're going to have a full-scale panic attack about what it means." She tilts her head. "Am I wrong?"

"I have rules," I say weakly.

"Babe." She puts a hand on my arm. "Rules are meant to be broken. Especially the dumb ones."

"It's not dumb. It's my career."

"Your career will survive. You're good at your job. One relationship isn't going to change that." Her expression softens. "The question is whether your heart will survive if you keep pushing away the first guy who's made you feel something in years."

I'm not sure what to say.

Because she's right. Zayden Bishop makes me feel things. Things I'd forgotten I was capable of feeling. Things I'd convinced myself I didn't need.

And that terrifies me more than any career risk ever could.

"I don't know what I'm doing," I admit quietly.

"Nobody does. That's the secret." Winnie squeezes my arm. "But I've seen you at your worst, Tori. After Jason, after all of it. I've never seen you light up the way you do when you talk about this guy."

"I don't light up."

"You absolutely light up. Like a dang Christmas tree. Your whole face changes. It's honestly kind of disgusting."

I laugh, even though my eyes are suddenly stinging. "I'm scared, Win. What if I mess this up? What if I'm not what he needs? What if Maisie gets attached and then I—"

"What if it works out?" She cuts me off gently. "What if he's exactly what you need, and you're exactly what he needs, and that little girl gets someone in her life who actually shows up?"

My throat tightens.

"You'd be good at it, you know," Winnie adds, softer now. "The mom thing. You've always been nurturing; it's in your DNA."

That's the thing about having a best friend.

They see all the best parts of you.

18

MIRACULOUS RECOVERY

Grayson Reed's hip injury is a medical marvel.

It flares up whenever I'm on shift and disappears completely when James covers for me—almost like it has access to my Google calendar.

Funny how that works.

This is the third "emergency treatment" he's needed this week. The first time, I gave him the benefit of the doubt. The second time, I was suspicious. Now I'm just annoyed.

He's also developed a habit of needing ice baths when I'm restocking the training room—ice baths that apparently require nothing but a pair of very snug black boxer briefs that leave absolutely nothing to the imagination. It's a lot. And he always has "quick questions" that turn into fifteen minutes of him leaning against doorframes in a towel, smiling like he's waiting for me to notice how charming he is.

I've noticed. I'm just not impressed.

"Right here," he says, pointing vaguely at his hip flexor. "It's been killing me."

I palpate the area. No inflammation. No tightness. No strain beyond what any athlete carries. His hip is perfectly fine, and we both know it.

"Feels normal to me." I step back from the table, frowning. "Ice if it bothers you, but honestly? There's nothing there."

"Maybe I just like the attention." He sits up slowly, watching me. "You've got good hands, Wells."

"It's my job."

"Still." He swings his legs off the table and stands, positioning himself between me and the door now, which I'm sure is just a coincidence, even if it feels a little odd. "We should grab a drink sometime. Celebrate my miraculous recovery."

"I don't think so."

"Come on." He takes a step closer. "One drink. What's the harm?"

"I don't date players." I keep my voice flat. Bored. "It's not personal."

"Everything's personal." Another step. He's close enough now that I can smell his cologne—something expensive and aggressive, like he bathed in it. "I've seen the way you look at Bishop."

My heart stutters, but I keep my face blank. "I don't know what you're talking about."

"Sure you do." His smile sharpens. "You've got a type. I'm just trying to figure out where I fit."

"You don't."

The words come out harder than I intended. Good.

His expression fades. The charming mask slips, just for a second, revealing something uglier underneath. Entitlement. Irritation. The look of a man who's not used to hearing no.

"That's not very friendly," he says softly.

"I'm not here to be friendly. I'm here to do my job." I grab my tablet from the counter and move toward the door. Toward him. "Now, if you'll excuse me—"

He doesn't move.

For a long, uncomfortable moment, we just stand there. Him blocking the exit. Me refusing to back down. The air between us thick.

"Reed." I keep my voice steady. "Move."

He holds my gaze for another beat. Then he steps aside, hands raised in mock surrender.

"Relax, Wells. I was just making conversation."

I push past him without responding. My shoulder brushes his chest as I go, and I hate how much I want to shower after that brief contact.

"See you around," he calls after me.

I don't look back. But I feel his eyes on me all the way down the hall, and the expression I glimpsed before I turned away?

It said this isn't over.

I shouldn't tell Zayden.

It's not his problem. We're not together—not really, not officially—and the last thing I need is him going full protective alpha and doing something stupid that gets him in trouble.

I can handle Grayson Reed. I've been handling guys like him my entire career.

But when I walk into the training room an hour later and find Zayden there—alone, stretching his shoulder, looking up at me with those dark eyes—it just spills out.

"Reed's been... a lot," I blurt out after our third round of stretches.

He goes still. Completely, unnaturally still, like a predator who's just caught a scent. "What do you mean, a lot?"

"Nothing I can't handle."

"That's not what I asked." His voice is low. Controlled.

I set my tablet down and lean against the counter, crossing my arms. "He asked me out. I said no. He didn't take it well."

"Didn't take it well how?"

"Blocked the door. Got in my space."

Zay's nostrils flare. "What the fuck?"

"And he mentioned you," I say finally. "Said something about how I've got a type."

Zayden's jaw tightens. A muscle tics near his temple. "What did you say?"

"It's fine," I add quickly. "I handled it. And he eventually backed off."

"For now."

"Zayden—"

"It's not fine." He stands, closing the distance between us in two steps. Close enough that I have to tilt my head back to meet his eyes. Close enough that I can feel the heat radiating off him, can see the tension coiled in every line of his body. "If he bothers you again—"

"You'll what? Punch him? And end up suspended?" I raise an eyebrow. "How exactly does that help me?"

He exhales. A long, slow breath, like he's physically forcing himself to calm down.

"It doesn't," he admits. "I know it doesn't."

"So don't."

"I'm trying." His hands are clenched at his sides. "But when you tell me some asshole is cornering you, blocking doors, making you uncomfortable—"

"I didn't say he made me uncomfortable."

"You didn't have to."

We stare at each other. The air between us charged with everything we're not saying.

"Tell Dana," he says finally. "Document everything. Dates, times, what he said. Create a paper trail."

"And if that doesn't work?"

"Then we figure out the next step. Together." He holds my gaze. "But if he touches you—if he puts his hands on you, even once—I don't care about suspensions. I don't care about headlines. Yeah?"

That soft "yeah" at the end. It shouldn't make me feel safe, seen, and cared for. But it does.

"Yeah," I whisper back.

He nods once. Then he reaches out and takes my hand—just holds it, his thumb brushing across my knuckles. The gesture is so simple, so steady, that it hits harder than any kiss would.

"I've got you," he says quietly. "You know

that, right?"

I do know that. That's what terrifies me.

"I know."

He drops his hand, steps back, and the loss of contact feels like a physical thing.

"Ice my shoulder?" he asks, and just like that, we're back to professional. Back to the roles we're supposed to be playing.

"Sit down," I say. "And stop getting into fights you can't win."

"Who says I can't win?"

"You'd win the fight and lose everything else. Suspension. Headlines. Who knows what else." I grab the ice pack. "Not worth it."

Zayden frowns, watching me with those dark eyes.

He's impossible. Protective and stubborn and way too intense for his own good.

And somehow, despite every rule I've ever made for myself, I'm in deep. Way too deep. That's the scariest part of all.

19

EMERGENCY CONTACT

Tori

My phone buzzes while I'm restocking supplies, and Zayden's name on the screen makes my stomach do a little flip.

Zayden

I need a favor.

Hannah's sick. Stomach bug. Can't pick up Maisie from school.

Flight from Jersey got delayed. I won't land until 4.

I tried the backup sitter, but she's not answering.

Three dots appear. Disappear. Appear again. I didn't travel with the team for this one—just an overnight trip to Jersey, quick turnaround.

Zayden

School gets out at 3:20.

I check the clock. 2:47.

Me

Send me the address. I'll head over now.

Zayden

You're sure?

Me

Already grabbing my keys.

Zayden

I owe you.

Me

You really don't.

Twenty minutes later, I'm standing in the pickup line at the elementary school, feeling distinctly out of place among the SUVs and minivans and the moms who clearly all know each other. A woman in yoga pants and a messy bun gives me a once-over, probably trying to figure out if I'm a nanny, an aunt, or some random kidnapper.

I give her a little wave. She does not wave back.

The doors open, and kids start streaming out—a flood of backpacks, lunch boxes, and high-pitched chatter. I scan the crowd until I spot her. Maisie, walking with her head down, her dinosaur backpack nearly as big as she is.

She looks up, sees me, and her whole face transforms.

"Tori?"

She breaks into a run, weaving through the other kids, and crashes into my legs hard enough to make me stumble. Her arms wrap around my waist and squeeze.

"Hey, Maze." I smooth a hand over her hair, something warm and dangerous blooming in my chest. "Surprise."

"Where's Hannah?"

"She's not feeling well, so I'm on pickup duty. That okay?"

She pulls back and looks up at me with those big brown eyes—Zayden's eyes—and nods solemnly. "That's very okay with me."

This kid. Seriously.

"Your dad said I could take you for ice cream if you want. Or we could go to the park. Your call."

"Ice cream," she says immediately. "Obviously."

"Obviously. Let's go."

The ice cream shop has too many flavors and a toppings case that would make a dentist weep. Maisie peers through the glass, studying her options.

"Cotton candy," she decides. "With rainbow sprinkles. And gummy bears."

"Solid choice."

I order her a kid's cup and get myself salted caramel because I'm a grown-up and I can. We grab a booth by the window, and Maisie attacks her ice cream like she hasn't eaten in days. There's a spot of blue on her nose within thirty seconds.

"So," she says between bites. "Are you my dad's girlfriend?"

I choke on my salted caramel.

"Um." I grab a napkin, buying time. "That's... we're... your dad and I work together."

"Hannah thinks you're his girlfriend."

"She does?"

"She said, 'I think she might be his girlfriend,' on the phone to someone." Maisie shrugs, unbothered by the eavesdropping admission. "I have good ears."

"Apparently."

"So are you?"

How do you explain situationship dynamics to a six-year-old? How do you explain them to yourself when you don't even know what's happening?

"Your dad and I are figuring things out," I say carefully. "We like each other. But it's complicated."

Maisie considers this, spoon hovering mid-air. "Because you work together?"

"Partly."

"What's the other part?"

"Grown-up stuff."

"That's what people say when they don't want to explain things."

"You're too smart for your own good."

She grins, and there's a chunk of gummy bear stuck to her front tooth. "Daddy says that too."

We eat in comfortable silence for a minute. The afternoon sun slants through the window, catching the glitter in her nail polish—purple, slightly chipped.

"Do you have kids?" she asks suddenly.

The question lands somewhere soft and unprotected. "No, I don't."

"How come?"

"I guess... I just haven't yet. I've been busy with school and work." I trail off, unsure how to finish.

"Do you want kids?"

I look at her—this earnest, curious girl with ice cream on her chin and questions that cut right to the bone—and something in my chest aches.

"Yeah," I admit quietly. "I do. Someday."

"You'd be a good mom."

The words hit like a sucker punch. I have to look away, blinking hard, focusing on the napkin dispenser until I'm sure I'm not going to cry in the middle of an ice cream shop.

"Thanks, Maze." My voice comes out rougher than I intended. "That's really sweet."

"It's true." She says it matter-of-factly, like stating the weather. "You let me get sprinkles *and* gummy bears. And you actually listen when I talk instead of looking at your phone."

"Of course I listen. You're interesting."

"And you don't make promises you don't keep."

That one lands heavily. I think about Sienna, showing up twice a year with expensive gifts and empty words, leaving Maisie to pick up the pieces.

"I try not to," I say.

Maisie nods, swirling her spoon through what's left of her ice cream, turning it into blue soup. "My mom says stuff but then doesn't do it. Like she said she'd come to my dance recital, but then she had a 'work thing.'" She makes air quotes with sticky fingers. "And she said we'd go to Disney, but that didn't happen either."

"I'm sorry, honey."

"It's okay. I'm used to it."

She says it so casually, like it's just a fact of her life, and that's somehow worse than if she'd cried.

"You shouldn't have to be used to it."

She looks up at me, head tilted. "You're better at this than my mom. The mom stuff, I mean."

I can't breathe.

I physically cannot draw air into my lungs because this six-year-old just said the thing I didn't know I needed to hear and also the thing that's going to wreck me completely.

"Maisie..."

"I'm not trying to be mean about her," she adds quickly. "I love my mom. I just..." She shrugs those little shoulders. "I'm glad you're here with me."

I reach across the table and take her hand. Her fingers are sticky with sugar, and she squeezes back with surprising strength.

I don't know what's happening with her dad, not when my career could implode if anyone finds out how deep I'm already in. But I can give her this moment. This afternoon. This version of me that shows up.

"Can we go to the park after?"

"Absolutely."

"And can you push me on the swings?"

"As high as you want."

"And can you not tell Daddy about the ice cream before dinner? He gets weird about sugar."

I laugh, and it comes out watery. "That might be hard. Your face is literally blue."

She grins and licks her spoon. "Worth it."

The park is mostly empty—a few kids on the climbing structure, a dad scrolling his phone on a bench, everyone bundled against the late afternoon chill. Maisie's got her purple puffer coat zipped to her chin and a colorful pom-pom beanie. She makes a beeline for the swings, and I settle into the familiar rhythm of pushing her higher while she kicks her legs and shrieks.

"Higher! Higher!"

"Any higher and you're achieving orbit."

"What's orbit?"

"Space. You'll fly into space."

"Cool!"

I push her again, watching her ponytail stream behind her. The late afternoon light is golden, and for a moment I let myself pretend this is my life. That I pick her up every day, that I know her favorite flavor and all her stuffed animals' names, that I get to watch her grow up.

Dangerous fantasy. I know that.

I let myself have it anyway.

My phone buzzes.

Zayden

Just landed. How's she doing?

Me

Currently attempting to defy gravity on the swings. I'm supervising.

Zayden

That tracks.

I can be there in 45. You're okay to stay?

Me

Of course.

Zayden

Thank you, Tori.

Three dots appear. Disappear. Appear again.

Zayden

For everything.

I pocket my phone and go back to pushing Maisie, trying not to think about how this feels more like home than anywhere I've been in years.

We're on the couch watching *Moana* when Zayden walks in.

Maisie's tucked against my side, singing along under her breath to "How Far I'll Go" while I pretend not to notice. There are goldfish crumbs on my shirt, her hair is escaping its ponytail, and she's got the blanket pulled up to her chin even though the living room is perfectly warm.

"This is the best part," she whispers loudly, like it's a secret. "Watch, watch, watch—"

Zayden stops in the doorway. Just... looks at us.

His face does something complicated. Soft and hungry and sad all at once, like he's seeing something he wants but doesn't think he's allowed to have.

"Daddy!" Maisie launches off the couch and barrels into him. He catches her easily, scooping her up like she weighs nothing.

"Hey, little shadow." He presses a kiss to her temple. "Good day?"

"The best." She's already talking a mile a minute. "Tori took me for ice cream and the park, and we watched *Moana*, and she knows all the words to the songs, and she can push really high on the swings, like really, *really* high—"

His eyes cut to me over her head, amused. "She knows all the words?"

"I have a lot of hidden talents."

"Apparently." He's smiling—really smiling—and it transforms his whole face. "Thank you. Seriously."

"Stop thanking me. It was fun." I rise from the couch. "I should go. Let you guys have dinner."

"Stay."

The word comes out fast, like he didn't plan it. We both freeze.

"I mean—" He runs a hand through his hair. "I'm ordering Italian. There's always too much. You should stay."

I should go. Maintain distance. Protect my heart from this man and his daughter and the life they're offering me one moment at a time.

"Okay," I say. "I'll stay."

Maisie cheers weakly from the couch, and Zayden's whole face lights up.

I am in so much trouble.

But when Maisie grabs my hand and pulls me toward the kitchen, chattering about her favorite noodles, I find I don't really care.

20

DINNER FOR THREE

Zayden

The Italian arrives in twenty minutes, which gives me eighteen minutes of Maisie talking Tori's ear off about her best friend Sophie's hamster, and two minutes of me standing in the kitchen pretending to get plates while actually just watching them.

They're on the couch together, with Maisie's legs draped across Tori's lap as if they've done this a hundred times. Tori nods along to the hamster saga with genuine interest, asking questions and laughing at all the right moments. Her hair is coming loose from its ponytail, and she looks more relaxed than I've ever seen her.

She looks like she belongs here.

The thought hits me square in the chest, and I have to turn away, gripping the edge of the counter until I regain my composure.

"Daddy, did you know hamsters can run eight miles in one night?" Maisie calls out.

"I did not know that."

"Tori says it's because they have lots of energy

and nowhere to put it. Like me."

Tori catches my eye over Maisie's head, a smile tugging at her mouth. "Her words, not mine."

"Accurate, though," I reply.

The doorbell rings, and I grab the food, tipping the delivery guy too much because I'm distracted. By the time I unpack everything on the table, Maisie has dragged Tori to the kitchen by the hand and installed her in the chair next to hers.

"You sit here," she instructs. "Daddy sits there. Those are the rules."

"I didn't know we had seating rules," I say.

"We do now."

Tori bites her lip, clearly fighting a laugh. "I guess I'm sitting here, then."

I pour wine for Tori and myself, apple juice for Maisie, and start dishing out pasta. It feels weirdly domestic—passing containers back and forth, twirling noodles onto forks, the clink of glasses— like we're a real family instead of whatever we actually are.

"This is really good," Tori says after her first bite.

"Sal's. Best carbonara in Brooklyn."

"Bold claim."

"I stand by it."

Maisie watches this exchange with the laser focus of a tiny detective. I know that look. It means she's about to say something that will either be hilarious or mortifying, with no in-between.

"Tori," she says, twirling her fork with exaggerated casualness, "do you think my dad is handsome?"

And there it is.

Tori chokes on her wine. I close my eyes briefly, wondering if it's possible to die of secondhand embarrassment.

"Um." Tori dabs at her mouth with a napkin. "That's... a very direct question."

"Hannah says he's handsome," Maisie adds, nodding.

Great. So my middle-aged nanny has apparently been checking me out. That's not uncomfortable at all.

"She told her friend on the phone that he looks like a 'romance novel cover,'" Maisie continues, making air quotes. "What's a romance novel?"

"Nothing," I say quickly. "Eat your pasta."

Hannah—sweet, matronly Hannah who bakes cookies and does crossword puzzles—discusses my looks with her friends. Cool. Great. Love that for me.

Tori's cheeks are pink, but she's smiling. "Your dad is... yes. He's handsome."

"Ha!" Maisie points her fork at me triumphantly. "I told you."

"You told me what? We've never discussed this."

"I told Sophie you were handsome, and she said her mom thinks so too, and I said obviously because you're my dad." She shrugs as if this is perfectly logical. "So I was right."

I take a very long sip of wine.

Tori's shoulders are shaking with silent laughter. When I catch her eye, she mouths *sorry* at me, but she doesn't look sorry at all.

"Do you have a boyfriend?" Maisie asks Tori, pivoting without warning.

"Maisie."

"What? It's just a question."

Tori sets down her fork, giving the question serious consideration. "No. I don't have a boyfriend."

"How come? You're really pretty."

"Thank you. I've just been... busy with work."

Maisie nods sagely, as if she understands the demands of a professional career. "Daddy doesn't have a girlfriend either. He says he's too busy, but I think he's just scared."

I'm going to ground this child until she's thirty.

The table goes quiet for a moment. Tori's eyes meet mine, and there's a whole conversation happening in that look—one we can't have out loud, not here, not with Maisie watching us like we're the most interesting show on television.

"More pasta?" I ask, because I'm a coward.

"Please."

I serve her another helping, and our fingers brush when I pass the plate. It's nothing—barely a touch—but I feel it everywhere.

"You guys keep looking at each other funny," Maisie observes.

"We're not looking at each other funny," I insist.

"You are. It's the same way Sophie's mom looks at Sophie's stepdad," she states before taking a big bite of pasta. "Right before they kiss."

I'm going to need more wine.

"So," Tori says brightly, clearly desperate for a subject change. "Maisie, tell me more about the recital. What are you dancing to?"

It works. Maisie launches into an elaborate description of her dance routine, complete with demonstrations of specific moves that nearly knock over her juice. By the time she's done explaining the "very important twirl at the end," the tension has eased, and we're back to something that feels almost normal.

Almost.

Because underneath the easy conversation, I'm hyper-aware of everything—the way Tori laughs at Maisie's jokes, the way she asks follow-up questions that prove she's actually listening, and the way she looks at my daughter like she matters— like her recital, hamster facts, and opinions about pasta shapes are worth paying attention to.

Sienna never looked at her like that. Not once.

My throat tightens.

Dinner continues. Maisie asks Tori her favorite dinosaur (T-Rex, though she admits the Pachycephalosaurus has "great energy"). She asks what Tori wanted to be when she grew up (a marine biologist, then a teacher, then a physical therapist). She asks if Tori can do a cartwheel (yes, but not indoors, a rule Maisie finds deeply unfair).

And through all of it, I just watch—watch Tori charm my daughter without even trying, watch Maisie open up in ways she rarely does with new people, and watch this connection forming between the three of us that I didn't plan for, didn't expect, and definitely don't know how to handle.

"I'm done," Maisie announces, pushing her plate away. "Can we have dessert?"

"You had ice cream two hours ago."

"That was a snack. This is dessert. Totally different."

"She's got you there," Tori says.

"Whose side are you on?"

"Hers. Obviously." She grins at me. "Girls stick together."

Maisie beams. "Yeah, Daddy. Girls stick together."

I'm outnumbered, and honestly? I don't hate it.

We compromise on half a cookie each—chocolate chip, from the batch Hannah made—and then it's cleanup time. Tori starts clearing plates before I can stop her.

"You don't have to do that."

"I want to." She's already at the sink, rinsing dishes. "You cooked. Well, you ordered. Same thing."

"It's really not."

"Close enough."

Maisie disappears to use the bathroom, and suddenly we're alone in the kitchen, standing side by side at the sink, and the air between us changes. It thickens.

"She likes you," I say quietly.

"I like her too." Tori hands me a plate to load into the dishwasher. "She's amazing, Zay. You've done such a good job with her."

The compliment lands somewhere soft. "I just try not to screw it up."

"You're not screwing it up." She turns to look at me, and we're close—too close for two people who are supposed to be figuring things out. "She's happy. She's confident. She knows she's loved. That's all you."

My hand finds her hip before I can think better of it. She doesn't pull away.

"Tori..."

"Daddy!" Maisie's voice echoes from the hallway. "I can't find my pajamas!"

We spring apart like teenagers caught making out.

"Check the dryer!" I call back, my voice only slightly strangled.

"Oh! Found them!"

Tori lets out a breath that's half laugh, half something else. "That was close."

"Story of our lives lately."

We finish the dishes in charged silence. Every accidental brush of shoulders, every time our hands touch while reaching for the same thing—it all feels significant. Weighted. Like we're both holding our breath, waiting for something to happen.

The dishwasher hums to life, and Tori dries her hands on the kitchen towel.

"I should go," she says. "Let you guys get to bath time."

"You could stay."

The words come out rougher than I intended. She looks at me, startled.

"Stay," I say again, softer this time. "I'll put her down, read her a story. It takes maybe thirty minutes. And then we can... talk. About everything."

She's quiet for a moment, and I can see her thinking, weighing her options. Wanting to say yes but afraid of what yes might mean. "I can't," she whispers. "Not tonight."

"Why not?"

"Because if I stay..." She swallows hard. "I'm trying to have some boundaries here. And being alone with you, in your home, after dinner with your daughter—" She shakes her head. "It's too much. I'll say yes to things I'm not ready to say yes to."

I want to convince her. But I look at her face and see the genuine uncertainty in her eyes—and I make myself step back.

"Okay," I say.

She stares at me for a long moment. Then she rises on her toes and presses a kiss to my cheek—soft and quick, her lips warm against my skin.

"Goodnight, Zayden."

"Goodnight."

Maisie comes barreling back into the kitchen carrying her dinosaur pajamas, her hair a tangled mess.

"Is Tori leaving?"

"Yeah, sweetheart. She has to go home."

Maisie's face falls for just a second before she recovers. "Will you come back? ... another time?"

Tori crouches down to Maisie's level—something I've noticed she does every time she talks to her, meeting her as an equal, not speaking down from above.

"I hope so," she says carefully. "I'd like that."

It's not a promise. I can tell she's choosing her words, protecting my daughter from the kind of guarantees that might not hold. And somehow that makes me fall for her even harder—that she cares enough to be careful with a little girl's heart.

Maisie considers this for a moment, then throws her arms around Tori's neck. "Okay."

Tori hugs her back, one hand smoothing over Maisie's hair. "I had a really good time with you today."

"Me too." Maisie pulls back and looks at her seriously. "You're my favorite of Daddy's friends."

Tori's laugh comes out a little watery. "Thanks, Maze. That means a lot."

"I'll walk you out," I say, my voice rougher than I intended.

We go to the door together, Maisie trailing behind us. In the hallway, Tori turns back one more time.

"Thanks for dinner," she says. "And for... everything."

"Thank you for saving my life today. The pickup, I mean."

She smiles—really smiles, the kind that reaches her eyes and makes my heart do something embarrassing.

"Goodnight, Zayden."

"Goodnight, Tori."

I watch her walk to her car and climb inside. Once it starts and pulls away, I go back inside, where my daughter is waiting with a look on her face that is way too knowing for a six-year-old.

"You really like her," she says.

"What makes you say that?"

"You kept looking at her all funny."

"I didn't look at her funny."

"You did." She takes my hand and tugs me toward the hallway. "It's okay, Daddy. I like her too."

"Yeah?"

"Yeah. She's nice. And she listens. And she's really pretty."

"Is she?" My lips twitch. "I hadn't noticed."

"*Dad!*" Maisie whines like I'm the most clueless person she's ever met.

"What?" I laugh. "You're the prettiest girl I know, Maze."

21

PLAYING THE GAME

We're careful.

Polite nods as we pass each other. *Kill me.*

Professional distance during team meals. *Slowly.*

No lingering looks when anyone might be watching. *Torture.*

No touching, even when my hand itches to find the small of her back. *The worst kind of torture.*

She treats me like any other player when we're around the team—professional, distant, all business.

At least, that's the plan.

The reality is messier. The reality is me tracking her across the hotel lobby like some lovesick idiot, pretending I'm checking my phone while I watch her talk to Dana about tomorrow's schedule. The reality is catching her eye for half a second and feeling it everywhere.

"You're staring," Banks says, dropping into the chair next to me.

"I'm not staring."

"You're absolutely staring." He doesn't even look up from his phone. "You've been staring since we landed." For a guy with the resting expression of someone plotting violence, Banks is annoyingly perceptive about other people's emotions.

"Mind your business."

"This is my business. You're my ride or die, Bish. If you crash and burn, I have to hear about it." He finally glances at me, one eyebrow raised. "You two being smart about this?"

"We're being careful."

"That's not what I asked."

I don't answer, because the truth is I don't know anymore. Smart would be keeping my distance. Smart would be waiting until the season's over, until she's not technically part of my medical staff, until there's no risk to her career.

Smart went out the window somewhere around the third time I kissed her.

"Just... don't get caught," Banks says quietly. "For her sake, if not yours."

"I know."

He nods once and goes back to his phone, and I return to not staring at Tori across the lobby.

She's wearing that gray sweater again. The soft one that slips off her shoulder sometimes. I want to put my mouth on that shoulder. I want to do a lot of things I shouldn't be thinking about in a hotel lobby surrounded by my teammates.

She glances over. Our eyes meet.

One corner of her mouth twitches—barely there. A secret meant just for me.

Then she turns back to Dana like nothing happened, and I remember how to breathe.

The in-between moments are where we live now.

The hotel hallway at midnight, when everyone else is asleep, and I "happen" to need ice from the machine near her room.

She opens her door on the second knock, wearing an oversized T-shirt and sleep shorts, her hair loose around her shoulders. Her eyes widen when she sees me.

"Zayden, what are you—"

I crowd her backward into the room, kicking the door shut behind me.

"Five minutes," I say, my hands already finding her waist. "Just give me five minutes."

"Someone could have seen you."

"No one saw me."

"You don't know that."

"Tori." I tip her chin up, forcing her to meet my eyes. "Five minutes. Then I'll go."

She stares at me for a long moment. Then her shoulders drop, and she fists the front of my shirt, pulling me closer.

"Five minutes," she says. "And then you're gone."

I kiss her before she can change her mind.

She tastes like toothpaste and something sweet, and when she sighs against my mouth, her whole body softens into mine. I forget every reason this is a bad idea. My hands slide up her back, pulling her flush against me, and she makes a quiet sound that I want to hear on repeat for the rest of my life.

"Missed you," I murmur against her lips.

"You saw me three hours ago."

"Too long."

She laughs, breathy and warm, and I walk her backward until her knees hit the edge of the bed. She sits, then scoots back, and I follow, stretching out beside her on the crisp hotel sheets.

For a moment, we just lie there, facing each other, close enough that I can count the flecks of gold in her brown eyes. Her hand comes up to rest on my chest, right over my heartbeat.

"This is dangerous," she whispers.

"Probably." I bring her hand to my mouth and press a kiss to her knuckles. "Can't seem to make myself leave."

She watches me with an expression I can't quite read. Then she shifts closer, tucking herself against my chest, and I wrap my arm around her like it's the most natural thing in the world.

We lie there for a while—her head on my shoulder, my fingers tracing lazy patterns on her arm. The room is dimly lit, except for the glow from the desk lamp and the city lights filtering through the curtains.

"Can I ask you something?" I say.

"Mm-hmm."

"Your rule. The no-players thing." I keep my voice soft. "Did that come from somewhere?"

She goes still against me—not pulling away, just... bracing.

"You don't have to tell me," I add. "I just figured—we're lying here in the dark, spilling secrets. Seemed like the right time to ask."

She's quiet for a long moment. Then she exhales, her breath warm against my chest.

After a beat, she says, "His name was Jason. He was the starting quarterback at my college."

I keep my arm steady around her.

"I played soccer," she continues. "Division I. We met at some athlete mixer freshman year. He was..." She laughs, but there's no warmth in it. "He was the golden boy. Charming, good-looking—everyone knew him, everyone loved him. I thought I was so lucky that he picked me."

My jaw tightens, but I stay quiet.

"It started small. A text I saw on his phone. A story that didn't add up. I confronted him, and he apologized, said it would never happen again." She exhales slowly. "And I believed him. Because I wanted to. Because it was easier than admitting I'd been stupid."

"You weren't stupid."

"I was. Because it happened again. And again. And every time, he'd apologize, promise to change, and I'd stay." Her voice goes flat. "For two years, I stayed. Watching him charm everyone while I made excuses, telling myself it would get better."

I want to find this guy and break every bone in his body.

"What finally made you leave?"

"I walked in on him with a freshman from the volleyball team." She shrugs against me, a small, tight movement. "Hard to make excuses when it's happening right in front of you."

"Tori..."

"But the worst part wasn't the cheating. It was what happened after." She finally looks up at me, her eyes dry but hard. "When I ended it, he told everyone I was the crazy ex—obsessive, jealous, making things up. And people believed him. Because he was Jason—star quarterback, the golden boy, everyone's favorite. And I was just the girl who dated him."

My arm tightens around her.

"I watched my reputation disappear overnight," she says quietly. "I wasn't Tori Wells, soccer player, good student, a person with her own life. I was 'the girl who dated Jason.' The cautionary tale. People looked at me with pity, as if I should have known better than to think someone like him would actually want someone like me."

"That's bullshit."

"Maybe. But it's also how the world works." She settles her head back on my shoulder. "That's when I made the rule: no athletes. No one who could turn me into a story instead of a person. No one with that kind of power over my reputation again."

I press my lips to the top of her head and hold them there.

"He was an idiot," I say against her hair. "A complete and total idiot who didn't deserve a single second of your time."

I tilt her face up to mine and press a soft kiss to her mouth.

She's quiet for a moment, her fingers tracing absent patterns on my chest. "There was something else, too."

"Yeah?"

"My first job out of grad school. A sports medicine clinic that worked with a college basketball team." She exhales slowly. "There was another trainer there—Carla. She was good. Really good. Better than me, honestly. She'd been there for years."

I wait, worried I know where this is going.

"She started seeing one of the players. Kept it quiet, thought she was being careful." Tori shrugs against me. "Someone found out. I don't even know who or how. But within a week, she was gone. No formal termination, no big announcement. Just... quietly removed. Like she'd never existed."

"What happened to the player?"

"Nothing." Her voice goes flat. "He finished the season, got drafted, moved on with his life. Meanwhile, Carla couldn't get a reference, couldn't explain the gap in her resume without the story following her. Last I heard, she had to take a demotion just to find another job."

My jaw tightens.

"This rule isn't just about protecting my heart. It's about protecting everything I'd worked for." She looks up at me. "Women in sports medicine— we're already fighting to be taken seriously. One wrong move and you're not the talented trainer anymore. You're the cautionary tale. The one who couldn't keep it professional."

I release a long, heavy exhale, hating that part of me knows she's right.

She stares at me, eyes searching. "Your turn,"

she whispers.

"My turn?"

"Fair's fair. I showed you mine."

I almost smile. Almost.

Then I think about Sienna, and the almost-smile dies.

"Maisie's mom... Sienna."

Tori waits. Her hand finds mine in the dark, fingers intertwining.

"We met at a charity event. She was beautiful, charming, knew all the right things to say." I stare at the ceiling. "I was twenty-two and naive, thinking I'd found the real thing."

"What happened?"

"She got pregnant. I thought that meant we were building something, you know? A family." The words come out flat. "Turns out we had very different definitions of that word."

"How so?"

"Sienna didn't want to be a mom. She wanted to be a hockey wife—the glamour, the money, the lifestyle. She thought a baby would be... I don't know, an accessory. Something cute for Instagram photos."

Tori's hand tightens on mine.

"When she realized that motherhood was actually hard—the sleepless nights, the crying, the mess—she checked out. She hired nannies and started traveling for 'work.'" I make air quotes in the dark. "She's an influencer now."

"And Maisie?"

"Maisie was an inconvenience, a complication in the brand. We broke up by the time Maisie was six months old." My voice grows rough. "I was terrified, I'd never spent any time around babies, but I figured it out. Sienna would show up twice a year with expensive gifts, make promises she never kept, then disappear again. Every time, Maze would wait by the window for days, thinking maybe this time Mom would come back."

"Zayden..."

"I got full custody when Maze was thirteen months old. Sienna didn't even fight it. She just signed the papers and posted a photo from Bali the next day." I finally look at Tori. "So that's my thing—I don't trust easily. I don't let people close because the last person I let in used me for my name and treated my daughter like she was disposable."

The room is quiet except for the hum of the air conditioner and the distant sounds of the city below.

Tori shifts, propping herself up on one elbow so she can look down at me. Her hand comes up to rest on my jaw, warm and steady.

"We're a mess," she says softly.

I turn my head and press a kiss to her palm. "We're healing."

She looks at me like no one has ever said that to her before. Like the word is foreign, like maybe she'd forgotten it was even an option.

"Yeah?" she whispers.

"Yeah." I pull her back down, tucking her against my chest, and she comes willingly, her body fitting into mine like she was made for this exact spot.

She's quiet for a moment, her fingers tracing

absent patterns on my chest. "Five minutes are up, lover boy," she teases.

I tighten my arms around her. "Five more."

She tilts her face up, and I meet her halfway for a kiss that's softer than the others. Slower. "It's already been twenty."

I smile into her hair. "I'm bad at math."

She laughs quietly, and I pull her closer.

I'll leave soon. I will. Just... not yet.

The treatment room with the door closed is our other refuge.

Legitimate sessions—my shoulder still needs work, and she's nothing if not thorough—that turn into something else when the last of the tension releases and her hands slow on my skin.

"You're healing well," she says, her voice pitched low even though we're alone. Professional words, but her fingers trace a path along my shoulder blade that has nothing to do with physical therapy.

"Yeah?"

"Mm-hmm." She leans closer, her lips brushing my ear. "Another few weeks, and you'll be back to full strength."

"And then what?"

"Then I won't have an excuse to touch you every day."

I turn my head and catch her mouth with mine. She makes a soft sound of surprise that melts into something warmer, and for a moment, we just stay there—her hands on my bare shoulders, my palm curved around her hip, stealing time we don't really have.

"We'll figure it out," I say when we break apart.

"Will we?"

"I'm not letting you go that easily, Wells."

She searches my face as if looking for the catch.

After a moment, something in her expression shifts. It softens.

"Okay," she whispers.

We're in Minneapolis for a two-game series against the Wild, and the arena is packed—twenty thousand fans, most of them here to watch us lose.

My shoulder feels solid. Not perfect—I don't know if it'll ever be perfect again—but stable. Strong enough to do what I need to do.

Tori caught me before warmups, her hands cool and professional on my skin as she ran through our pre-game routine. Stretches. Range of motion, the same thing she does with every player.

But when she finished, her fingers lingered on my shoulder just a second longer than necessary.

"You've got this," she said quietly. "Go show them."

Now I'm on the ice in the second period, and we're tied 2-2 with the Wild pressing hard. My line's been solid—good possession and a few quality chances—but nothing's fallen in yet.

Coach calls a timeout, and I skate to the bench, breathing hard.

"Bishop." He catches my eye. "Next shift, I want you crashing the net. None of this perimeter bullshit. Get in there and make something happen."

"Got it."

The timeout ends. I take a long drink of water and scan the crowd while I wait for my next shift.

I don't mean to look for her. I've trained myself not to—too risky, too obvious, too easy for someone to notice where my attention goes.

But my eyes find her anyway.

She's in the section reserved for team staff, a few rows up from the glass. Black sweater, hair pulled back, tablet in her lap as if she's tracking something official.

Her face is carefully neutral. Professional. The same expression she wears in the training room when others are watching.

But her eyes are bright. Focused. And fixed on the ice.

On me.

"Bishop! You're up!"

I hop the boards and hit the ice, legs fresh, lungs clear. Logan's on my wing, Banks anchoring the defense behind us.

The play develops fast. Logan wins the faceoff, kicks it back to Banks, who finds me with a stretch pass at center ice. I take it in stride, crossing the blue line with speed.

The Wild's D-man steps up to meet me. I fake left, cut right, and he bites it hard, his momentum carrying him past me. Suddenly, I've got a lane— not much, but enough.

I drive to the net. Their goalie squares up,

tracking the puck. I wind up as if I'm going high glove—my bread and butter—and he commits, getting into position.

At the last second, I change the angle. Quick release. Five-hole.

The crowd explodes. Logan crashes into me, whooping, and then Banks is there, slapping my helmet, grinning that rare Banks grin.

But I'm already looking for her.

I find Tori in the stands. She's on her feet with everyone else, tablet forgotten, both hands pressed to her mouth.

Her eyes meet mine.

She's not cheering. She's not even smiling, not really. But the look on her face—

Pride. Joy.

That's for you, I think. *All of it.*

I give her nothing. No nod, no wave, no acknowledgment that could be caught on camera or noticed by anyone watching. Just a half-second of eye contact before I skate back to the bench.

But she knows.

I can tell by the way she sits back down, pressing a hand to her chest as if trying to steady her heartbeat.

Yeah. She knows.

We win 4-3 in overtime.

I don't score the winner—that's Logan—but I do get the assist, a sweet cross-ice pass that he buries top shelf.

The locker room is chaos afterward. Music blasting, guys yelling, the usual post-win energy that never gets old, no matter how many times you've felt it.

I shower, change, and answer the required questions from the media with my standard non-answers. Yes, shoulder felt good. Yes, the team played well. No, I'm not thinking about playoffs yet, just taking it one game at a time.

Finally, I escape.

The hallway outside the visitor's locker room is mostly empty. A few equipment managers are packing up, and some arena staff are starting the cleanup.

And there's Tori.

She's leaning against the wall near the exit, arms crossed, pretending to look at her phone. When she sees me, she straightens.

"Good game," she says. Casual. Professional.

"Thanks." I stop in front of her, close enough to smell her shampoo. "Shoulder held up."

"I noticed." A smile tugs at her mouth. "That second goal was nice."

"Just nice?"

"I'm not going to inflate your ego, Bishop. It's big enough."

I step closer and lower my voice. "I was looking for you. After the goal."

Her breath catches. "I know."

"Did you like it?"

"Zayden—" Her cheeks flush. "We're in public."

"So?"

"So anyone could see—"

"I don't care." The words come out rougher than I intended.

She stares at me, lips parted, eyes wide.

Then the locker room door bangs open.

I step back so quickly that I nearly trip over my own feet. Tori is already moving, putting professional distance between us as her expression smooths into something neutral.

Logan bounds in, bag slung over his shoulder, still riding the high from his goal. "Bish! You coming out with us? Found this sick rooftop bar—" He pauses, glancing between us. "Oh, hey Tori. You coming too?"

"I can't," she replies, her voice so steady it's almost impressive. "Game reports."

"Lame." Logan grins, utterly oblivious. "Zay?"

"Gotta FaceTime Maze before bedtime."

"Double lame. You guys are no fun." He starts walking backward toward the exit. "Banks! Wait up!"

And then he's gone, the door swinging shut behind him, leaving us alone again.

Except we're not really alone. Anyone could walk out at any moment. This whole building is crawling with people.

Tori exhales slowly. "That was—"

"Close," I finish.

She nods, not quite meeting my eyes. "I should go."

"Yeah." I shove my hands in my pockets to avoid doing something stupid like reaching for her. "Yeah, okay."

Then she's gone, and I'm left standing in an empty hallway, heart pounding, wondering how the hell I'm supposed to sleep tonight.

22

ROOM 421

Zayden

I t's eleven-thirty, and I'm lying in my hotel bed, staring at the ceiling like it has all the answers. The FaceTime with Maisie was a nice distraction—she showed me a drawing she made of us at the park, filled with stick figures and purple crayon. It stirred that familiar ache in my chest that comes from loving someone so much it physically hurts.

But now she's asleep, and Hannah sent me a thumbs-up emoji. I've got nothing to do except think about the woman three doors down.

I shouldn't go.

I know I shouldn't go, but the team is out celebrating and likely won't be back anytime soon. I get up and pull on my shoes.

The hallway is empty. Most of the team is still out, and the coaching staff is on a different floor. I count the doors like I don't have her room number memorized—like I haven't walked past it four times today, finding excuses.

I knock before I can talk myself out of it.

There's shuffling inside, followed by the click

of the lock. When the door opens, Tori stands there in leggings and a tank top that's just thin enough to make my mouth go dry, her hair twisted up in a claw clip, face freshly washed.

Her eyes widen. "Zayden. What are you—"

"I know I should give you space." I step closer, and she instinctively backs up, allowing me into her room. The door swings shut behind me. "I know the rules. I know what's at stake. But I can't do this anymore."

I move closer. She doesn't back away. "I can't think straight. I can't sleep. I played a whole hockey game tonight, and half my brain was on you in the stands."

"You scored twice."

"Imagine what I could do if I wasn't distracted."

She almost smiles. Almost.

"You're driving me crazy." My hands find her hips before I can stop them, fingers pressing into the soft fabric of her leggings, pulling her closer. She sucks in a breath.

"Zayden..." Her voice is barely a whisper, but she's not pulling away.

"Tell me you don't feel this." My voice comes out rough. "Tell me it's one-sided, that I'm imagining things, and I'll leave right now. I'll go back to my room and pretend this never happened."

Her hands come up to rest on my chest, and I don't know if she's planning to push me away or pull me closer. "You know I can't tell you that."

"Then stop fighting this." One hand slides around to the small of her back, pressing her against me so she can feel exactly what she does to me.

She looks at me for a long moment. I can see the war playing out on her face—fear versus want, rules versus need, everything she's built to protect herself...

Then she rises on her toes and kisses me.

I lift her off the ground, and she wraps around me instantly—legs around my waist, arms around my neck, kissing me like she's been starving for it. Like the last few days of careful distance have been as torturous for her as they were for me.

I walk her backward until her shoulders hit the wall, and she gasps against my mouth. I swallow the sound, chasing it with my tongue, and she makes this noise—half whimper, half moan—that rushes south.

"Off," she breathes, tugging at my hoodie. "Take this off."

I let her go just long enough to pull it over my head, and then her hands are on my chest, sliding under my T-shirt, palms flat against my stomach. Her touch is cool and electric, and I'm going to lose my mind.

"You too," I manage, already reaching for the hem of her shirt. "Fair's fair."

She laughs and lifts her arms. The shirt comes off and—

Fuck.

She's not wearing a bra.

My brain short-circuits. For a solid three seconds, I just stare, taking her in—all soft curves, warm skin, and more beautiful than I imagined. And I've imagined this a lot.

"You're staring," she whispers.

"Damn right I am." I crowd her back against the wall, my mouth finding her neck, her collarbone, the curve of her shoulder. She arches into me, fingers sliding into my hair and gripping tight. "You're gorgeous. Do you know that? Every time I look at you, I forget how to breathe."

"Zayden—"

I kiss my way back to her mouth, slower this time, savoring. Her hips roll against mine, and I groan, one hand sliding down to grip her thigh, pulling her closer.

"Bed," she pants. "Now."

I don't need to be told twice.

I lift her again—she weighs nothing, or maybe adrenaline is turning me into a superhero—and carry her to the bed, laying her down on the duvet. She pulls me down with her, and for a moment we just look at each other.

Her hair is fanned out on the pillow. Her lips are swollen from my kisses. She looks at me like I'm something she wants to devour.

I know the feeling.

"Tell me to stop," I murmur, lowering myself over her, "and I will."

"Don't you dare stop."

I grin against her throat. "Yes, ma'am."

My mouth traces a path down her neck, across her collarbone, lower. She's making sounds that will be permanently etched into my memory—little gasps and sighs and my name.

Her fingers are in my hair, nails lightly scraping my scalp. My hands are everywhere—her waist, her hips, sliding up and over her perky breasts. She hooks a leg around my hip, pulling me closer, and the friction makes us both groan.

"Zayden," she breathes. "Please—"

A loud knock on the door.

We freeze.

"Tori?" Banks' voice, muffled through the wood. "You awake? Dana's looking for you. Something about game reports?"

We stare at each other in horror.

"Shit," she whispers.

I drop my forehead to her shoulder, breathing hard. "Of course."

"One second!" she calls out, her voice impressively steady for someone who was just writhing underneath me. "Just—give me a minute!"

We untangle with frantic efficiency. She grabs her shirt from the floor, yanking it over her head. I'm searching for my sweatshirt.

"Window?" I ask.

"We're on the third floor," she hisses.

"Behind the curtains?"

"This isn't a heist movie, Zayden."

"Then I'm hiding in the bathroom."

I'm already moving, scooping up my hoodie and ducking behind the bathroom door. Through the crack, I watch her finger-comb her hair, take a breath, and open the door.

"Hey." Her voice is casual. Normal. Like she wasn't half-naked thirty seconds ago. "What's up?"

"Dana needs the reports from tonight's game." Banks' voice is flat, but there's something in it—suspicion, maybe, or just his usual grumpiness.

"Said she texted you."

"Oh, uh—" Tori glances toward the nightstand, where her phone is presumably turned to silent. "Yeah, sorry. I was already asleep. I'll email them to her in five minutes."

"You okay?" A pause. "You look flushed."

"Hot shower. You know how hotels crank the heat."

Another pause. Longer this time. My heart is pounding so loudly I'm sure he can hear it.

"Alright," Banks finally says. "Get some sleep. Bus leaves at eight."

"Got it. Thanks."

The door closes. I wait, barely breathing, until I hear Banks' footsteps fade down the hall.

Tori opens the bathroom door. She's got a hand pressed to her chest, eyes wide, and she's fighting a smile.

"That was close."

"Too close." I lean against the doorframe, still trying to catch my breath. "You were very smooth, by the way."

"Years of practice lying to my mother about parties." She shakes her head. "God, if he'd come five minutes later—"

"Let's not think about that."

"I can't stop thinking about it."

We look at each other. The heat is still there—of course it is, it never really goes away—but now there's something else too. Reality is creeping back in.

"We can't keep doing this," she says quietly.

"I know."

"Someone's going to find out."

"I know."

"So what do we do?"

I cross to her, cup her face in my hands, the same way I did earlier, before everything went sideways.

"We figure it out. After the road trip. When we're back home and I can think straight." I brush my thumb across her cheekbone.

"Okay. After the road trip."

"After the road trip," I repeat.

I kiss her forehead, soft and sweet, letting my lips linger. Her eyes close.

"You should go," she whispers.

"I know."

"Before someone else shows up looking for game reports."

"I know." But I don't move. I can't seem to make myself.

She opens her eyes and smiles, just a little. "Go, Zayden."

I steal one more kiss—quick, chaste, nothing like what we were doing ten minutes ago—and force myself to step away.

I slip into the hallway, check both directions, and walk back to my room on legs that don't feel entirely steady.

The cold shower I take doesn't help at all.

23

RUMOR HAS IT

Tori

The week after we get back feels like I'm holding my breath underwater.

Every interaction with Zayden is measured, calculated, filtered through the lens of *who might be watching*. We've become adept at it—the professional nods, the way we never stand too close or let our eyes linger. He calls me Wells. We pretend we're nothing more than player and trainer, and most days, I almost believe it.

But at night, my phone lights up with his texts. Stupid things, small things. A photo of Maisie's latest art project. A complaint about the hotel coffee. A single *thinking about you* that makes me smile into my pillow like a teenager.

We agreed to figure things out after the road trip. We just... haven't yet.

And I'm trying not to read into it.

Now it's Thursday morning, and something's off. I notice it the moment I walk into the facility—the way conversations seem to stutter when I pass, the way eyes slide away from mine a beat too late. James gives me a weird half-nod at the coffee machine and practically speed-walks in the opposite direction, which is strange because James usually corners me for a twenty-minute breakdown of whatever true crime podcast he's binging.

I tell myself I'm being paranoid. That I'm projecting my own guilt about Zayden onto perfectly normal interactions. That nobody knows anything because there's nothing to know—just some kissing and hand-holding and one very interrupted almost-more in a Minneapolis hotel room.

But the feeling doesn't go away. It follows me through my morning sessions, through the staff meeting where barely anyone makes eye contact, through lunch in the break room where two trainers stop talking the second I sit down. What in the world?

By two o'clock, I'm wound so tight I could snap.

Logan's shoulder assessment is my 2:30. He bounces in with his usual golden retriever energy, already talking about some TikTok he saw, and I let myself relax a little. Logan's easy. Uncomplicated. The kind of guy who says exactly what he's thinking at all times, which is either refreshing or exhausting, depending on the day.

"Okay, let's see your range of motion," I say, guiding him through the standard tests. "Any pain when you—"

"So, uh." He drops his arm. "Can I tell you something?"

My hands freeze on his shoulder. "What?"

"It's just—okay, look." He turns to face me,

and his expression is uncharacteristically serious. "It's really not my business, and I'm not here to yuck on someone's yum, but I just thought you should, uh, know."

My stomach bottoms out. "Spit it out, Logan."

"There's some stuff going around. About you and Bish."

No, no, no, no.

The blood drains from my face. "What kind of stuff?"

"Reed's been running his mouth. He says he saw you two at the hotel in Minneapolis late at night. He also claims you've hooked up here in the training room." Logan scratches the back of his neck, looking genuinely uncomfortable. "I don't know if it's true, and I don't care if it is—Zay's a good dude, and you're cool; whatever makes people happy, you know? But I figured you'd want to know before it gets to the wrong people."

I'm going to be sick. I'm actually going to throw up right here in the training room.

"How many people have heard this?"

"I mean..." Logan winces. "A lot? Reed's not exactly subtle. He was telling anyone who'd listen in the locker room this morning."

Grayson. Of course it's Grayson. The guy I rejected, the one with the miraculous disappearing hip injury, the guy who told me I had a "type" and that he was just trying to figure out where he fit. This is payback. This is him making sure that if he can't have me, no one can—or at least, not without consequences.

"Tori?" Logan watches me with concern. "You

okay? You look like you're gonna pass out."

"I'm fine." The words come out automatic and hollow. "I just—I need a minute. Can you ice for ten? I'll be right back."

"Yeah, of course. Take your time."

I make it to the supply closet before my legs give out. I lean against the shelving unit, surrounded by boxes of KT tape and bottles of massage oil, pressing my palms against my temples and trying to breathe.

This is bad. This is really, *really* bad.

My phone buzzes. Then again. Then a third time. I wrench it from my pocket and dare a look.

Winnie

Hey, are you okay? Derek's cousin works at MSG and said there's some hockey gossip going around about a trainer and a player??

Please tell me that's not about you.

Tori???

I don't respond. I can't. My hands are shaking too hard to type.

The rest of the afternoon is a blur. I finish Logan's assessment on autopilot, smile and nod through two more sessions, and pretend everything is fine while the whispers follow me through every hallway. By three o'clock, even the equipment managers are giving me looks.

I don't see Zayden. He had a light practice this morning and left early—something about Maisie's school. Part of me is relieved. Part of me desperately wants to warn him, to figure out our story together, to not be alone in this.

At 4:15, my phone buzzes with a different kind of message.

Dana

Three words. No context. I feel like I might hurl.

I finish my notes, log out of my computer, and walk down the hall toward Dana's office on legs that feel like they belong to someone else. The hallway has never seemed this long, and every step feels like I'm walking toward my own execution, which is dramatic but also kind of accurate.

Her door is open. She's sitting behind her desk, reading something on her laptop, and she doesn't look up when I knock on the doorframe.

"Close the door," she says. "Sit down."

I do both. The chair across from her desk is uncomfortable—hard plastic, no cushion. I've sat in it before, during my initial interview and quarterly reviews. It's never felt this much like an interrogation.

Dana finally looks up, her expression neutral and professional, but there's something in her eyes that makes my chest tight. "I'm going to ask you something, and I need you to be honest with me."

"Okay."

"Is there something going on between you and Zayden Bishop?"

My heart pounds so hard I can feel it in my throat. I think about lying, about all the ways I could spin this, minimize it, make it sound like nothing. But Dana hired me because she trusted me, and I've never lied to her before.

"We haven't—" I start, then stop. I try again. "Nothing has happened that compromises my work. His treatment has been completely by the book. Every protocol followed, every session documented, every decision based purely on his medical needs."

Dana's expression doesn't change. "That's not what I asked."

I know it's not. I was hoping she'd let me get away with it anyway. She doesn't.

"I need you to be honest with me."

I take a breath. "There's… something," I admit, and the words feel like glass in my throat. "I don't know what to call it. But yes. There's something."

Dana leans back in her chair, and for a long moment, she just looks at me. I can't read her thoughts. Disappointment? Anger? Resignation? All three?

"How long?"

"A few weeks. Maybe longer, depending on how you count." I twist my hands in my lap. "It started during the road trips. Proximity, I guess. And then it just… kept happening."

"Have you slept with him?"

My head snaps up. "Excuse me?"

Dana's expression doesn't waver. "It's a straightforward question."

"It's an *invasive* question." The words come out sharper than I intend, but I don't take them back.

"I'm asking because I need to know what we're dealing with. If this is just flirtation, that's one thing. If it's gone further—"

"It hasn't." My face is burning—embarrassment, anger, and the sheer audacity of being interrogated about something so personal. "No, I haven't slept with him."

The word hangs there, ugly and raw. I've never felt more vulnerable—in front of my boss, no less.

Dana sighs—a long, heavy exhale that seems to carry the weight of every similar conversation she's probably had in her career. "I believe you about maintaining professional boundaries during his treatment. You're good at your job, Tori. One of the best I've ever hired. I've never had a reason to question your judgment before now."

"But?"

"But this league runs on optics. It doesn't matter what actually happened; it matters what people think happened. And right now, people think you're sleeping with one of our star players." I flinch, because hearing it out loud makes it sound so much worse. "If this becomes a story," Dana continues, "it won't just reflect on you. It will reflect on the whole program. On me. On every woman who's ever tried to build a career in sports medicine without being reduced to someone's girlfriend or conquest."

"I know." Tears sting my eyes, and my voice comes out barely above a whisper. "I know that."

"Do you?" Dana is quiet for a moment, then stands, walks to the window, and stares out at the parking lot. "I'm not going to tell you how to live your life. You're an adult. You're allowed to make your own choices, even the messy ones."

"But?"

She turns around. "But I need you to make a choice. Him or your career here. Because you can't have both. Not without consequences."

The words land like a blow to the chest. I knew this was coming—somewhere in the back of my mind, I've known since the first time he kissed me that this moment was inevitable. But knowing it and hearing it are very different things.

"What kind of consequences?"

"Well, it's not entirely up to me, I need to run this up the chain of command. But if this becomes public—and it will become public; these things always do—you'll be reassigned. Off his care, obviously. Probably off the team entirely. I'll do my best to find you a position somewhere else in the organization, assuming you're open to relocation, but I can't promise it'll be anything close to what you have now."

"And if I end it?"

"Then we weather this storm. The rumor dies down, people move on to the next scandal, and you keep building the career you've worked so hard for."

She makes it sound so simple. So clinical. Like feelings are just another variable to factor into a cost-benefit analysis.

"How long do I have to decide?"

"By the end of the day tomorrow." Dana's expression softens, just slightly. "I'm sorry, Tori. I know this isn't fair. But fair isn't really how this industry works."

"No," I agree quietly. "It's not."

I stand on legs that feel shaky and unreliable,

but I make it to the door without stumbling.

"Tori."

I turn back. Dana is watching me with what might be sympathy.

"For what it's worth," she says, "I hope he's worth it. Whatever you decide."

I don't respond because I don't know if he is. I don't know if anyone could be worth this.

I make it to my car before I fall apart. The tears come out of nowhere—big, ugly sobs that shake my whole body, tears I couldn't stop even if I wanted to. I press my hands over my face and cry in the front seat of my Honda, mourning everything I'm about to lose no matter which door I choose.

Because that's the thing, isn't it? There's no version of this where I win. I either lose him or I lose my career. I either break my own heart or I dismantle everything I've spent years building. The rule existed for exactly this reason—because I knew, I *knew*, that getting involved with a player would end exactly like this.

And I did it anyway.

24

CRISIS MANAGEMENT

Zayden

ori hasn't texted me back in three hours.

I'm not the kind of guy who stares at his phone waiting for a reply. I have a kid to raise, a career to maintain, and better things to do than refresh my messages like a teenager with a crush.

And yet here I am, sitting in my kitchen at 4 PM, staring at my phone as if it owes me something.

Me (1:47 PM)

Hey. You okay? You seemed off this morning.

Me (3:33 PM)

Starting to worry. Just let me know you're good.

Me (4:15 PM)

Tori?

Nothing. Radio silence. Three blue check

marks stare back at me, which means she's seen them but is choosing not to respond.

That's... not like her.

Maisie's at gymnastics until five, so I've got a little while to spiral in peace. I make an energy drink I don't need, pace the length of my living room, and check my phone eleven more times. I'm probably winding myself up over nothing. She's busy. She's working. She's got patients, paperwork, and a hundred things more important than reassuring her... whatever I am.

Boyfriend? That feels presumptuous. We haven't had that conversation.

Guy she's been sneaking around with? Accurate but depressing.

Man who's falling so hard for her he can barely see straight? Unfortunately also accurate.

My phone buzzes, and I nearly drop it grabbing for it, but it's not Tori. It's Banks.

Banks

You home?

Me

Yeah. Why?

Banks

I'm coming over. Don't argue.

I don't get a chance to argue. Ten minutes later, there's a knock on my door, and when I open it, Banks is standing there looking like someone stole his girlfriend. Which is concerning, because Banks doesn't have a girlfriend, and his default expression is already pretty grim.

"What's wrong?" I step back to let him in. "Did something happen?"

He walks past me into the living room, then turns around with his arms crossed. "Sit down."

"I'm not sitting down. You're freaking me out. Just tell me—"

"There's a rumor going around." His voice is flat, careful. "About you and Tori."

The floor drops out from under me.

"What kind of rumor?"

"The kind where Reed's been telling anyone who'll listen that he saw you two at the hotel in Minneapolis. Middle of the night. Her room. Door closing." Banks holds my gaze. "It's spread through the whole facility. Dana knows."

I'm going to kill him.

I'm going to find Grayson Reed, wrap my hands around his throat, and squeeze until that smug little smile disappears forever. I'm going to—

"Zay." Banks steps closer. "Breathe."

"He's been after her for weeks." My voice comes out rough, barely recognizable. "She turned him down, and this is—this is retaliation. This is him being a petty, vindictive piece of—"

"I know what it is."

"And now she's going to pay for it? Her career is going to suffer because some entitled asshole couldn't handle rejection?"

"That's how it usually works, yeah."

I'm pacing now, unable to stand still, my hands clenching and unclenching at my sides. All I can think about is Tori's face this morning—the way she smiled at me across the training room, careful and secret, like we had all the time in the world to figure this out.

We didn't. We don't.

"Dana pulled her into her office about an hour ago," Banks continues. "I don't know what was said, but James saw her leaving, and she looked..." He pauses. "Bad. She looked bad."

That's why she hasn't texted back. She's been getting interrogated about us while I sat here refreshing my phone like an idiot.

"I have to talk to her."

"You will. But first, you need to calm down and think about what you're going to do."

"What I'm going to do?" I stop pacing and stare at him. "I'm going to fix this. I'm going to march into Dana's office and tell her it was all me. That I pursued Tori, that she tried to maintain professional boundaries and I pushed past them, that if anyone should face consequences, it's—"

"And then what?"

"Then she keeps her job. Her reputation. Everything she's worked for."

Banks shakes his head slowly. "And you get what? Suspended for conduct violations? Fined? Benched during a playoff push?"

"I don't care about any of that."

"You should." His voice hardens. "Think about Maze, Z. You get suspended for misconduct, you miss games—that affects custody optics. Sienna's been quiet lately, but what if that changes, you really think her lawyers won't jump on something like this? 'NHL player suspended for inappropriate relationship with staff member'—that's exactly the kind of ammunition they'd love to have."

I freeze.

Maze. Always Maze.

Everything comes back to her—every decision, every risk, every choice I make gets filtered through the lens of what it might cost my daughter. And I wouldn't have it any other way, except right now it feels like a trap. Like I'm being forced to choose between protecting Tori and protecting Maisie, and there's no version of this where everyone comes out okay.

"So what am I supposed to do?" My voice cracks on the question. "Let Tori take the fall? Let her lose everything while I skate by because I've got more leverage?"

"No." Banks moves to stand in front of me, blocking my pacing path. "You let Tori decide what she wants. You talk to her, figure out your options together, and deal with the consequences like adults. Not like some knight in shining armor who thinks he knows what's best for everyone."

"I'm not—"

"You are. You're already planning to throw yourself on the grenade without even asking her if that's what she wants." He raises an eyebrow. "You ever think maybe she'd like a say in her own future?"

I open my mouth to argue, then close it.

He's right. I hate that he's right, but he is.

This isn't my decision to make alone. Whatever happens next, it has to be something we choose together. That's what being partners means—both people facing the mess side by side.

"When did you get so wise?" I mutter.

"I've always been wise. You just don't listen." Banks claps a hand on my shoulder. "Call her. Go see her. But don't do anything stupid until you've talked it through."

"Define stupid."

"Punching Reed. Storming into Dana's office. Making grand declarations that you'll regret tomorrow." He almost smiles. "Basically, don't be you."

"Helpful."

"I try." He heads for the door but pauses with his hand on the knob. "For what it's worth, I think you two are good together. Tori's solid. Smart. She doesn't take your crap, which God knows you need."

"Thanks?"

"I'm just saying—whatever you have to do to make this work, it's probably worth doing." He meets my eyes. "Some things are more important than avoiding a PR headache."

Then he's gone, and I'm alone with my phone, my racing thoughts, and the growing certainty that my whole life is about to change.

I pull up Tori's contact and type out a message.

Me

Hey we need to talk. You okay?

I wait, stare at the screen, and force myself to keep typing even though my hands want to shake.

Me

I can come over after I pick up Maze.

Still nothing. The silence is deafening.

Me

Whatever happens, we figure it out together. Yeah?

My screen stays dark.

Then I grab my keys and head out to pick up my daughter, because no matter what's falling apart in the rest of my life, Maisie still needs her dad. She still needs normal. She still needs to believe that the people who love her will show up, even when everything else is chaos.

I can fall apart later.

Right now, I have a kid to raise and a woman to fight for.

And God help anyone who tries to stand in my way.

25

RETREAT

Tori

I make it home on autopilot.

Keys in the door, shoes kicked off, I head straight to the couch where I curl up in a ball and stare at the wall as if it might tell me what to do. My phone buzzes in my pocket every few minutes with texts I can't bring myself to read.

Dana's words echo in my mind: *Him or your career. You can't have both.*

The truth is, I already know what I'm going to do. I've known since I walked out of her office with my heart in my throat and my future in pieces on the floor. I'm going to end it. I'm going to tell Zayden we can't do this anymore, that it was a mistake, that I need to focus on my career and he needs to focus on Maisie. We should just... stop.

It's the smart choice. The safe choice. The choice that protects everyone.

So why does it feel like I'm about to rip out my own heart?

A knock on my door makes me jump.

I know who it is before I even look through the

peephole. I mentioned my building once—complained about the fourth-floor walkup after a long shift—and apparently that was enough for him to find me. Zayden stands in the hallway, still in his workout clothes, looking like he drove straight here from the gym. His jaw is tight, his eyes worried, and he's so unfairly beautiful it makes my chest ache.

I open the door.

"Hey." His voice is rough. "You weren't answering your phone."

"I know. I just..." I step back to let him in because I don't know what else to do. "It's been a day."

"Yeah. I heard." He moves past me into my apartment, taking it all in—the tiny galley kitchen, the bookshelf overflowing with anatomy textbooks and romance novels I'd die before admitting to, the plants on the windowsill that I somehow keep alive despite everything. His eyes land on the fuzzy blanket bunched up on my couch, where I planned to curl up and die tonight. It's nothing compared to his place with the big windows, the chef's kitchen, and the room for Maisie to run around. But it's mine.

He turns to face me. "Banks told me about the rumors. About Dana pulling you in."

"Of course he did."

"Don't be mad at him. He was trying to help." Zayden's eyes lift to mine and his expression hits me right in the chest. "Are you okay?"

"Just peachy."

"Tori." He takes a step closer. "Please. Talk to

me." His voice is steady, but the rest of him isn't. There's a crease between his eyebrows that I want to smooth away with my thumb.

"Dana gave me an ultimatum. You or my career." I force myself to meet his eyes, but the rehearsed words get tangled on the way out. "I've been sitting here trying to figure out how to do the right thing. For both of us."

"The right thing." He repeats it flatly.

"The smart thing. The responsible thing." I wrap my arms tighter around myself. "Maybe we should just... stop. Before this gets any harder. You go back to your life, I go back to mine, and we pretend—"

"No."

"Zayden—"

"I said no." He closes the distance between us, and suddenly he's right there, close enough that I can see the gold flecks in his eyes. "You don't get to make this decision for both of us."

"Someone has to be rational here."

"This isn't rational. This is you running scared."

"I'm trying to protect—"

"I don't need protection. I need you to stop shutting me out." His voice cracks on the last word, and something in my chest cracks with it. "I'm not willing to walk away from this without seeing where it could go. Are you?"

I don't answer. I can't.

"Tori." He takes my hands, and his are shaking slightly. Or maybe mine are. "Let me fix this. Let me talk to Dana. The team leadership. Whoever I need to talk to. I need to know your job is safe before we make any decisions."

"You can't just—"

"I can try." His grip tightens on my fingers. "I'm not asking you to choose me over your career. I'm asking you to let me fight for a world where you don't have to choose at all."

I sway, resolve loosening. "What if it doesn't work?"

"Then at least we'll know we tried." He brings one hand up to cup my face, his thumb brushing my cheek. "But I need you to promise me something."

"What?"

"Don't give up on me. Not yet." His eyes search mine, desperate, hopeful, and terrified all at once. "Can you do that? Can you give me a chance to make this right?"

I should say no. I should tell him it's too risky, too complicated, too much. I should protect myself the way I always have.

But I'm so tired of protecting myself.

"Okay," I whisper.

"Okay?"

"Okay. I won't give up on you." A tear slips down my cheek. "Not yet."

Something in his expression breaks open—relief, maybe, or hope—and then he's kissing me. Soft at first, almost tentative, like he's asking permission. I respond by pulling him closer, my fingers curling into the fabric of his shirt, and the kiss deepens into something desperate, aching, and real.

When we finally break apart, we're both breathing hard.

"I have to go," he murmurs against my lips, pressing his forehead to mine. "I'm going to figure this out." He sounds more confident than I feel.

"Okay."

One more kiss—quick, fierce, a promise—and then he's stepping back, letting go of my hands like it physically hurts him to do it.

He pauses at the threshold, looking back at me with an expression that makes my heart stutter.

"Goodnight, Tori."

"Goodnight."

The door clicks shut behind him, and I lean against it, pressing my palm flat against the wood as if I can still feel him on the other side.

I don't know if he can fix this. I don't know if anyone can.

But for the first time today, I have something I didn't have before.

Hope.

I don't sleep that night.

The next morning, there's a knock on my door at 7 AM. When I open it—still in my pajamas, hair unwashed, looking like a cautionary tale about poor life choices—my mother stands there with a bag of bagels and an expression that says she's not leaving until she gets answers.

"Mom. What are you—"

"You've been ignoring my calls." She pushes past me into the apartment. "The last time you ignored my calls, you'd failed organic chemistry and were convinced your life was over."

"I didn't fail. I got a C-minus."

"Same thing, in your mind." She sets the bagels on my counter and turns to face me. "So. What happened?"

"Nothing happened."

"Victoria."

I hate when she uses my full name. It makes me feel twelve years old again, unable to lie under that steady maternal gaze.

"I don't want to talk about it."

"Too bad." She pulls out a chair and sits. "I drove two hours. You're going to talk about it."

So I do. I tell her everything—Zayden, Maisie, the rumors, Dana's ultimatum—and by the time I finish, my cheeks are wet and she's holding both my hands across the table.

"So that's it," I say. "I either choose him and lose my career or choose my career and lose him. There's no option where I get both."

"Are you sure about that?"

"I don't know," I admit.

Zayden said he'd talk to team leadership, that he'd... go to bat for me. The thought is both sweet and mortifying. I never wanted to be *that* girl. The one who caused a rift and needed a man to clean up her mess. The one people whispered about in the break room.

"Okay. So let me ask you something else." My mom tilts her head. "This job—does it make you happy?"

"Of course it does." I nod. "I'm good at it, and it makes me feel accomplished," I say carefully.

"Helping athletes."

She nods, like it's the answer she expected. "And Zayden? How does he make you feel?"

"Terrified," I whisper. "Out of control. Like I'm standing on the edge of a cliff."

"That's not all, though. Is it?"

"No." I swallow hard. "He also makes me feel... seen. Like I don't have to be perfect to be enough."

"And Maisie?"

The mention of her name sends warmth through me. "She's the sweetest little girl, Mom. And I want it. Not just kids in general, but that life. With them."

"Then why are you running?"

"Because what if I ruin it? What if I give up everything and it still falls apart?"

My mom cups my face in her hands. "Victoria. Listen to me. You've spent your entire adult life building walls. After what happened with Jason, you decided you'd never let anyone have that kind of power over you again. But at some point, the walls that protect you become the prison that traps you."

She wipes a tear from my cheek.

"This man isn't trying to break down your walls. He's standing outside them, knocking gently, asking if you might want to let him in."

"What if I let him in and he hurts me?"

"He might. Love is a risk." She says it simply. "But it's also the greatest, most beautiful thing in the world."

Her words unlock something inside me.

"I need to call him," I say.

"Probably." She stands, pressing a kiss to my head. "But first, shower. You smell like regret and dry shampoo."

"Mom."

"And eat a bagel." She's already pulling plates from my cabinet. "You're going to need your strength for whatever comes next."

I pick up a bagel and give her a grateful look. "Thanks for coming, Mom."

"I'm always here, love."

26

FIGHTING FOR HER

Zayden

I'm outside Dana's office at 7:45 AM.

She doesn't get in until eight—I know because I asked her assistant, who looked at me like I'd grown a second head. Players don't usually show up at the administrative wing before practice. Players definitely don't show up looking like they haven't slept and asking to speak with the Director of Athletic Performance about "a personal matter."

But here I am. Coffee in hand, leg bouncing, rehearsing what I'm going to say for the hundredth time.

I thought about calling my agent first. He would probably tell me to stay out of it, let the lawyers handle it if it comes to that, and not to make waves during a playoff push. Smart advice. The kind of advice I'd normally take.

Too bad I'm done being smart about this.

The elevator dings, and Dana steps off with her own coffee and a leather bag over her shoulder. She spots me immediately, and something flickers across her face—surprise, then wariness, then the carefully neutral expression of someone who's been in management long enough to see everything.

"Bishop." She stops in front of me. "This is unexpected."

"I need to talk to you. About Tori."

"I figured." She studies me for a moment, then sighs. "Come in. Let me at least put my bag down first."

I follow her into the office and close the door behind me. It's a nice space—windows overlooking the practice facility, framed photos of championship teams on the walls, and a desk that's intimidatingly organized. Dana settles into her chair and gestures for me to sit.

I stay standing.

"Before you say anything," she starts, "you should know that I've already spoken with Tori. She's aware of the situation and the options available to her."

"I know. She told me."

"Then you know this isn't really your conversation to have."

"With respect, I disagree."

Dana raises an eyebrow. "Go on."

I take a breath. This is it. The moment I either fix this or make it a hundred times worse.

No pressure.

"The rumors going around—the ones Reed started—they're about me as much as they're about Tori. More, actually, since I'm the one who pursued her." I hold up a hand before she can interrupt. "I know what you're thinking. That I'm just trying to protect her. And yeah, I am. But I'm also telling you the truth. I have no incentive to lie right now. And the truth is, she tried to keep things professional. She had rules. I'm the one who kept pushing."

"Bishop—"

"I'm not done." The words come out harder than I intended, and I force myself to soften. "Sorry. I just—I need you to hear this."

Dana leans back in her chair, arms crossed. "I'm listening."

"Tori is the best PT I've ever worked with. And I've worked with a lot. She's the reason my shoulder is ahead of schedule. She's the reason I'm going to make it through this season without surgery." I grip the back of the chair in front of me. "She's also the most ethical person I know. She agonized over this—over us. Tried to fight it. Tried to keep her distance. But I didn't make it easy for her."

"So you're saying this is your fault."

"I'm saying if anyone should face consequences, it should be me. Not her."

Dana is quiet for a long moment. I can't read her expression, and it's making me want to crawl out of my skin.

"That's very noble," she finally says. "But it doesn't change the facts. There's a policy. It exists for good reason. And whether you initiated things or not, she made choices too."

"I'm not asking you to pretend nothing happened." I move around the chair and sit, leaning forward with my elbows on my knees. "I'm asking you to consider the context. Reed started these rumors because Tori rejected him. He's been harassing her for weeks—showing up for fake injuries, blocking doorways, making comments. This is retaliation, pure and simple."

Something shifts in Dana's expression. "I had no idea."

I figured as much. My jaw tightens. "You want to talk about conduct violations? Start with him."

"Reed's behavior is a separate issue."

"Is it? Because from where I'm sitting, it looks like the same issue. A woman does her job, turns down the wrong guy, and suddenly she's the one facing consequences while he gets to keep running his mouth in the locker room."

Dana's eyes narrow, but not in anger. More like she's reassessing something. Considering it from an angle she hadn't before.

"What exactly are you asking for, Mr. Bishop?"

"I'm asking for a solution that doesn't destroy Tori's career." I hold her gaze. "Reassign her off my case—fine. I get it. Optics matter. But don't push her out of the organization. Don't make her pay for something that was as much my doing as hers."

"And what about you? What consequences are you willing to accept?"

"Whatever you need. A fine. A statement. Sensitivity training." I almost laugh at that last one. "I'll sit through a hundred HR seminars if it means Tori keeps her job."

Dana taps her pen against her desk, thinking. The silence stretches long enough that I start to wonder if I've completely miscalculated.

"You care about her," she says finally. It's not a question.

"Yeah." There's no point in denying it. "I do."

"Enough to risk your own reputation? Your standing with the team?"

"Enough to be standing in your office at eight in the morning begging you to give her a chance. So yeah. I'd say so."

There's another long pause. Dana sets down her pen and folds her hands on the desk.

"Here's what I can offer. Tori gets reassigned— off your care, effective immediately. James will take over your treatment for the remainder of the season. She stays with the organization, but in a reduced capacity until the noise dies down. No formal disciplinary action goes in her file."

"What exactly does reduced capacity mean?"

"I'll move her off the active roster for now. She'll work with the guys rehabbing long-term injuries, prospects coming through. No road trips. Same pay. Same hours. But a little more behind the scenes."

Relief floods through me, but I force myself to stay focused. That might work out okay. She'd probably be off Reed's radar for a little while too. "And after the season?"

"If things have settled, we revisit. I can't make promises, but I can tell you that I value her work. I don't want to lose her any more than you do."

"What about us? Tori and me?"

Dana sighs. "I'm not going to pretend I can control what you do in your personal lives. But I'd strongly suggest keeping things... discreet. At least until the playoffs are over. The last thing any of us needs is more fuel for the rumor mill."

"I can do discreet."

"Can you?" She raises an eyebrow. "Because showing up at my office first thing in the morning to plead your case isn't exactly subtle."

Fair point.

"I'll be more careful," I say. "We both will."

Dana studies me for another moment, then nods slowly. "Alright. I'll talk to Tori this morning and let her know the new arrangement. But Bishop—" She fixes me with a look that makes me feel like I'm back in the principal's office. "If this blows up, if there's any more drama or any reason for me to think this is affecting the team, I won't be as generous next time. Understood?"

"Understood."

"Good." She picks up her pen again, a clear dismissal. "Now get out of my office. You have practice in an hour."

I stand but hesitate at the door. "Dana?"

"What?"

"Thank you. For hearing me out."

Her expression softens, just slightly. "For what it's worth, I think she's lucky to have someone willing to go to bat for her like this. Not everyone would."

"She'd do the same for me."

"I don't doubt it." She waves a hand toward the door. "Go. Before someone sees you leaving my office and we have a whole new set of rumors to deal with."

I go.

The hallway is still empty, the administrative wing quiet this early in the morning. I pull out my phone and stare at Tori's name in my contacts, thumb hovering over the call button.

I should let Dana tell her first. That's the professional thing to do. The appropriate thing.

But I need her to know it's going to be okay. I need her to stop worrying, stop spiraling, stop thinking she has to give up everything she's worked for.

I type out a text instead.

Me

I talked to Dana. I'll call you after practice.

Three dots appear almost immediately.

Tori

What did you do?

Me

The same thing you would have done for me.

I pocket my phone and head for the elevator, already running through what I need to do before practice. Get my gear, warm up my shoulder, and try not to think about how badly I want to see Tori's face when she finds out—

"Bishop."

I recognize that voice. Every muscle in my body goes tight.

Grayson Reed is leaning against the wall near the stairwell, arms crossed, smirk firmly in place. Like he's been waiting for me.

"Heard you were up here early." He pushes

off the wall and strolls toward me with that cocky swagger that makes me want to put my fist through his face. "Meeting with Dana? Let me guess— damage control?"

I don't respond; I just keep walking toward the elevator.

"Come on, Bish. Don't be like that." He falls into step beside me. "I'm just making conversation. The locker room's been buzzing all week about you and the hot PT. Gotta say, I didn't think you had it in you."

My jaw is so tight it aches. "Walk away, Reed."

"Or what?" He laughs. "You gonna run to Dana again? Cry about how unfair everything is? Must be nice having management wrapped around your finger because you're screwing the staff."

I stop walking and turn to face him.

He's still smirking, but something flickers in his eyes when he sees my expression. Good. He should be nervous.

"She rejected you." I keep my voice low and controlled. "And you couldn't handle it. So you spread rumors like a little boy throwing a tantrum on the playground."

"I told people what I saw."

"You told people what you wanted them to believe. There's a difference." I take a step closer. He holds his ground, but barely. "What's the matter, Reed? Is your ego that fragile? A woman turns you down, and you have to try to destroy her career?"

His smirk slips. "She's not that special."

"Yeah, she is." Another step. "And you know it. That's why it stung so badly when she wanted nothing to do with you."

His face darkens. "I don't know what she told you, but—"

"She told me everything. I saw it—the fake injuries, the way you'd find excuses to be in the training room whenever she was on shift, the way you'd corner her after sessions." I take another step closer, and he takes a step back. Interesting. "Dana knows now too, by the way. All of it. So whatever story you've been spinning? It's done."

For the first time, real concern flashes across his face. "You told Dana?"

"I told her everything: the harassment, the retaliation, the fact that you spread rumors because a woman had the audacity to turn you down." Another step forward, and he backs into the wall. "How do you think that's going to play out for you?"

"It's her word against mine."

"No. It's her word, my word, and whatever paper trail she's been keeping." I'm close enough now to see the worry lines appearing on his forehead. "You really think she's been putting up with your crap for weeks without documenting it? She's smarter than you on your best day, Reed."

He opens his mouth—probably to say something stupid—when footsteps echo down the hallway.

Banks rounds the corner, takes one look at the scene, and stops. His eyes move from me to Grayson to the approximately three inches of space between us.

"Problem?" he asks, his voice flat.

"No problem." I don't take my eyes off Grayson. "Reed and I were just having a conversation about professional conduct. Weren't we?"

Grayson's gaze darts to Banks—six-four, built like a brick wall, with a permanent scowl currently directed right at him—and whatever bravado he had left evaporates.

"We're done here," he mutters, trying to slide along the wall toward the stairwell.

I let him get two steps before I speak again.

"Hey, Reed."

He pauses but doesn't turn around.

"If I hear you've so much as looked at her wrong—" I step closer, and Reed's back hit the wall. Good. "—if she tells me you've been any-where near her, if you so much as breathe in her direction—" I let him see exactly what's coiled be-hind my eyes. The thing I kept leashed on the ice. The thing that would very much enjoy an excuse. "There won't be a conversation next time. Banks won't be around to stop me. There won't be wit-nesses. There'll just be you, trying to explain to the trainers how you broke your own face. We clear?"

He doesn't answer. He just shoves through the stairwell door and disappears.

The door swings shut behind him, and I finally let out a breath.

"You good?" Banks asks.

"Yeah." I roll my shoulders, trying to release some of the tension still coiled in my body. "Yeah, I'm good."

"You weren't actually going to hit him, were you?"

"I was thinking about it."

"Don't." Banks falls into step beside me as we head for the elevator. "He's not worth the suspension."

"I know." I punch the button for the locker room level. "But it would've felt really satisfying."

Banks almost smiles. Almost. "Can't argue with that."

The elevator doors open, and we step inside.

"For what it's worth," Banks says as the doors close, "I've been wanting to deck that guy since training camp. So if you ever change your mind about the suspension thing, let me know. I'll hold him down."

I laugh—actually laugh—for the first time in days. "I'll keep that in mind."

27

FIGURING IT OUT

Tori

Dana's office feels different this time.

The last time I was here, I sat in this same uncomfortable chair, forced to choose between my career and my heart. Now I'm back, summoned by a two-word text—*My office*—with no idea what's waiting for me.

I expect anger, disappointment, maybe even a formal termination letter.

What I don't expect is Dana looking at me with something that might be respect.

"Close the door," she says. "Sit down."

I do both, my heart hammering against my ribs.

"I had an interesting visitor this morning," she starts. "Before practice. Zayden Bishop showed up outside my office, looking like he hadn't slept, asking to talk about you."

My stomach drops. He texted me this morning, but I have no idea how their conversation turned out.

Dana leans back in her chair. "He told me the whole thing was his fault. That he pursued you, that you tried to maintain professional boundaries, and that if anyone should face consequences, it should be him."

I close my eyes. That idiot. That sweet, stubborn, impossible idiot.

"He also told me about Reed," Dana continues, her voice sharpening. "The fake injuries. The comments. The fact that this whole situation started because you rejected him, and he decided to retaliate."

"I don't want to cause problems," I say quickly. "I just—"

"I wish you had reported it." Dana sighs. "That's a separate conversation, and one we'll be having with HR. But for now, let's focus on you."

I brace myself. Here it comes.

"I'm reassigning you off Bishop's care, effective immediately. James will take over his treatment for the rest of the season."

I nod. I expected that much.

"You'll stay with the organization," she continues, "but I'm moving you off the active roster for now. You'll work with players rehabbing long-term injuries and prospects coming through the system. Same pay, same hours—just a little more behind the scenes until this blows over."

I blink. "I'm... not fired?"

"No, Tori. You're not fired." Dana's expression softens slightly. "You're a damn good PT. I don't want to lose you over something like this. But I need you to be smart. Keep things discreet—until the season is over. No public displays, no drama, nothing that gives the rumor mill more fuel. Can you do that?"

"Yes." The word comes out breathless. "Yes, absolutely."

"Good." She picks up her pen, a clear dismissal. "That's all. You can go."

I stand on shaky legs but pause at the door. "Dana?"

"What?"

"Thank you."

She gives me a warm smile before turning back to her computer.

I walk out of her office in a daze.

He showed up for me. Before I could fall on my own sword, before I could sacrifice everything to protect him, he marched into Dana's office and took responsibility. He fought for me.

No one's ever done that before.

Not Jason, who threw me under the bus the second things got hard. Not anyone since, because I never let anyone get close enough to have the chance.

But Zayden did. Without being asked. Without expecting anything in return.

I make it back to my office—my tiny, cramped, glorified closet of an office—and sink into my chair, pressing my hands over my face. I'm not going to cry. I'm not.

A knock on the door makes me jump.

I know who it is before I even look up. Zayden's filling the doorway, still in his practice gear, hair damp with sweat. He must have come straight from the ice.

"Hey." His voice is soft. Uncertain. "Dana said

she talked to you."

"She did."

"And?"

"And I still have a job." I stand up, moving toward him. "Because of you."

He shrugs, but there's a hint of a smile playing at the corner of his mouth. "You would've done the same for me."

"Maybe." I stop in front of him, close enough to touch. "But no one's ever done it for me before."

Something shifts in his expression. He reaches for me, his hand cupping my jaw, thumb brushing my cheek.

"Get used to it," he murmurs.

I want to kiss him. I want to grab him by the front of his jersey and pull him into this office to show him exactly how grateful I am.

Instead, I take a step back.

"Discreet," I remind him. "Remember?"

He groans, dropping his hand. "Right. Discreet." He glances at his watch, then back at me. "It's almost lunchtime."

"Okay?"

"Can you leave?"

I blink. "What?"

"Come to lunch with me." He says it like it's the most obvious thing in the world. "There's a place around the corner with really good sandwiches."

"You want to go get sandwiches?"

He grins. "I want to kiss you and since you just pointed out that I can't do that here, yes. Let's go get sandwiches."

The sandwich place is a hole in the wall three blocks from the facility. Plastic tables, paper napkins, a counter where you order by number. It's the least romantic setting imaginable.

I love it.

We grab a booth in the back corner—discreet, as promised—and unwrap our food. Zayden got the Italian sub. I got chicken salad on sourdough. We're eating out of paper baskets like teenagers on a lunch break.

"You know," I say, popping a chip into my mouth, "this is technically our first date."

Zayden pauses mid-bite. "This is not a date."

"We're sitting across from each other, eating food, having a conversation. That's a date. Plus… you insisted on paying."

"This is a plastic basket and fluorescent lighting. This is not a date." He sets down his sandwich, looking almost offended. "When I take you on a date—a real date—there will be candles. And wine. And food that doesn't come with a number."

A smile tugs at my lips. "That sounds very romantic."

"I'm serious." He reaches across the table and takes my hand. "I'm going to do this right, Tori. Dinner reservations. Flowers. The whole thing."

"You don't have to—"

"I want to." His thumb traces circles on my palm. "You deserve to be taken out properly. Not snuck around with. Not hidden. Properly."

My chest tightens. "Zayden…"

"Tomorrow night," he says. "I'll pick you up at seven. Wear something nice."

"Where are we going?"

"It's a surprise." He grins. "But I promise it won't involve a pickup counter."

I laugh, and it feels like the first real laugh I've had in days. Maybe weeks. "Fine. Tomorrow. Seven o'clock."

"It's a date." He lifts my hand and presses a kiss to my knuckles. "A real one this time."

We finish our sandwiches, talking about nothing important—his skate this morning, the game tonight, my new assignment, whether Italian subs are superior to meatball subs (they are, and I will die on this hill). It's easy. Normal. The kind of conversation couples have all the time, except we've never been a normal couple. We've been stolen moments, secret texts, and constant fear of getting caught.

Maybe we can finally be something else.

Zayden reaches across the table and wipes a smear of mayonnaise from the corner of my mouth. "You're a mess," he says, but he's smiling.

"Your mess, apparently."

"Apparently." He leans in, and I meet him halfway, our lips brushing in a soft, quick kiss that still manages to make my toes curl. "We should head back."

"Probably."

Neither of us moves.

My phone buzzes, breaking the moment. I glance down, expecting Dana, James, or some work emergency.

It's Winnie.

Winnie

I broke up with Derek.

I stare at the screen. Holy plot twist.

Winnie

Or he broke up with me. Not sure. Either way, it's over.

I'm fine. I think. Maybe. Can we talk later?

"Everything okay?" Zayden asks.

"Yeah, I..." I look up at him, then back at my phone. "Winnie just texted. She and Derek broke up."

"The guy with the strong opinions about everything?"

"That's the one."

"Good." Zayden shrugs. "She can do better."

He's not wrong. But the timing feels strange—my life finally coming together while Winnie's falls apart. Like the universe only has so much happiness to go around, and I just used up her share.

Me

I'm so sorry. Yes, let's talk. Tonight? Wine at my place?

Winnie

Perfect. Bring tissues. I might cry.

Or I might celebrate. Haven't decided yet.

A thought hits me. Winnie and Derek live together. Have for almost a year now. His name is on the lease.

Me

Wait. Do you have a place to stay?

Winnie

TBD. My friend Megan offered her couch, but she has a cat that hates me.

Me

You can stay with me. As long as you need. Bring a bag tonight!

Winnie

Tori, your apartment is the size of a shoebox.

Me

A shoebox with a very comfortable couch. And no cats that hate you.

Winnie

You sure?

Me

Positive. We'll drink wine, trash-talk Derek, and figure out the rest tomorrow.

Winnie

I love you, you know that?

I pocket my phone, making a mental note to pick up her favorite rosé—and maybe some extra pillows—on the way home.

"You okay?" Zayden asks again.

"Yeah." I reach across the table and squeeze his hand. "Winnie and Derek live together. Lived together. She needs a place to crash."

"So she's staying with you?"

"For a while, yeah." I smile. "My tiny apartment is about to get a lot more crowded."

"You're a good friend."

"She'd do the same for me." I pause. "She has done the same for me, actually. After Jason. Let me sleep on her floor for two weeks while I got my head on straight."

Zayden nods slowly. "Then I guess it's your turn."

I guess it is.

28

DUFFEL BAG AND ROSÉ

Tori

Winnie shows up at my door with a duffel bag, a bottle of wine, and mascara streaks down her cheeks.

"I grabbed what I could while he was at the gym," she says by way of greeting. "I'll have to go back for the rest of my stuff later, when he's not there."

"Get in here." I pull her into a hug, and she sags against me for a long moment before straightening up and wiping her face with the back of her hand.

"Sorry. I'm a mess."

"You're allowed to be a mess." I take the wine and usher her inside. "That's what tonight is for."

My apartment looks even smaller with two people in it, but we make it work. Winnie drops her duffel by the couch while I grab glasses and a corkscrew. By the time I'm pouring, she's already kicked off her shoes and curled up in the corner of my couch, knees pulled to her chest.

"Okay." I hand her a very full glass. "Tell me everything."

She takes a long sip. Then another.

"I ended it," she says finally. "Yesterday. After he told me I was being 'too emotional' about the fact that he made plans on my birthday."

"What do you mean, made plans?"

"My birthday's in two weeks. I mentioned maybe doing dinner, something nice for once, and he said he couldn't because his fantasy football league is doing their draft that night." She laughs, but there's no humor in it. "When I got upset, he said I was overreacting. That I could just celebrate on a different day. Like my birthday is flexible."

"Are you kidding me?"

"And the thing is—" She takes a long sip of wine. "Maybe it would have been fine if he'd sat me down and said, 'Hey, my friends planned this thing on your birthday. Obviously, my priority is celebrating you, so I can skip it. But if you're okay with it, we could do your birthday another night. Whatever you want.' That's a conversation. That's considering my feelings."

"But that's not what he did."

"No. He just informed me he had plans and that I needed to deal with it. And when I didn't deal with it the way he wanted, suddenly I'm the problem." She shakes her head. "That's when I realized—I've been overreacting to everything for two years, according to him. My feelings are always too big, my needs are always too much, and I'm always the one who has to apologize for wanting basic human consideration."

"Win..."

"So I told him I was done. And he said—" She

pauses, jaw tightening. "He said 'fine, but you're the one who has to find somewhere else to live, because I'm not leaving my apartment.'"

"His apartment? You've been paying half the rent!"

"I know. But his name's on the lease, and apparently that's all that matters." She drains half her glass. "So now I'm homeless, single, and drinking wine on my best friend's couch. Really living the dream, here."

I scoot closer and wrap an arm around her shoulders. "You're not homeless. You're staying here as long as you need."

"Tori, your apartment is literally one room."

"A very cozy room." I squeeze her. "Besides, I like having you here. It'll be like college, except with better wine and fewer questionable life choices."

She snort-laughs, which is exactly what I was going for. "I don't know about fewer questionable life choices. I did just blow up my entire life."

"You didn't blow it up. You escaped." I pull back and look at her seriously. "Win, I've been watching you shrink yourself for two years. Every time we hang out, you're a little quieter, a little more careful about what you say. Like you're always bracing for him to criticize you."

Her eyes fill with tears. "Was it that obvious?"

"Only to people who love you."

She sets down her wine and drops her head into her hands. "I kept telling myself it would get better. That he was just stressed, or that I was being too sensitive, or that every relationship has rough patches." She looks up at me. "But it wasn't a rough patch. It was just... how he is. And I finally realized I can't fix that."

"You can't. And you shouldn't have to."

"I know." She wipes her eyes and takes a shaky breath. "The worst part is, I don't even feel that sad. I feel... relieved? Is that terrible?"

"That's not terrible. That's your gut telling you that you made the right call."

She's quiet for a moment, processing. Then she reaches for her wine again, and I notice something I didn't see before. Her shoulders are looser. Her jaw isn't clenched. Even with mascara smeared under her eyes and her life in chaos, she looks lighter than she has in months.

"What are you going to do now?" I ask.

"I don't know. Figure out the living situation first, I guess. I'll eventually need to find an apartment of my own." She makes a face. "And then there's work."

"What about work?"

Winnie sighs. "Derek and I both teach at the same gym. Or, we did. After yesterday, things are... tense."

"How tense?"

"It's a small place, Tori. Like, twelve employees small. Everyone knows everyone's business." She picks at the edge of her blanket. "We were the cute couple who met at work. Now we're the messy breakup everyone has to tiptoe around."

"That sounds awful."

I sip my wine, already thinking. The staff meeting this week—Dana mentioned they've been talking about bringing in a yoga instructor for the team. Flexibility training, injury prevention, mental wellness. The guys have been resistant to it, but management is pushing hard.

"Win," I say slowly. "How would you feel about teaching somewhere else?"

"Like where? Another gym?"

"Like... the Knights facility."

She stares at me. "What?"

"The team's been talking about hiring a yoga instructor. For the players. It came up in a staff meeting this week." I grab my phone. "I could talk to Dana. Put in a good word. Send her your resume."

"Tori." Her eyes go wide. "Are you serious?"

"Dead serious."

"That would be—I mean, that's a professional sports team. That's a completely different level." She sets down her wine glass. "You really think they'd consider me?"

"I think you're exactly what they need. You're good, Win. Really good. And these guys desperately need someone to work on their flexibility. Half of them can barely touch their toes."

"Oh my God." She presses her hands to her cheeks. "That would be amazing. Like, life-changing amazing. No more tiny gym, no more Derek poisoning everyone against me, no more—" She stops, looking at me with something like hope for the first time all night. "You'd really do that for me?"

"I'm already drafting the email in my head." I grin. "Send me your resume tonight. I'll get it to

Dana first thing tomorrow."

"You're the best. You know that, right? Literally the best friend anyone has ever had."

Winnie takes a long sip, then narrows her eyes at me over the rim. "Okay, enough about my disaster. What's going on with you? I feel like I've barely seen you in weeks, and you've got that look."

"What look?"

"The look of someone who has news and is waiting for me to ask."

I laugh, but she's not wrong. "Things have been... eventful."

"Eventful how?"

"Well... the team found out about me and Zayden."

Winnie's eyes go wide. "Oh shit. What happened?"

"Grayson Reed—the guy who wouldn't leave me alone—saw us at the hotel in Minneapolis and spread it around the whole facility." I take a long drink of my own wine. "My boss, Dana, called me in. It was... not fun."

"Did you get fired?"

"No. But I got reassigned." I pick at the label on the wine bottle, not quite meeting her eyes. "I'm off the active roster, only working with guys rehabbing long-term injuries and prospects now. No more road trips."

"So, like... a demotion?"

"They're calling it 'reduced capacity until things settle down.'" I shrug. "Same pay, same hours. Just less visible. Less important."

"Tori." Winnie reaches over and squeezes my

hand. "That sucks. I'm sorry."

"It could have been worse. Zayden went to Dana before I could—like, showed up at her office at the crack of dawn to take responsibility. He told her about Reed harassing me, defended me, and offered to take whatever consequences they wanted to throw at him." I smile despite myself. "He went to bat for me. No one's ever done that before."

"Okay, that's annoyingly romantic."

"I know." I roll my eyes.

"So you two are...?"

"Officially? Keeping things 'discreet.'" I make air quotes. "But we're going on a date tomorrow night. A real one. Reservations and everything."

"Your first real date?"

"We've done everything completely backwards. I've met his daughter, almost slept with him in a hotel, and nearly lost my job over him—but we've never actually been on a date."

Winnie laughs. "That's the most chaotic relationship timeline I've ever heard. I love it."

"It's been a lot." I lean back against the couch cushions. "But it's good. He's good. Even with all the mess, I don't regret it."

"You shouldn't." She clinks her glass against mine. "To messy, chaotic love. And to both of us figuring our shit out."

"I'll drink to that."

We polish off the rest of the bottle, and later, I help her set up the couch with sheets and pillows. It's not glamorous—my couch is about six inches too short for a full-grown adult to sleep comfortably—but Winnie doesn't complain. She just wraps herself in the blanket and sighs.

"Thank you," she says quietly. "For all of this. I don't know what I'd do without you."

"Probably sleep on Megan's couch and get peed on by a cat."

"Probably." She smiles. "Goodnight, Tori."

"Goodnight, Win."

I turn off the lights and head to my bed—which is really just a slightly elevated section of the same room, separated by a bookshelf that serves as a makeshift wall. The joys of studio apartment living.

But as I lie there in the dark, listening to Winnie's breathing even out, I'm not thinking about the cramped quarters or the chaos of the last few days.

I'm thinking about tomorrow night.

My date with Zayden, him taking me somewhere with candles and wine and food that doesn't come with a number.

I've never been the girl who gets giddy about dates. After all the horrible first dates I've been on, I've trained myself not to. Expectations lead to disappointment, and disappointment leads to heartbreak, and I'd had enough of that to last a lifetime.

But this feels different. Zayden feels different.

I fall asleep smiling, and for the first time in a long time, I don't dream about everything that could go wrong.

I dream about everything that could go right.

29

FINALLY

Zayden

I change my shirt three times.

This is ridiculous. I'm a grown man. I've played hockey in front of twenty thousand screaming fans—sick, injured, and I've given post-game interviews with blood drying on my face. I've handled custody negotiations, contract disputes, and a six-year-old's meltdown over the wrong color popsicle.

But somehow, getting dressed for a date with Tori Wells has me standing in front of my closet like a teenager before prom.

"Daddy, you look handsome."

I turn to find Maisie in my doorway, already in her pajamas even though it's only 6:30. Hannah's downstairs getting dinner ready, and Maze is supposed to be washing her hands, but apparently my fashion crisis is more interesting.

"You think so?"

"Mm-hmm." She walks over and studies me with the critical eye of a six-year-old fashion consultant. "But maybe not that shirt."

"What's wrong with this shirt?"

"It's boring."

"It's navy blue. Navy blue is classic."

"It's boring," she repeats, then marches to my closet and starts rifling through hangers. After a moment, she pulls out a dark green button-down I forgot I owned. "This one. It brings out your eyes."

"Where did you learn that phrase?"

"Hannah. She said it once about my sweater." Maisie thrusts the shirt at me. "Trust me, Daddy."

I take the shirt. At this point, I'm willing to trust anyone's judgment over my own.

"Are you going to kiss Tori tonight?" Maisie asks while I change.

I nearly choke on my own spit. "Why would you ask that?"

"Because that's what people do on dates. Sophie's mom told her."

"Sophie's mom talks about kissing with her six-year-old?"

"Sophie's mom tells her everything." Maisie sits on my bed, swinging her legs. "So? Are you?"

"That's... not really something we discuss, Maze."

"But you like her, right? Like, *like-like* her?"

"I like-like her," I admit, because there's no point in lying to a child who can smell dishonesty from a mile away. "Very much."

Maisie beams. "Good. I like-like her too." She hops off the bed and heads for the door. "Don't mess it up, Daddy!"

"Thanks for the vote of confidence, shadow." I shake my head.

"You're welcome!"

She disappears down the hall, and I finish getting ready with her words echoing in my head.

Don't mess it up.

No pressure.

I pull up to Tori's building at 6:55.

Five minutes early because I'm pathologically punctual, but also because I've been ready for an hour, and sitting at home was making me insane. I check my hair in the rearview mirror, grab the flowers from the passenger seat—colorful gerbera daisies, because she mentioned once that roses felt too cliché—and head inside.

Fourth floor. No elevator. By the time I reach her door, I remember why she complained about this walk-up.

I knock, and when she opens the door, I forget how to breathe.

She's wearing a deep red dress that stops just above her knees—simple but stunning. Her hair falls in soft waves around her shoulders, and she's adorned with earrings I've never seen before—small gold hoops that catch the light when she moves. She's wearing lipstick. I've never seen her in lipstick before—and it's distracting as hell. She's a knockout.

"Hi," she says, sounding almost shy.

"Hi." I hold out the flowers. "These are for you."

"They're beautiful." She takes them, and her

whole face softens.

She looks up at me, and for a moment, we just stand there, grinning at each other like idiots.

"I should put these in water," she says. "Come in for a second?"

I follow her inside and notice the woman on the couch.

She's curled up under a blanket, laptop open, hair piled in a messy bun on top of her head. She looks up when we walk in, and I realize this must be Winnie—the best friend, the yoga instructor, the one who just left her boyfriend. *Yikes.*

"Oh." She sits up straighter, her eyes widening a bit. "Hi."

"Winnie, this is Zayden. Zayden, Winnie." Tori gestures between us while heading toward the kitchen. "I need to put these in water."

"Hey." I give an awkward wave. "Uh, sorry about the breakup."

Winnie blinks. "Thanks?"

"Tori mentioned it. The guy sounds like a jerk."

"He is a jerk." She almost smiles. "A very large, fantasy-football-obsessed jerk."

"I could kick his ass if you want. I know people."

Now she actually laughs. "I appreciate the offer, but I think public humiliation via word of mouth will be more satisfying than physical violence."

"Fair enough. But the offer stands."

Tori reappears from the kitchen, flowers now arranged in a tall glass that's definitely not a vase. She sets them on the counter and grabs her clutch from the coffee table.

"Don't wait up," she tells Winnie.

"Wasn't planning on it." Winnie waggles her eyebrows. "Have fun, you two. Don't do anything I wouldn't do."

"That leaves a lot of options," Tori replies dryly.

"Exactly."

"Okay." Tori turns to face me. "I'm ready."

"You look incredible."

"You already said that—with your eyes, when I opened the door."

"I'm saying it again—with words this time." I offer her my arm. "Shall we?"

She takes it, and we head out into the night.

The restaurant is a hidden gem in Brooklyn, tucked between a laundromat and a bakery. There's no sign out front, just a wooden door with a brass number. Inside, it's all exposed brick, candlelight, and tables tucked into cozy corners. The host leads us to a booth in the back, and I slide in across from Tori, trying to memorize the way she looks in this light.

"This place is beautiful," she says, looking around. "How did you find it?"

"Archer told me about it. He brought Bree here for their anniversary." I open the menu, then set it down. "I've been saving it."

"Saving it?"

"For someone worth bringing."

She ducks her head, but I catch the smile.

"That's very smooth, Bishop."

"I have my moments."

The waiter arrives, and we order wine—a red she chooses because I tell her I trust her judgment—and way too much food. Neither of us seems to care. When he leaves, Tori props her chin on her hand and studies me.

"I just realized something weird."

"Weird?" I lift an eyebrow.

She nods. "We've done everything out of order. I've seen your medical history. I know your resting heart rate. I've met your daughter." She pauses. "But I don't know where you grew up or if you have siblings. Basic stuff."

"I was born in Montreal. A little suburb outside the city." I take a sip of wine. "Moved to Colorado when I was ten for my dad's job—he was an engineer and got transferred. I did one year of college in Minnesota before getting drafted."

"So you're barely Canadian."

"Don't ever say that to my mother. She'd disown me." I smile, but it fades a little. "She's back in Montreal now, actually. Moved home a few years ago after my dad passed."

Tori's expression softens. "I'm sorry. I didn't know."

"Heart attack. It was quick, which I guess is a blessing, but..." I shrug. "Maisie was only two when it happened. She doesn't remember him at all."

"That's hard."

"Yeah." I clear my throat. "Anyway, my mom wanted to be near her sisters, so she went back. My older sister Elise lives there too—she's got twin boys, so Mom's busy being the world's most devoted grandmother."

"You have a sister?"

"She's three years older. Bossy as hell. Calls me every Sunday to make sure I'm eating my vegetables and not letting Maisie watch too much TV." I grin. "You'd like her. She doesn't take any of my crap either."

Tori laughs. "I already like her."

"What about you? Where did you grow up?"

"Connecticut. Suburbs. Very white picket fence." She takes a sip of wine. "My parents are still married. My dad's an accountant, and my mom teaches third grade. I have two older brothers who made my life hell until I learned to fight back."

"Two brothers?"

She nods. "They're both married now, with kids. I'm the cool aunt who shows up at Christmas and teaches their children bad words."

I laugh. "Oh, you're very cool."

"Well, not according to my mother. Apparently, I'm not getting any younger, and she has started asking about my love life on almost every phone call. 'Meet any nice boys, Victoria? You're not getting any younger, Victoria.'" She rolls her eyes. "I'm twenty-six. She acts like I'm running out of time."

"My mom's the same way. Except she's less subtle. Last time I visited, she literally handed me a newspaper clipping about a local girl who was 'very nice and looking for a good Catholic boy.'"

"Did you call her?"

"The girl? No. My mom? Yes, to tell her to stop."

Tori laughs, and the sound does something to my chest, loosening a knot I didn't know was there.

The appetizers arrive—burrata with tomatoes and some kind of stuffed mushroom—and we eat while we talk about our childhoods, our families, and the dreams we had when we were young and foolish, convinced we knew everything.

"I wanted to be a marine biologist," Tori admits, "until I realized it involved a lot more chemistry than swimming with dolphins."

"I always planned to be a hockey player. There was never a backup plan." I twirl pasta around my fork. "Which is terrifying in retrospect. What if I'd gotten injured? What if I wasn't good enough?"

"But you were good enough."

"I got lucky. Right place, right time, right genetics." I set down my fork. "But it's made me think a lot about what comes next. I can't play forever—another five years, maybe, if my body holds up. Then what?"

"What do you want to do?"

"I don't know. Coaching, maybe. Or something with kids—hockey camps, youth programs. Something that gives back." I've never said this out loud to anyone before.

"That could be cool."

"What about you? Where do you see yourself in ten years?"

She's quiet for a moment, swirling her wine. "I used to have this whole plan: career ladder, accomplishments, titles. Be the head of a sports medicine department by thirty-five. Open my own clinic by forty."

"Used to?"

"I still want those things. But lately, I've been thinking about other aspects of life too—things I always told myself would come 'later.'" She meets my eyes. "Family. Kids. A life that isn't just about work."

"And what does 'later' look like now?"

"I don't know. That's the scary part." She laughs softly. "I spent so long protecting myself, keeping people at arm's length, that I never really thought about what I actually wanted—just what I didn't want."

"Which was?"

"To be hurt. To be the cautionary tale. To need someone and have them leave." She sets down her glass. "But you can't build a life around avoiding things. At some point, you have to choose what you're running toward instead of what you're running from."

I reach across the table and take her hand. "For what it's worth, I'm glad you stopped running."

"Me too." She squeezes my fingers. "Even if you did make it very difficult to maintain professional boundaries."

"I have no idea what you're talking about."

She laughs, and I think I could spend the rest of my life trying to make her laugh like that.

Dinner stretches into dessert, dessert into coffee, and by the time we leave, the restaurant is nearly empty. I've learned more about Tori Wells in three hours than I did in three months of treatment sessions.

I learn that her favorite movie is *The Princess Bride*, and she can quote the entire sword fight scene from memory. She stress-bakes when she's anxious and once made seven loaves of banana bread during finals week. It's random and odd, and I love it.

I discover that she's afraid of disappointing people and sometimes lies awake at night wondering if she's good enough. (She definitely is.) I find out that she wants kids, which sends warmth spreading through my chest.

We linger over the check, neither of us making a move to leave. The restaurant has emptied around us, candles burning low, and I'm not ready for this to end.

"So," I say, signing the receipt, "I should probably get you home."

"Probably." She doesn't move.

"Or..." I set down the pen. "Hannah's with Maisie until midnight. I could pay her, send her home, and we could... talk. At my place."

Tori raises an eyebrow. "Talk."

"Among other things." I hold her gaze. "If you want."

She's quiet for a moment, and I can see her thinking—the implications, the step we'd be taking. Then something shifts in her expression. A decision made.

"I want to."

Three words. My heart slams against my ribs.

"Yeah?"

"Yeah." She reaches across the table and

threads her fingers through mine.

Hannah is waiting in the living room when we walk in, her crossword puzzle abandoned on the coffee table. She stands when she sees us, and her eyes flick to Tori with obvious curiosity.

"Hannah, this is Tori. Tori, Hannah—she's the reason I haven't completely fallen apart this season."

"Oh, stop." Hannah waves a hand, but she's smiling as she extends it to Tori. "It's so nice to finally meet you. Maisie talks about you constantly."

"She does?" Tori sounds genuinely surprised.

"Are you kidding? It's Tori this, Tori that. Tori knows all the dinosaur names. Tori let me paint her nails. Tori's going to teach me to do a cartwheel." Hannah laughs. "I was starting to think she made you up."

Tori's cheeks go pink, and I love it. "She's a pretty great kid."

"She is." Hannah's expression softens as she looks between us. "And it's nice to see this one smiling for a change. He's been a grump for months."

"I have not been a grump."

"You've been a grump," Hannah confirms. She grabs her bag and coat. "Maisie went down easy, by the way. Out like a light by eight."

"You're a lifesaver."

"I know." She pauses at the door, looking between me and Tori with a knowing twinkle. "You two have fun."

Then she's gone, and we're alone.

The house feels different at night—quieter. The city lights glow through the windows, casting everything in soft shadows. Tori moves to the living room, running her fingers along the back of the couch, looking at the photos on the wall.

"That's Maisie's first hockey game," I say, pointing to a picture of her in a tiny jersey, face painted with team colors. "She was three. Cried for the first twenty minutes because the noise scared her."

"She looks so little."

"She was. She still is, but sometimes she seems so grown-up it scares me."

Tori turns to face me. "You're a good dad, Zayden."

"I try to be."

"You are." She steps closer.

I can't help it. I kiss her.

It starts soft—a question more than a statement—but she answers by pressing closer, her hands sliding up my chest to curl around the back of my neck. I pull her against me, one hand in her hair, the other at the small of her back, and the kiss deepens into something hungrier.

She tastes like wine and chocolate and everything I've wanted for months.

"Upstairs," I murmur against her mouth. "My room. Unless—"

"Yes." She doesn't let me finish. "Yes."

I take her hand and lead her up the stairs, my heart pounding, barely able to believe this is actually happening. At the top, I pause to check Maisie's room—door cracked, nightlight glowing, the soft sound of her breathing confirming she's asleep.

Then, I pull Tori into my bedroom and close the door behind us.

She looks around, taking in the space—the big bed with the gray comforter, the stack of books on my nightstand that I always mean to read. Her gaze returns to me, and the desire in her eyes makes my mouth go dry.

"Hi," she says.

"Hi." I cross to her, cupping her face in my hands. "We can slow down if you want. We don't have to—"

She kisses me to silence my words.

And then we stop talking altogether.

30

WORTH THE WAIT

Tori

The door clicks shut behind us, and suddenly we're standing in Zayden's bedroom, surrounded by dim light and anticipation.

He doesn't rush. Despite the heat that's been building all night—during dinner, during the drive, during the thirty seconds it took to pay Hannah and usher her out the door—he takes his time now, looking at me as if he wants to memorize this moment.

"You okay?" he asks softly.

"Nervous," I admit.

"We don't have to—"

"Don't you dare finish that sentence." I step closer, pressing my palm flat against his chest. His heart is pounding just as hard as mine.

"Come here," he murmurs, and then his mouth is on mine.

The kiss starts slow, almost careful, but it doesn't stay that way. His hands find my waist, pulling me against him, and I melt into the heat of his body.

My fingers find the buttons of his shirt, and I start working them open. He pulls back just enough to watch me, a smile playing at the corner of his mouth.

"In a hurry?"

"We've been waiting months for this. Yes, I'm in a hurry."

He laughs, low and warm, and helps me with the last few buttons. The shirt falls open, and I push it off his shoulders, then—

Oh.

Oh, this is a lot.

I've seen him shirtless before—dozens of times. I've had my hands on this body in a purely professional capacity more times than I can count.

But this is different. This is Zayden in the low light of his bedroom, looking at me like I'm the only thing he's ever wanted, and I am absolutely not prepared for the full impact of him.

Broad shoulders that seem to go on forever. A chest that's all hard planes and defined muscle. A dusting of dark hair trails down his stomach to where his belt sits low on his hips. There's a scar on his left side—an old injury I know the history of—and I want to trace it with my tongue.

"You're staring," he says.

"You're very stareable."

"That's not a word."

"It is now."

He grins, reaching for the zipper at the back of my dress. "May I?"

I turn around, lifting my hair off my neck. His fingers brush my spine as he pulls the zipper down, and I shiver at the contact. The dress loosens, then falls, pooling at my feet in a whisper of fabric.

I stand before him in nothing but a black lace bra and matching underwear—thank God I planned ahead—and suddenly I feel very exposed. Very seen.

He makes a sound, low and almost pained. "Tori." My name comes out rough. "You're..."

I lift my eyes to his, waiting.

"I had a whole sentence planned. It's gone now." He shakes his head slowly, his eyes traveling over me. "You broke my brain."

I laugh, and just like that, the nervousness fades. This is us—heat and humor and something real underneath it all.

"Get over here," I tell him.

He doesn't need to be told twice.

We tumble onto the bed in a tangle of limbs and laughter, and then his mouth is everywhere—my neck, my collarbone, the curve of my shoulder. I arch into him, fingers digging into the muscles of his back, trying to pull him closer even though there's no space left between us.

He kisses his way down my body, taking his time, and I'm going to lose my mind. Every touch feels amplified, electric—like my nerve endings have been waiting for exactly this.

When he reaches the edge of my underwear, he looks up at me.

"Still good?"

"Zayden. If you ask me one more time if I'm okay, I'm going to—"

"Going to what?"

"I don't know, but it'll be dramatic."

He grins, and then he stops asking and starts showing me exactly why he's been worth the wait. His mouth trails across sensitive skin, and I arch into him.

"You have no idea," he murmurs against my thigh, "how long I've been thinking about this."

"How long?" I pant.

"Since the first time you put your hands on my shoulder and told me to stop being a baby about the ice bath."

"That was week one."

"I'm aware." He kisses my hip bone, and I gasp. "Drove me crazy. This gorgeous woman with her hands all over me, completely professional, while I'm lying there trying not to embarrass myself."

"You hid it well."

"I'm an athlete. I'm used to hiding pain." He lifts his head, grinning. "Among other things."

I pull him back up, kissing him hard, and his hands start to wander. Down my sides, over my hips, hooking under my thigh to pull my leg up around him. The contact makes us both groan.

"Wait," I breathe. "Too many clothes. You're still wearing pants."

"Valid point."

He pulls back long enough to deal with his belt, and I take the opportunity to unhook my bra and toss it somewhere over the side of the bed. I hear the rustle of fabric, the soft thud of pants hitting the floor, and then—

When he looks back at me, he actually stops moving. Just freezes, staring.

"What?"

"Give me a second. I'm committing this to memory."

"Zayden."

"I'm serious. This image is going to get me through a lot of long road trips."

I throw a pillow at him. He catches it, laughing, and then he's back—pressing me into the mattress, skin against skin, nothing between us but heat and want.

"Better?" I manage.

"So much better." He kisses me deeply, thoroughly, until I'm dizzy with it. "You feel incredible."

His hand slides down my stomach, and I stop thinking altogether.

He takes his time with me—learning what makes me gasp, what makes me arch off the bed, what makes me say his name like a gasp. He's patient and thorough and devastating, and by the time he finally pulls away to reach for the nightstand drawer, I'm trembling for entirely different reasons.

"Good?" he asks, hovering over me.

I pull him down by the back of his neck. "Very."

He presses into me slowly, giving me time to adjust. My breath catches. He's big—I knew that, objectively, but knowing and experiencing are very different things.

"Okay?" His voice is strained, like it's taking everything he has to hold still.

"Yeah." I wrap my legs around him, pulling him deeper. "More than okay."

He starts to move, and it's—

It's everything.

Slow at first, finding our rhythm, learning how we fit together. Then faster, deeper, as the tension builds between us. His forehead drops to mine, breath ragged, and I can feel him holding back.

He pauses above me, and something raw crosses his face. "I haven't—" He swallows hard. "It's been a long time since anyone—"

I cup his jaw, feeling the muscle tick beneath my palm. "Don't," I tell him.

"Don't what?"

"Don't hold back. I want all of you."

Something flashes in his eyes—dark, hungry—and then he's not holding back anymore. He hooks my leg higher on his hip and changes the angle, and I actually cry out because it's so good.

"There?" he asks, and the smugness in his voice should be annoying, but it's really, really not.

"There. Right there. Don't stop."

"Never."

He keeps his word—over and over—until I'm clutching at his shoulders, until I'm making sounds I'll probably be embarrassed about later, until I feel the pressure building to something I can't contain.

"Zay—I'm going to—"

"I know." He kisses me hard. "I've got you. Let go."

I do.

It crashes through me in waves, and I'm pretty sure I say his name, or maybe just a string of incoherent sounds. He follows a moment later, groaning against my neck, hips stuttering before he collapses half on top of me.

For a long moment, neither of us speaks. Just breathes. His weight is heavy but I don't want him to move.

"I think you killed me," I finally manage.

He laughs against my neck. "You okay?"

"I am much better than okay." I trace a finger down his jaw. "I might need a minute before I can feel my legs again."

"Take all the time you need." He presses a kiss to my shoulder. "I'm not going anywhere."

Later—much later—we're lying in a tangle of sheets, my head on his chest, his fingers tracing lazy patterns on my bare shoulder. I can hear his heartbeat under my ear, gradually slowing back to normal.

We lie there in comfortable silence for a while, and I'm just starting to drift toward sleep when something occurs to me.

"Zayden?"

"Mm?"

"Did you lock the door?"

A pause. A very long pause.

"I... think so?"

"You think so?"

"I'm pretty sure I—"

And then, as if the universe has been waiting for exactly this moment, there's a small knock on the door.

"Daddy?"

We both freeze. I've never moved so fast in my life—scrambling for sheets, for clothes, for any-thing to cover myself while Zayden nearly falls off the bed trying to find his boxers.

"One second, Maze!" His voice comes out strangled. "Just—stay there, okay?"

"I had a bad dream."

"I know, baby. One second."

I'm under the covers now, blanket pulled up to my chin, watching Zayden hop around trying to get his legs into his boxers. He bangs his shin on the bedframe and bites back a curse.

"Smooth," I whisper.

"Not helpful."

He finally gets them on and cracks the door open, slipping out into the hallway. I hear murmured voices—Maisie's small and sleepy, his low and soothing—and then footsteps padding away toward her room.

I lie there, heart pounding, caught somewhere between mortification and hysterical laughter.

This is my life now—sneaking around like a teenager, hiding under the covers while my... boyfriend? Whatever he is... puts his daughter back to bed.

It should feel strange. Complicated. Maybe a little scary.

Instead, it just feels right.

Zayden comes back ten minutes later, closing the door softly behind him—and this time, I hear the lock click.

"Is she okay?"

"Bad dream about a dinosaur eating her homework." He slides back into bed, pulling me against him. "I told her dinosaurs are extinct and also don't care about first-grade math."

"Solid parenting."

"I try." He settles back against the pillows with a sigh. "Sorry about that. Not exactly the romantic ending I had planned."

"Are you kidding? That was perfect."

He looks down at me, confused. "How is my kid almost walking in on us perfect?"

"Because it's real." I prop myself up on my elbow. "It's you—your life, your daughter, all of it. I don't want some sanitized version that pretends complicated things don't exist. I want this—the messy, interrupted, real thing."

He stares at me for a long moment, something shifting in his expression.

"What?" I ask.

"Nothing. Just..." He reaches up, tucking a strand of hair behind my ear. "I'm falling hard for you. You know that, right?"

My heart does something complicated in my chest. "Yeah?"

"Yeah." He pulls me down for a kiss—soft this time, tender. "Stay tonight?"

"What about Maisie?"

"Well… we could sneak you out in the morning." He presses a quick kiss to my lips. "But I think she'd be happy to see you again."

I settle against his chest, letting my eyes drift closed. "Okay."

His arm wraps around me, warm and solid and safe, and I fall asleep listening to his heartbeat.

And for the first time in longer than I can remember, I'm not scared of what comes next.

I'm excited for it.

31

CALLED OUT

Zayden

I'm in the best mood I've been in for months.

Maybe years.

The locker room smells the same as always—sweat and industrial soap and the sharp bite of menthol from someone's muscle rub—but even that can't drag me down today. The fluorescent lights hum overhead, casting their usual unflattering glow, and the tile floors are cold under my bare feet as I pad toward my stall.

None of it matters. I woke up this morning thinking of Tori, and I haven't stopped smiling since.

Apparently, it shows.

"Okay, what's going on with you?" Logan drops onto the bench next to me, already half-dressed for practice. "You're smiling. It's freaking me out." He's got a protein bar hanging out of his mouth and his practice jersey on inside out—classic Logan—but his eyes are sharp as he studies me. The kid misses nothing when it comes to team dynamics. It's annoying as hell.

"I smile."

"You don't smile. You brood. You glare. You occasionally smirk when you score a goal." He squints at me. "This is different. This is like... happy smiling. It's unnatural." He narrows his eyes.

"Maybe I'm just having a good day."

"Uh-huh." Logan's not buying it. He turns to Banks, who's lacing up his skates two stalls down. "Banks. Tell him he's being weird."

Banks glances over, takes one look at my face, and returns to his skates. "He got laid."

I choke on nothing.

"What? No. I—"

"You definitely got laid." Banks doesn't even look up. "You've got that look."

"What look?"

"The look of a man who's finally gotten what he's been pining after for months." Now he does look up, one eyebrow raised. "Congratulations. It's about time."

Heat creeps up the back of my neck. I want to deny it—should deny it—but the memory of last night floods through me unbidden. Tori in my bed, her hair spread across my pillow, the sounds she made when I—

I clear my throat and focus very intently on strapping on my shin guards.

Logan's head swivels between us like he's watching a tennis match. "Wait. Wait wait wait." His eyes go wide. "Is this about Tori? Did you and Tori finally—"

"Keep your voice down," I hiss, glancing around the locker room. The last thing I need is this spreading through the whole team.

"Holy crap." Logan's grin is enormous. "I knew it. I knew it! I called this like two months ago. Didn't I call this?" He turns to Banks. "I called this."

"You called it," Banks confirms, sounding bored.

"I said, 'Those two are going to end up together,' and everyone was like, 'No, Logan, she's his PT, it's professional,' and I was like, 'Watch. Just watch.'" He's practically bouncing. "And now look! I was right!"

"You want a trophy?"

"I want acknowledgment of my superior observational skills."

Archer appears from the shower area, towel slung over his shoulder, steam still rising off his skin. His hair is damp and pushed back from his face, and he's got that calm, steady energy he always carries—the goalie zen that makes him unflappable in the crease.

He catches the tail end of the conversation and raises an eyebrow. "What are we acknowledging?"

"Zay finally made a move on his PT," Banks says.

"The hot one who doesn't take his crap?" Archer grins. "Good for you, man. She seems solid."

"She is solid." The words come out before I can stop them, and I sound like an idiot, but I don't care. "She's... yeah. She's great."

Great doesn't even begin to cover it. She's brilliant and funny, and she's great with Maisie. She fits into our life like she was always supposed to be there.

And God, the way she—

I cut off that train of thought before it shows on my face. Too late, judging by the way Logan's grinning.

"Oh no. He's got it bad. Look at his face."

"Shut up." I catch a glimpse of myself in the mirror mounted on the inside of my locker door. He's right. I look... different. Softer around the edges. The permanent furrow between my eyebrows has smoothed out.

"You're all soft and mushy. It's disgusting." But he's smiling when he says it. "Seriously though, I'm happy for you. You've been wound so tight lately I was worried you'd snap."

"I wasn't that bad."

Three voices say, "You were that bad" in unison.

This startles a laugh out of me—a real laugh, the kind that comes from somewhere deep in my chest. Banks looks mildly surprised at the sound, like he's never heard me make it before.

He probably hasn't. Not like this.

"Okay, fine." I hold up my hands in surrender. "Maybe I was a little tense."

"'A little tense,'" Logan mimics. "Bro, you nearly took Henderson's head off last week for breathing too loud during film review."

"He was breathing loud. It was distracting."

"You need to get laid more often. You're way more tolerable like this."

Okay, maybe I was that bad.

Archer settles onto the bench across from me,

pulling on his pads. "So what's the situation? You guys official? Keeping it quiet?"

"Keeping it quiet for now. At least until the season is over." I run a hand through my hair. "Dana knows. She's... handling it. Tori got reassigned off my case, but she's still with the team."

"That's good. Could've been worse."

"Yeah." It could've been a lot worse. I'm still grateful every day that Dana listened, that she gave us a chance instead of just following policy to the letter.

"How's Maisie taking it?" Banks asks, and the question catches me off guard. Not because it's intrusive, but because he remembered. Because he thought to ask.

Banks doesn't do small talk. Doesn't ask questions he doesn't care about the answers to. The fact that he's wondering how Maze is doing—says more about our friendship than a hundred locker room conversations.

I feel a sudden surge of gratitude for these guys. This team. The family I've built here without even realizing I was doing it.

"She's, uh... she's good. Really good, actually." I can't help the smile that creeps across my face. "She's been asking when Tori can come over for dinner again. Apparently, I'm 'boring' and Tori knows all the words to the *Moana* songs."

"Brutal," Logan says. "Upstaged by a Disney soundtrack."

"You have no idea. Last week, Maisie informed me that Tori's grilled cheese is better than mine. Which is insane because I use three kinds of cheese."

"Maybe it's not about the cheese," Archer says, and there's something knowing in his voice. "Maybe it's about who's making it."

I don't have a response to that. Because he's right. It's not about the sandwich. It's about Maisie seeing someone who shows up, who keeps promises, who fits into our little two-person world like she was always meant to be there. It's about her finally having a positive maternal figure who's not just her nanny.

"She's good for you," Banks says quietly. "Tori. I've noticed."

"Noticed what?"

"You're different when she's around. Less..." He waves a hand vaguely. "Clenched."

"Clenched?" My eyebrows dart up. That's not a pleasant word. Is that really what my teammates thought of me?

"You know what I mean. You're always carrying everything yourself. The kid, the career, the pressure. Like you're afraid to let anyone help." He shrugs. "With her, you seem like you actually breathe."

I don't know what to say to that. Banks isn't exactly known for his emotional insights—or for sharing them, at least. The fact that he's noticed, that he's saying something, means more than I know how to express.

"Thanks, man."

He nods, and that's the end of it. No big moment, no lengthy heart-to-heart. Just acknowledgment between two guys who've been in the trenches together.

Logan, of course, has to ruin the moment. "So when do we get to officially meet her? Like, as your girlfriend? Because I have a lot of questions about your medical history that I feel she could answer."

"Absolutely not."

"Come on. Just a few questions. Like, what's his pain tolerance really? Because he acts all tough, but I saw him limping for twenty minutes after that love tap from Boston's third liner."

"That was not a love tap. He caught my knee, you dick."

"Dude, my grandma hits harder than that guy." Logan shakes his head. "And don't even get me started on the tape incident yesterday."

"There was no tape incident."

"You yelped, Zay. Out loud. When you ripped the tape off your socks."

"It pulled my leg hair."

"You're literally missing a tooth from blocking a shot and you're crying about leg hair?"

Archer laughs, and even Banks cracks a smile, and I realize something that catches me off guard.

These idiots. They give me endless crap, chirp me about everything from my tape job to my love life, and half the time I want to strangle them. That's the funny thing about hockey players—we don't do the emotional stuff. No big declarations, no deep conversations about our feelings. But they show up when it matters, and that's enough.

I spent so long thinking I had to do everything alone. That needing people was weakness, that letting anyone in was a risk I couldn't afford. But sitting here in this locker room, surrounded by idiots who won't stop making fun of me, I realize I already have what I was so afraid of losing.

A family.

Not just Maisie. Not just Tori now. But this—the brotherhood, the trust, the knowledge that these guys have my back no matter what.

"Hey." Logan snaps his fingers in front of my face. "You're doing the thing again."

"What thing?"

"The soft mushy thing. You're gonna make me emotional."

"God forbid."

"I'm serious. If you start crying, I'm going to start crying, and then Banks is going to make fun of both of us."

"I would," Banks confirms.

"See? So pull it together, Bishop. We've got practice."

He claps me on the shoulder and heads toward the tunnel, and the moment passes. But the feeling doesn't. That warmth in my chest, that sense of belonging—it stays.

Archer pauses next to me on his way out. "Hey. For real though. I'm glad you found someone. After everything with Sienna, with Maisie... you deserve something good."

"Thanks, Arch."

"Just don't screw it up."

"Helpful."

"I try." He grins. "Now come on. Coach is going to murder us if we're late."

I grab my helmet and follow him out, but I'm

still smiling.

Not because everything's perfect. It's not. There's still the playoff push, still the pressure, still a hundred ways this could all go sideways.

But for the first time in a long time, I'm not facing it alone.

And that makes all the difference.

32

DINOSAUR PANCAKES

Tori

It's Sunday morning, and I'm standing in Zayden's kitchen making pancakes.

Not just any pancakes—dinosaur pancakes. Maisie informed me very seriously that round pancakes are "boring" and dinosaurs are "scientifically superior." She's currently perched on a stool at the counter, supervising my technique with the intensity of a tiny Gordon Ramsay.

"The T-Rex needs bigger arms," she says.

"T-Rexes have tiny arms. That's their whole thing."

"But he looks sad with tiny arms."

"Maybe he *is* sad. It's hard being an apex predator who can't reach things."

She considers this. "Can you give him a friend? So he's not lonely?"

I add a blobby shape next to the T-Rex that's supposed to be a triceratops but looks more like a lumpy potato with horns. "There. Now he has a buddy."

"Perfect."

Zayden appears in the kitchen doorway, hair still damp from the shower, wearing gray sweatpants that should be illegal and a faded Canadiens T-shirt. He takes in the scene—me at the stove, Maisie on her stool, batter splattered across the counter—and a tender look crosses his face.

"Please tell me there's coffee and that one of those dinosaurs is for me."

"Of course," I answer.

"Tori's teaching me about dinosaur feelings," Maisie adds.

"Dinosaur feelings." He reaches for a coffee mug, brushing up against me.

"They have them, Daddy. Even the scary ones."

He catches my eye over her head, and I shrug. "She's not wrong. Emotional intelligence is important across all species."

"Even extinct ones?"

"Especially extinct ones. They never got closure."

He laughs—that low, warm sound I'm becoming addicted to—and crosses to the coffee maker. His hand brushes the small of my back as he passes, casual and intimate, and I feel it everywhere.

Part of me still can't believe this is real. That I'm standing in Zayden Bishop's kitchen, covered in pancake batter, falling deeper every day.

My phone buzzes on the counter. I flip the triceratops—*nailed it*—and check the screen.

Winnie

GUESS WHO OFFICIALLY STARTS MONDAY

Dana just emailed. I'm in. Team yoga instructor. This is real life!!!

I'm going to throw up. In a good way.

I grin and type back a quick response.

Me

You're going to be amazing. The guys don't know what's coming for them.

Winnie

Challenge accepted.

I pocket my phone, still smiling. Winnie starting with the team is the best news I've heard all week. She'll be brilliant—she's always been brilliant—and maybe now she can rebuild everything Derek tried to tear down.

"Good news?" Zayden asks, handing me a cup of coffee made exactly how I like it. He remembered. Of course he remembered.

"Winnie got the job. She starts Monday."

"The yoga thing?"

"The yoga thing." I take a sip. "Fair warning though—she's going to make your life very uncomfortable. Lots of stretching. Lots of breathing exercises."

Maisie tugs on my shirt. "Is Winnie your best friend?"

"She is."

"Is she nice?"

"She's very nice. She's going to teach the hockey players how to do yoga."

Maisie wrinkles her nose. "Daddy can't do

yoga. He's too big and clunky."

"Hey." Zayden sounds genuinely offended. "I'm not clunky."

"You knocked over the lamp last week with your elbow," she reminds him.

I bite back a laugh as Zayden sputters. He's got no defense, and he knows it. Maisie just watches him with those big brown eyes, completely unimpressed with her father's athletic credentials.

"I could do yoga if I wanted to," he mutters.

"Sure you could." I pat his arm consolingly.

Once the pancakes are ready, we settle at the table with an ease that still surprises me. Maisie chatters about her friend Sophie's new puppy, about the book they're reading in class, and about whether mermaids are real (she's convinced they are, just very good at hiding). Zayden listens to every word, asking follow-up questions, nodding seriously at her theories.

After breakfast, Maisie announces that we're building a blanket fort. This is apparently non-negotiable.

"It has to be big enough for all three of us," she instructs, already pulling cushions off the couch. "And it needs a door. And windows. And maybe a chimney?"

"How would a blanket fort have a chimney?" Zayden asks.

"I don't know. You're the adult. Figure it out."

Twenty minutes later, we've constructed something that looks less like a fort and more like a fabric explosion in the middle of the living room. But Maisie's delighted, crawling inside with her stuffed dinosaur and a flashlight, and that's all that matters.

"Come in, come in!" She waves us through the "door"—a gap between two couch cushions. "There's room!"

There is not room. Not for two adults, anyway. Especially not when one of them is as large as Zayden, but we squeeze in anyway, and suddenly I'm pressed against Zayden's side in a tiny space that smells like laundry detergent and maple syrup, with a six-year-old shining a flashlight directly in my face.

"This is cozy," I manage.

Zayden chuckles beside me, flashing me a conspiratorial grin.

"Isn't it?" Maisie beams. "Okay, now we tell secrets. That's what you do in forts."

"It is?"

Maisie nods. "Sophie told me. She knows everything about forts."

"Sophie sounds like an expert."

"She really is." She settles cross-legged, looking between us expectantly. "Daddy, you go first."

Zayden shifts, trying to find a position where his shoulder isn't jammed against a dining chair. "Uh. Okay. My secret is... I sometimes eat cereal for dinner when you're at your grandma's."

"That's not a secret. I knew that already." She turns to me. "Tori's turn."

I think for a second. "My secret is that I'm thinking about starting my own business. A sports medicine clinic where I'd be the boss."

Zayden's head turns toward me. "You are?"

"Maybe. I've been looking into it." I haven't

told anyone this yet—not even Winnie—but it's been bouncing around in my head for weeks. All the upheaval with Dana, the reassignment, the realization that I don't want to spend my career at the mercy of someone else's policies. "I could work with athletes from any sport. Set my own rules. Build something that's actually mine."

"Tori, that's amazing." He smiles, like he can envision the whole thing.

"It's just an idea right now. I'd need funding, a business plan, a location—"

"You'll figure it out." He says it with complete certainty, like there's no doubt in his mind. "You're the most capable person I know."

Something warm blooms in my chest. "Thanks."

"Okay, okay." Maisie waves her flashlight impatiently. "My turn for a secret."

"Go ahead, little shadow."

She's quiet for a moment, fiddling with her dinosaur's tail. When she looks up, her expression is serious.

"My secret is that I used to wish for a mom."

The air goes still. Zayden tenses beside me, and I don't dare move.

"Like, a real mom," Maisie continues. "Not my mom, because she's... she's fine, but she doesn't really do real mom stuff. So I would wish on stars and birthday candles and on pennies thrown into fountains for someone who wanted to do real mom stuff with me."

"Maze..." Zayden's voice is rough.

"But I stopped wishing," she says, "because

wishes are for things you don't have yet."

I can't breathe. I literally cannot draw air into my lungs because I know what's coming, and I'm not ready for it.

Maisie looks directly at me, her brown eyes—Zayden's eyes—wide and earnest.

"I don't have to wish anymore. Because now there's Tori."

The words hit me like a physical blow. My vision blurs, and I realize I'm crying—actual tears sliding down my cheeks—in the middle of a blanket fort on a Sunday morning.

"Maisie." I have to stop, swallow, my voice breaking. I pull her to me, and she climbs into my lap like it's the most natural thing in the world.

"I just wanted you to know," she whispers, "so you won't leave."

"I'm not going anywhere."

"Promise?"

I look at Zayden over her head. His eyes are red-rimmed, his jaw tight with emotion. He gives me a small nod, barely perceptible.

"I promise," I whisper into her hair. "I'm staying."

She relaxes against me with a sigh, and I hold her tight—this little girl who wished on stars for someone to show up, who guards her heart because she's learned the hard way that people leave, who just handed me something precious and fragile and trusted me not to break it.

Zayden's hand finds mine under the blanket, his thumb tracing across my knuckles. When I glance at him, he's watching us with an expression that makes my chest ache in the best way.

We stay like that for another few minutes, Maisie warm and heavy in my lap, the three of us tangled together in this ridiculous structure made of couch cushions and dreams.

Then Maisie squirms.

"It's really hot in here." She's already crawling toward the exit. "I'm getting sweaty. Can we get out now?"

So much for the moment.

Zayden laughs, that low rumble I love, and starts dismantling our "door" so we can escape. Maisie bursts out into the living room like she's been trapped for hours instead of minutes.

I crawl out after her, my knees protesting from too long on the hard floor, and Zayden follows with a groan, stretching his back like he's aged thirty years in the last hour.

"I'm too old for blanket forts," he mutters.

"You're twenty-nine."

"Trust me, in hockey years, that's ancient."

I watch Maisie dig through her toy bin, already onto the next thing, the fort forgotten behind us in a heap of blankets and pillows. And I think about all the years I spent building walls instead of forts. All the rules I made to keep myself safe from exactly this—Sunday mornings with pancake batter on the counter and a little girl who wished on stars for someone like me.

I never expected this. Never let myself want it.

But it's here anyway, and I'm so grateful.

Zayden's arms wrap around me from behind, his chin coming to rest on top of my head. "I love you," he murmurs, low enough that only I can hear.

I lean back into him, into the solid warmth of his chest, into this life I somehow stumbled into when I wasn't looking.

"I love you too."

Maisie glances up from her toys. "Are you guys being mushy again?"

"Extremely," Zayden confirms.

She rolls her eyes—a move she's definitely picked up from me—and goes back to her dinosaurs.

And I just stand there, wrapped in his arms, watching his daughter play, feeling safe and loved and happier than I thought possible.

This is it? This is what I was so afraid of?

Turns out, it feels a lot like home.

33

SKYWRITING AND OTHER BAD IDEAS

Zayden

ONE MONTH LATER

"**W**hat about skywriting?"

Banks stares at me like I've suggested we rob a bank. "Skywriting."

"Yeah. You know, the plane thing. Writes words in the sky." I motion with my finger.

"I know what skywriting is, Zay. I'm questioning your sanity for suggesting it."

We're sitting in a booth at an overpriced steakhouse downtown, supposedly having a "guys' lunch," but really, I'm interrogating my best friend about romantic gestures because apparently, I have no idea what I'm doing.

"What's wrong with skywriting?"

He lifts one brow. "Besides the fact that it's tacky, weather-dependent, and she might not even be looking up at the right moment?" Banks takes a long sip of his water. "Nothing. It's perfect. Go for it."

"You're not being helpful."

"You asked for my opinion. My opinion is that skywriting is stupid."

I slump back against the booth. "Okay, fine. What would you do?"

"I wouldn't."

"Wouldn't what?"

"Propose." He shrugs. "Marriage isn't really my thing."

"That's incredibly unhelpful, Banks. I'm asking you to use your imagination."

"My imagination is telling me to order another steak."

I drag a hand down my face. This was a mistake. I should have asked Archer—he's married, he's done this before. But Archer talks too much, and the last thing I need is the whole team knowing I'm planning to propose before I actually do it.

Banks was supposed to be the safe option. The vault. The guy who doesn't gossip or get emotional or make a big deal out of things.

Turns out he's also the guy with zero romantic instincts whatsoever.

"Okay, let's try this differently," I say. "What do women like?"

"How would I know?"

"You've dated women."

"I've slept with women. That's different."

"Banks."

"What? I'm being honest." He leans back, arms crossed. "Look, I'm not the guy you come to for this stuff. I don't do feelings. I don't do grand gestures. I show up, I do my job, I go home. That's it."

"You showed up at my house to warn me when

the rumors started."

"That was different."

"How?"

"That was crisis management. This is—" He waves a hand vaguely. "Romance. Not my department."

I'm about to argue when movement near the entrance catches my eye. The hostess is leading someone toward the back of the restaurant, and I recognize the blonde hair immediately.

Winnie. Tori's best friend. The yoga instructor Dana hired a few weeks ago—she's been finishing up some training thing, but she starts with the team on Monday.

She spots me and waves, changing course toward our table.

I've met Winnie a handful of times now. Objectively? Yeah, she's gorgeous—tall, blonde, the kind of impossible-to-ignore pretty that's going to cause problems when she starts working with a locker room full of hockey players. Not my problem, obviously. I'm so gone for Tori it's almost embarrassing. But I'm already bracing myself for the chaos.

"Hey, Zayden!" She's all warmth and energy, even in the middle of a Tuesday. "Fancy seeing you here. Is Tori with you?"

"Nah, I wish. She's at the new clinic. Grand opening prep." I gesture across the table. "This is Banks. Banks, this is Winnie—she starts with the team on Monday. Yoga and flexibility training."

Winnie turns to him with that megawatt smile. "Nice to finally meet you. Tori talks about you guys all the time."

Banks opens his mouth.

Nothing comes out.

I watch, genuinely fascinated, as the most stoic man I've ever known completely short-circuits. He just... stares at her. Jaw slightly slack. Eyes a little too wide.

Winnie's smile falters, just a flicker of uncertainty. "Um. Hi?"

"Hi." Banks's voice comes out like sandpaper. He clears his throat. "I'm—yeah. Banks."

"So I heard." She laughs, a little awkward now. "Well, I guess I'll be seeing you Monday. Should be fun."

Banks nods. Just nods. Like he's forgotten how words work.

"Okay then." Winnie glances at me, and I catch the question in her eyes—*is he okay?*—before she recovers. "I'm meeting a friend, so I should run, but tell Tori I said hi!"

"Will do."

She gives one last little wave and heads toward the back of the restaurant. Banks watches her go. For way too long.

"Dude."

He blinks. "What?"

"You didn't say a single coherent thing just now."

"I said hi."

"Barely."

"I'm not—" He stops. Picks up his water. Drains half of it. "She caught me off guard."

"Uh-huh."

"She did."

I don't push it. But I file it away because I've known Banks for six years, and I've never seen him rattled by anything. Not enforcers, not play-offs, not contract negotiations.

But a five-foot-six yoga instructor with a nice smile just turned him into a malfunctioning robot.

Interesting.

"Can we get back to your proposal?" Banks growls. "Since that's supposedly why we're here?"

"Right. The proposal." I pull out my phone and scroll to the notes app where I've been keeping a list of ideas. "Okay, so we've ruled out skywriting. What about... a flash mob?"

"Absolutely not."

"Jumbotron at a game?"

"She'd murder you."

"Hot air balloon?"

He considers this one, then shakes his head. "You're afraid of heights."

I sigh and scratch my temple. Banks just looks at me. That flat, unimpressed stare he's perfected over years of shutting down reporters and overea-ger fans.

I take a sip of my water. "Okay, so I have a healthy respect for heights. There's a difference."

Banks continues his unimpressed stare.

"Fine. No hot air balloon." I scroll further. "What about something simple? Cook her dinner, candles, get down on one knee?"

"Now you're talking." He nods once.

"Really?"

"Yeah." He shrugs. "Tori's not flashy. She

doesn't need a production. She just needs you to show up and mean it. Make it genuine and from the heart."

"That's... actually really insightful."

"Don't sound so surprised."

"I'm just saying, for a guy who claims to have no romantic instincts—"

"I observe. I don't participate." He signals the waiter for the check with a subtle raise of his hand. "There's a difference."

There's something almost wistful in his voice. I file it away but don't push. Banks shares when he's ready, which is basically never, and pushing just makes him clam up tighter.

My phone buzzes. It's a text from Tori, with a photo attached.

It's her standing in front of her new clinic—Wells Sports Medicine, the sign reads—grinning like she just won the lottery. The grand opening is this weekend, but she's been over there every day this week, setting up equipment, meeting with potential clients, making sure everything is perfect.

Tori

Look what came in today!

Another photo. Business cards with her name on them. *Victoria Wells, DPT, Owner.*

Me

Those look amazing. You look amazing.

Tori

Flattery will get you everywhere, Bishop.

Me

That's the plan.

Tori

Maisie's asking if you can pick up gold-fish crackers on the way home. The pizza ones, not the regular ones. She was very specific.

Me

Tell her I'm on it.

Tori

My hero.

I'm smiling at my phone like an idiot, and I don't even care.

"You're disgusting," Banks says.

"Jealous?"

"Of that dopey look on your face? Hard pass."

But there's something in his voice that makes me glance up. He's looking toward the back of the restaurant again, where Winnie is sitting with someone I don't recognize—a woman, probably a friend—laughing at something on her phone.

"You sure about that?" I ask.

"Positive." He stands, tossing cash on the table. "Now let's go. Some of us have things to do."

I follow him out, but not before catching one last glimpse of Winnie. She looks up at the exact wrong moment, catching Banks staring, and something passes between them—electric and brief—before he turns away.

Yeah. He's definitely screwed.

But that's a problem for another day. A problem for Banks to figure out, whenever he's ready to admit he has one.

Right now, I've got goldfish crackers to buy, a proposal to plan, and a woman waiting for me who somehow turned my whole life upside down and made it better in the process.

I pull out my phone and jot a note in my proposal planning list:

Cancel skywriting.

Then, after a moment:

Simple. Genuine. From the heart.

Show up and mean it.

Banks might claim to be useless at romance, but he's not wrong about this. Tori doesn't need grand gestures. She doesn't need skywriting or jumbotrons or hot air balloons. She just needs to know I'm not going anywhere.

My phone buzzes again.

Tori

Also Maisie says to tell you she loves you. And that you're "the best daddy in the whole world." Direct quote.

My throat goes tight. I blink against the sudden sting in my eyes, standing on a Manhattan sidewalk like an idiot, completely undone by a secondhand message from my six-year-old.

Me

Tell her I love her too. And that she's the best daughter in the whole world. Also a direct quote.

Home.

I pocket my phone and head for the car, a smile stretching across my face that I couldn't suppress if I tried.

I've got a woman who somehow turned my whole life upside down and made it better in the process. A daughter who thinks I'm the best daddy in the world. A future that looks nothing like I planned and everything like I never knew I wanted.

And I'm going to spend the rest of my life proving I deserve every bit of it.

epilogue

Tori

Something's going on.

I can tell because Maisie keeps giggling every time she looks at me, and Zayden has checked his phone approximately forty-seven times in the last hour. They're both terrible at keeping secrets—a trait I find endlessly endearing—and whatever they're hiding, it must be big.

"You're being weird," I tell him as he sets the table for dinner. "Both of you."

"We're not being weird," Maisie says, way too fast. "We're being normal. This is normal."

"Totally normal," Zayden agrees, avoiding my gaze. "Just a regular Friday dinner."

"Uh-huh."

I let it go because the clinic's grand opening is tomorrow, and I'm too tired to interrogate them properly. The past month has been a blur of paperwork, equipment deliveries, and marketing meetings, and I still can't quite believe it's real or that it happened so quickly. But a lease on a perfect building was available, and I jumped at the chance. My name on the door. My business. Mine.

Dinner is spaghetti—Maisie's favorite—and we eat at the table like we always do now. The three of us. This little family we've somehow become.

"Tori," Maisie says, pushing a meatball around her plate. "Can I ask you something?"

"Sure, Maze."

She glances at Zayden, who gives her a tiny nod. My stomach flutters. Whatever this is, they've rehearsed it.

"Remember when we built the blanket fort?" she asks. "And I told you my secret?"

My throat tightens. "I remember."

"About how I used to wish for someone to do mom stuff with me?"

"Yeah, honey. I remember."

She sets down her fork and looks at me with those big brown eyes—so serious and earnest it makes my chest ache.

"I was thinking," she says carefully, like she's reciting lines she's practiced. "That maybe... you could be that person. For real. Forever."

I can't breathe.

"Maisie—"

"Not like a pretend mom or a sometimes mom." She slides off her chair and comes around the table to stand next to me, and that's when I notice movement out of the corner of my eye.

Zayden. Pushing back from the table. Lowering himself to one knee.

My heart stops.

"A real one," Maisie continues, reaching for my hand. "The kind that stays."

Zayden pulls a small velvet box from his pocket, and Maisie steps aside, her job done, grinning like she just pulled off the world's greatest heist.

"She's been practicing that for three days," Zayden says, his voice rough. "Wouldn't let me help. Said she had it handled."

I laugh, but it comes out watery. "She did."

"My turn now." He opens the box. The ring catches the light—a stunning oval diamond on a gold band. It's bigger and more beautiful than anything I would have picked for myself. "Tori, I had this whole speech prepared. About how you walked into my life and everything started to make sense. How you made me want to be better—for you, for Maisie, for myself."

"Zayden—"

"But she's right. You're already our family. And I know this is fast, but I'm not confused about where this is going. Not even a little." He reaches for my hand, his thumb brushing over my knuckles. "I want to watch you build your clinic into something incredible. I want to be the one by your side through all of it."

His eyes are bright, and I realize with a start that he's close to tears too. This man who guards everything, who holds the world at arm's length—he's kneeling in front of me with his whole heart on display.

"I'm all in, Tori. I have been since the beginning." His voice cracks slightly. "So will you be my wife. Be ours—forever?"

"Say yes!" Maisie whisper-shouts from somewhere behind him. "You have to say yes!"

I'm crying. Full-on ugly crying, tears streaming down my face, and I don't even care. I look at this man—this stubborn, guarded, impossibly tender man who fought for me when I was too scared to fight for myself—and I wonder how I ever thought I could walk away from this.

"Yes." The word comes out thick and watery. "Yes, of course yes."

His whole face transforms. That rare, real smile breaks through as he slides the ring onto my finger—and it fits perfectly, because of course it does; he pays attention to everything.

Then he's on his feet, pulling me up with him, and his mouth finds mine in a kiss that tastes like tears, promise, and finally.

"Group hug!" Maisie barrels into us, wedging herself between our legs until we break apart laughing. "I did good, right? I didn't mess up my lines?"

"You did perfectly, little shadow." Zayden scoops her up with one arm, keeping the other around me.

Later—after dinner and ice cream and cleanup, after Maisie finally falls asleep; and after we've migrated to the couch with the lights low and my head on his shoulder—I look at the ring on my finger and try to remember the last time I felt this happy.

I can't. Because I've never felt this happy.

"Do you like it?"

I glance up. "What?"

"The ring." He's watching me with an expression I can't quite read—nervous, almost. "It's an oval cut, just over two carats. The band is platinum with pavé diamonds—that means the little ones on the side. The jeweler said the clarity is—”

“Zayden.”

“—VS1, which is apparently very good, and the color is—”

“Zayden.”

“—but if you don’t like it, we can exchange it. We can get something different—whatever you want. A different shape, a different setting, bigger, smaller—”

I silence him the most effective way I know how—by kissing him.

When I pull back, he blinks at me, slightly dazed. “So... that’s a yes on the ring?”

“I love the ring.” I hold up my hand, watching the diamond catch the light. “I love that you know what pavé means. I love that you picked it. I love everything about it.”

The tension drains from his shoulders. “Yeah?”

“Yeah.”

He pulls me closer, pressing a kiss to the top of my head. We sit there for a while, his fingers tracing lazy patterns on my arm, the city humming outside the window.

“Hey,” Zayden murmurs.

“Hey.”

“You okay?”

I twist to look at him. “I’m perfect. Why?”

“You’re quiet. You’re never quiet.”

“I’m just... thinking.” I settle back against him. “About how different everything is. A few months ago, I had my rule, my five-year plan, and this whole life mapped out. And now...”

"Now?"

"Now I have you. And Maisie. And a clinic with my name on the door." I laugh softly. "None of this was in the plan."

"Is that bad?"

"No." I find his hand and thread my fingers through his. "It's just funny. I spent so long trying to control everything. And then you came along and blew it all up."

"In my defense, you blew up my life too. In the best way." His hand intertwines with mine.

"Fair."

We sit there for a while, not talking, just breathing. His thumb traces circles on my palm. The city hums outside the window. Everything feels exactly right.

"Thank you," I say quietly.

"For what?"

"For not giving up on me. Even when I was trying really hard to push you away."

He shifts, tilting my chin up so I'm looking at him. "I told you, Tori. I'm not going anywhere."

"I know." I smile. "But thank you anyway."

He kisses me—slow, sweet, full of promise—and I sink into it. Into him. Into this life I never planned but somehow ended up exactly where I'm supposed to be.

The woman with the ironclad rule and the five-year plan, engaged to a hockey player.

My mother is going to lose her mind. But that's a problem for tomorrow.

Tonight, I'm just going to be here. In this moment. With my family.

The one I never knew I was wishing for.

***

You're not going to want to miss what's coming next! Banks & Winnie's story continues in book two—where the team's broodiest defenseman meets his match in a sunshine yoga instructor who doesn't take no for an answer.

Banks doesn't do relationships. Doesn't do feelings. Doesn't do yoga.

Winnie's about to change all that.
Ice Cold Chemistry is a grumpy-sunshine hockey romance, and oh... it's going to get spicy.

Ice Cold Chemistry

She's the distraction the team can't afford.
He's the solution no one saw coming.

Winnie Garrett is done with men. After a toxic relationship left her second-guessing everything, she's focused on one thing: her dream job as the New York Knights' new yoga instructor.

Banks Callahan doesn't do relationships. Or feelings. Or anything that requires letting people get close. Growing up in the foster system taught him not to need anyone—and definitely not to want something he could lose.

So when the team's new yoga instructor becomes an unexpected locker-room distraction threatening their playoff focus, Banks comes up with a solution so ridiculous it just might work.

Fake dating.

If the guys think Winnie is *his*, they'll back off. It's simple locker room code: you don't touch what's claimed—like calling dibs on the last slice of pizza.

The problem?

Nothing about Winnie Garrett is simple.

She's warmth and laughter and everything Banks has spent years convincing himself he doesn't need. She makes him want things he can't have. Makes him feel things he doesn't understand.

He was never supposed to fall for her.

But somewhere between fake hand-holding, pretend nicknames, and very real late-night moments, the line between "just for show" and "dangerously real" starts to blur.

Acknowledgements

To my husband, John, and my two wonderful sons—you're my heart. Thank you for loving me through the chaos, for putting up with my endless plotting, and for reminding me what truly matters. I adore you more than words.

To the best marketing guru an author could wish for, *thank you* to Alyssa Garcia for all the things!

To my besties — thank you for every lunch date, happy hour, girl's trip, and set of matching pajamas. I'm so lucky to have you in every chapter. You're my favorite side characters!

To my readers—thank you, thank you, *thank you!* You're the reason these stories exist, and I hope you enjoyed this. I'm so grateful to every single one of you for joining me on this journey. Here's to more stories, more characters to fall for, and more books to share with you.

About the Author

Kendall Ryan is a *New York Times*, *Wall Street Journal*, and *USA Today* bestselling author of flirty, feel-good romance filled with heart, heat, and plenty of banter. An American author who has lived all over the world, her books have sold millions of copies and been translated into multiple languages. She writes swoony heroes, bold heroines, and stories that make you laugh, blush, and fall in love. When she's not dreaming up new plotlines, she is a proud mom to two amazing sons and the wife of her real-life hero.

Other Titles by Kendall Ryan

Main Character Energy
Filthy Beautiful Lies
The Room Mate
Dirty Little Secret
Baby Daddy
Love Machine
Flirting with Forever
Playing for Keeps
The Rebel
The Forever Formula
A Beginner's Guide to Forever

For a complete list of Kendall's books, visit:
www.kendallryanbooks.com/books